A NOVEL BY

ELLEN RUDERMAN

iUniverse, Inc.
New York   Bloomington

Chasing the Red Car

This is a work of fiction. All of the characters, names, incidents, organizations, and dialogue in this novel are either the products of the author's imagination or are used fictitiously.

iUniverse books may be ordered through booksellers or by contacting:

iUniverse
1663 Liberty Drive
Bloomington, IN 47403
www.iuniverse.com
1-800-Authors (1-800-288-4677)

ISBN: 978-1-4502-6718-2 (sc)
ISBN: 978-1-4502-6719-9 (dj)
ISBN: 978-1-4502-6720-5 (ebk)

Library of Congress Control Number: 2010915434

Printed in the United States of America

iUniverse rev. date: 10/26/2010

Dedications

When all is said and done, it is the relationships in our lives—the beauty of family and rich friendships—that fully enhance and sustain us.

To Herb

Adam and Vanessa

Marcia and Barbara

To my Writers Group—Kathy Checchi, Joan Jackson and Paty Kouba— my deep appreciation for your commitment, ideas and suggestions. This novel's development and completion is a reflection of all you have given me. To Gretchen Henkel, my editor and friend, my gratitude for the enrichment your skillful editing brought to *Chasing the Red Car.*

Acknowledgments

The subject of this book aroused in many I encountered a willingness to share their McCarthy Era stories. My profound thanks to the following people for sharing their personal connection to this unique time in history and bringing to life the tragic reality of McCarthyism:

Alice Powell, educator and social activist, who recalled her journey as an involved progressive during a repressive era;

Linda Shapiro, whose memories of her childhood as a "red diaper baby" underscored the fear and hysteria of the Cold War period and the anxieties she and her family experienced;

Joy Schary, who shared recollections of living in a Hollywood family and the intrusive effects of the "tones" and "tensions" of the time of the Red Scare;

Norma Barzman, (author of *The Red and the Blacklist*, and married to Sam Barzman, one of the Hollywood Ten) for verbally bringing to life the disruptive effects of blacklisting she and her family experienced;

The late Miriam Harriss, my friend and office suite mate, who was a stewardess on the 1947 flight carrying Hollywood luminaries to Washington, D.C. to protest the HUAC hearings, for the unforgettable photo in the book depicting that flight.

So many people came forward and offered their generous support for this project. I extend my heartfelt thanks to:

Kayvan Kardan, an excellent graphic designer, for your patience and professionalism, your guidance through the process and for executing a remarkable cover for the book; and to Karen Kardan, for your helpful suggestions;

Julia Mass, Staff Attorney for the ACLU of Northern California, for reading and offering comments on certain chapters of the book, and for providing me with such a fine review for the cover;

Michael Theobold, author: your skillful and no-nonsense commentaries led me to restructure and modify portions of the book, which greatly benefited it;

Joan Jackson, for going the extra mile with your contributions to writing and editing, all of which greatly enhanced my book;

Paul Cholodenko, my cherished friend, for your wonderful ideas, and for the excellent book cover concept;

Marcia Cholodenko, for your enthusiasm and support, and for reading, editing, and offering suggestions, no matter how much time it took;

Barbara Rittenberg, for your generosity of time spent reading and improving this novel and for your help in reworking its title. Your enthusiasm and support meant so much;

Amy and Howard Mass, for your ongoing encouragement, and many helpful suggestions along the way;

Rosalyn Benitez-Bloch: you were among the first to read my early manuscript, offer valuable suggestions and encouragement. Thank you also for a wonderful book review;

Helen Landgarten, for reading my manuscript, and for your help always—in friendship and in writing;

Billie Lee Violette, for your support, for your help in launching the book, and for your vibrant ideas which brought a deeper understanding of the "progressive" personality;

Cindy Olnick, Director of Communications, Los Angeles Conservancy, for your generosity in sending me a copy of the July, 2006 Feasibility Study for the Resurrection of the Red Car Trolley Services in the Los Angeles Downtown Area;

Joan Rankin, my appreciation for your support and suggestions; and to Howard Ballon for connections to promote the book;

Karen Redding, for supporting my efforts and helping me to expand my vistas in promoting the book; and to Ed Kaufman for his helpful suggestions;

Sandra Santini, for your support and for introducing me to Gretchen; and to Marvin Victor for valuable information about the Red Car and the early San Fernando Valley;

Judy Chaikin of One Step Productions, for sending me the excellent documentary you directed, *Legacy of the Hollywood Blacklist,* which was so helpful to my book;

Barbara Lovenheim, author of *Survival in the Shadows,* for taking your time to read and comment on my early chapters; and to Carole Bender, for introducing us;

Richard Walter, for your discussions with me about writing and writers, and for encouraging me to call Carolyn See; and to Pat Walter for your support;

Carolyn See, author of *There Will Never Be Another You,* for your ideas about the publishing scene and for your wonderful article in the *Los Angeles Times,* "Streetcar Desire," which was so well timed;

John Lang, for reading the early manuscript, for your thoughtful edits and comments; and to Lisa Halotek for your support;

Barbara Powell, for your helpful edits in the early stages of the book;

Paula Shatsky, for your emails about America's political landscape, past and present, which were so helpful;

Paula and Sid Machtinger, my appreciation for your support and your paving the way for communication with Ramona Ripston of the ACLU;

Eileen Gallo, coauthor with John Gallo of *Silver Spoon Kids*, for sharing so much with me about writing, publishing and promotion, and for talking with John about ways to help me promote the book;

Phyllis and David Rothman, for your support, the early pictures of the Red Car and for helping me to launch the book.

Herb and Mary Ann Karlow, Jane Rubin, and Bob Gerstein, who have been boosters for my efforts and keep the "liberal" spirit alive; and

Finally, the staff at iUniverse, for your invaluable help in shepherding me through the publication process.

Chapter 1

1947

It was a hot day in the Bronx. I could feel the sweat dripping down the backs of my knees—and it wasn't even noon yet. As I turned on the spigot to get some water, I noticed that the tar on Bolton Street was starting to bubble. I carried a little pan of water to the concrete stoop and splashed it all over the steps so my friends and I could sit comfortably on the wet stairs.

As we settled on the stoop, I remained perched on the top step of what looked like a pyramid of friends in front of the eight-story apartment building where my family lived.

I was slender and quite tall for a nine-year-old, with a mop of long dark brown curly hair, tufts of which would fall in front of my eyes. I pulled my knees up close to my chest, pushed back a few strands of hair, and began to tell them about my family's plans to drive in Aunt Winnie's car tomorrow on a highway called Route 66. My mock bravery about the long trip my family was going to take the next morning seemed to be working. My friends were enthralled. I could sense the magic that California held for them. They smiled, their faces in rapt attention, as I spoke of the many far-off places my family would visit on our trip. I could tell some of them wished they could come along.

1

"You get to go to California," shouted Stuey, a short dark-haired boy with glasses and a rumpled plaid shirt, his eyes wide and his face all lit up. "No one I know in the Bronx has ever been there." I suspected that he must be conjuring up images of his favorite movie and television cowboys. And sure enough, he burst out again: "I just saw a Hopalong Cassidy movie on Saturday at the RKO Pelham! Hoppy is my favorite!"

Rita Goldman, my very best friend since we were three years old, her blond braids glistening in the hot sun, said, "Well, I like Dale Evans and Roy Rogers." Then with a serious expression on her face, Rita turned to me. "Do you think Trigger is alive?"

"Well, he better be," I said, "because when I get out there I'm going to ride him." They all laughed, imagining me on a huge white horse on some ranch in the wilderness. I pushed away the wave of sadness that was threatening to get in.

Jimmie Snyder, who had had a crush on me since first grade, moved closer to me. "Do all the horses look like the ponies at the Bronx Zoo?" His question triggered a wistful memory of the day we climbed through the hole that he and Stuey dug under the chain link fence at the nearby Bronx Zoo so we wouldn't have to pay the ten-cent entrance fee.

The thrill of connecting that place out west with cowboys in big Stetson hats and sizzling cactus bushes faded as I looked around me. *I'll probably never see any of you again! We'll never play stick ball and ring-a-levio and mother-may-I again. We'll never go to Rapps Candy Store for a two cents plain and an egg salad sandwich. Or sled together out on the street in the freezing weather, or hold hands while we walk to P.S. 105 on winter mornings.* The sadness that had been lingering in me each day our trip got closer made me want to beg my parents to change their minds about the move.

And anyway, why *were* they moving? I was perfectly happy with all my friends here. Yes, my mother complained a lot about how cramped the apartment was and how her fingers and toes nearly froze in the Bronx winters. But so what? Summers came and we were outside a lot, and the heat of the summer made up for the coldness of the winter. I also felt a pang of guilt. I suspected that we were moving permanently, but I'd told Rita that we were only going to be gone for three months. I also told the rest of my friends that we were going on a long vacation. I guess I just couldn't bear to admit that I wouldn't be coming back and I might never see any of them again. *And all because Lila wants a larger and warmer place to live. Sometimes, Lila is a pain!*

"Arthur," Lila would plead, "the apartments here are the size of postage stamps. We're all banging into each other. It's not civilized. How can we live this way? One bathroom for all of us?"

Arthur is my father, and Lila is my mother. My sister Jonna and I call them by their first names, because in their crowd, which they call "progressives," they said that's what people do. So, whenever Lila complained, Arthur would tell her, "Count your blessings; it's not that bad. Look at the Greenes. They're making do with one bathroom for six people. Now, how about if we go out for Chinese tonight, and give you a rest from cooking?"

Over at the next stoop, my sister Jonna, who had just turned seven, sat chatting with her friend, eight-year-old Harry Landsman. Her little hands were moving in many directions. She seemed kinda cute, I thought. But it was going to be so hard for Jonna to leave Harry, her only close friend.

Although I had been talking about "the trip" with my friends for over two months, I kept pushing it out of my mind. So when my family was gathered last week at the oak table in our kitchen finishing dinner, Arthur's announcement that we'd be off to California in less than a week came as a rude shock for Jonna and me. "That's the way they always do things," I muttered to myself. No time was ever allowed for discussion. Decisions were handed down as proclamations and they didn't seem at all interested in what we felt.

Pipe hanging from one side of his mouth, Arthur pranced around the room, actually hopping every other step. "They want me, Lila. The position I've been offered has come through. The University wants me to come out for an interview with the President…the *President* of the college! Lou Allenson, my buddy at CCNY, says it's in the bag. Lou also says that Los Angeles City College has quite a good reputation for a community college. They're doing great things out there in California— new things, dynamic things—and he says if they've already set up the meeting with the President, I'm as much as on the faculty."

Rarely had I seen my mother smile the way she did that night. Her face was radiant as she listened to Arthur talk about what might be a brighter future for him as well as for all of us. I could barely remember a time in all my almost ten years when my mother and father seemed this close and so happy together. Maybe things would really change in California.

But while they were beaming at each other, Jonna was looking out the large window that took up almost one whole wall of the kitchen, now wide open to allow for a breeze that might miraculously appear. She looked so sad, and began to whine. "Who cares where you teach, Daddy? I don't want to go away from here. I like my best friend Harry. I want to stay here with him." Jonna's lips were trembling.

I came out of my idyllic reverie about change. Crestfallen, I gazed at Jonna and realized what a terrible loss this would be for her. She was so shy it was hard for her to make friends. Harry was like her treasure.

Lila's smile transformed into a tight-lipped frown. She slammed her plate down hard on the table and glared at Jonna. "You'll get used to it. You have no choice. Your father needs a good job. At least a better one than he has here at City College of New York! He's had nothing but trouble here. They've done nothing but hound him about his politics. This move will be better for all of us."

Jonna slid down in her seat. Since she was terrified of Lila's temper, I moved closer to her, protectively placing my hand on her shoulder. Lila knew my unspoken message: if you snap and need to vent your wrath, you'll have to do it to both of us. Sometimes that stopped her in her tracks. But not always.

Lila was the bane of our existence. She was so volatile. When she really lost control, she'd throw whatever was in front of her, like ash trays or plates. Once she threw a whole bowl full of steaming spaghetti across the room, barely missing us. We learned very early in our lives to stay out of her way when she was in that furious state. If we didn't, we'd fall prey to her anger. Lila would pull our hair, slap us, or sometimes even land a punch or two. At these times, she looked demonic to me. Then, her mood would suddenly shift and she was calm as a cucumber. *Maybe, the hot weather in California will change Lila.*

The warm spell, the thawing of the tension, now returned to the familiar ice-storm we were all used to. No one spoke, as we glumly sat finishing Lila's dinner of burnt lamb chops, an undercooked baked potato, and dry green beans.

The gloomy silence continued. I watched warily as Jonna secretly funneled a portion of her meat into her pants pocket, which would end up behind the radiator. Jonna knew that I'd clean out the food scraps the next day, another desperate attempt to protect my sister. Some mornings I would go to school with two paper sacs, one for my lunch, and the other for Jonna's droppings that I would deposit in the first available trash can.

I often wondered what would happen if Lila finally discovered Jonna's deposits and learned that the cockroaches gathering at the foot of the radiator were preceded by a gracious invitation from Jonna. She stuffed crumbs, chewed chunks of meat, cream of wheat, or vanilla junket, as if to say, "Please, cockroaches, eat," to hide the evidence.

"So would you kids like to go to California and live in a house with a swimming pool?" Arthur's eyes twinkled as he smiled at Lila, hoping to restore her enthusiasm and coax her out of her angry mood. He got everyone to clear the rest of the dishes, then opened a large map of the United States, unfurled it across the now cleared kitchen table and proceeded to show us the route we would take across the country.

Now, sitting here on the stoop, I repeated Arthur's words to my friends, naming cities we'd visit: Chicago, St. Louis, Oklahoma City, Gallup, Kingman, Barstow and, finally, North Hollywood, the place where we would wind up. I didn't say "our future home." I continued my secret fantasy that we would soon be back. So, just as Arthur had done, I painted the trip on Route 66 as the grandest of adventures. To be traveling by car was exciting in itself. None of the families in my Bronx neighborhood had a car. They didn't need one in the city and besides, no one could afford a car. My friends were impressed, and thought I was "so, so lucky" to be going.

Time went by too quickly. Soon the echoing voices of my friends' mothers, leaning out their apartment windows calling them to dinner, broke the stillness which now surrounded me and my Pelham Parkway friends.

"Stuey, your father and I are sitting down to dinner. Get up here, now!"

"Okay, Ma, I'm coming!" Stuey got up very slowly and awkwardly reached out his hand to me. "Well, I hope I'll see you soon. I mean, come back real soon. And also, write if you can." He quickly crossed the street and, without turning around, waved with the back of his hand.

Next, it was Beth Huber, Willie Eiler, and Jimmy Snyder's turn to answer the call. Ever since I could remember, my three friends had dinner together on the weekend. Their mothers worked overtime on the assembly line at the heat-treating plant. Lila told me they had helped to make guns and airplanes to fight Hitler during the war and they were called "Rosie the Riveter" ladies. But when Mollie Snyder injured her arm falling on the ice one winter, she stayed home to cook for the other mothers' kids. Every weekend, Willie told me, the three of them went to his house for dinner. Now, each of them turned and looked up in the direction of Mollie's voice.

"Okay, you three, time for chow," she roared. "On the double!"

"Rita, Rita Goldman, this is your mother calling!"

Rita, her voice choking, was ready to cry. Sounding like a sheep, she responded: "Maaah, waydda minute." She turned to me, "I don't know who I'm going to talk to while you're away, Kim. Ask your parents if you could stay here and live with me and my folks while they go." With that, she reached down, picked up her Gimbels bag from her last shopping trip and pulled out a shoebox filled with her treasured trading cards of the latest movie stars. She handed the whole box to me, her hand so unsteady that the smiling faces of Judy Garland and Clark Gable went wafting to the ground. "Now, you have to come back soon cause I'll miss you and I'll miss these!" My eyes began to well up as I thanked her in a muffled tone. She turned away in tears.

My friends drifted away to three different apartment houses, leaving me alone at the top of my stoop. *I'll never see them again. Maybe I can come back next summer. Who knows what will happen? But California is so far away.*

That night, on the eve of our departure, the evening turned cool, finally making the apartment more bearable. All four of us were in the living room, Lila busily packing, Jonna lying on the floor drawing in her coloring book, and Arthur finishing the letter he had been writing for the past two days. I approached him, careful not to make too much noise.

He looked up when I tapped him on the shoulder. "Arthur, why *are* we going to California? I know it'll be fun and everything, but I'll miss my friends and when winter comes, I won't be able to go sledding with them. And anyway, why can't we go with Aunt Hedy to the lake this year?"

Lila frowned when I mentioned Kiamesha Lake, but she didn't look up. Like other apartment dwellers in the Bronx, we made the exodus during July and August, when the heat and humidity were at their worst. For eight weeks each summer, we shared the duplex that Lila's sister and her family rented. Jonna and I loved our two-month summer vacations with our fun-loving Aunt Hedy, who was the polar opposite of our mother. Hedy was lively, permissive, and soft spoken. We spent hours walking on the shore of the lake with our cousins, collecting flowers, or singing with Aunt Hedy songs from *Carousel* and *Oklahoma*, our two favorite Broadway musicals.

"Maybe we could go to California just for a vacation and forget about staying?" I pleaded.

Both Arthur and Lila looked up at me at once. "There are no ifs, ands or buts about our going for good," Lila said sternly.

I retreated to the little bedroom I shared with my sister. Jonna now sat at the table staring forlornly out the window. Maybe she wished that Harry would come and whisk her away so she wouldn't have to take this trip after all!

Listlessly, I started to put some of my treasured books and diaries into a box, when I heard a faint tap on the door. Arthur, looking a little sheepish, stuck his head into our room. "I need to go out to Rapps Candy Store. Do you want to come, Kim?" I felt badly leaving Jonna behind, but saw this as a chance to speak to my father alone, and continue to plead my case.

Arthur and I walked up Bolton Street and turned left on Lydig Avenue. As we walked, we chatted, often raising our voices over the noisy Pelham Parkway El, the elevated train speedily roaring above us. Even though it was early evening, heat still radiated off the concrete pavement. When we got to Rapps, we settled into the comfy red leather bar stools in front of the long soda fountain counter. Arthur gave me a wink. "How about an egg cream?" He knew that besides black licorice, I could live my entire life on egg creams, the concoction of a glob of Fox's U-Bet chocolate syrup, a little milk and a lot of seltzer, well fizzed. How could I leave the Bronx and egg creams, the world's greatest delicacy?

Arthur ceremoniously ordered our drinks. I waited for him to finish chattering about the forthcoming trip. "Arthur, I don't know if you know this, but I'm very worried about Lila and Jonna."

He shifted uncomfortably in his seat. "What is there to worry about?" His eyes glazed over as I tried to pursue the subject. He looked away and struck up a conversation with the waitress. I waited patiently until I felt I had his attention again.

"Arthur, I'm worried. Lila doesn't do anything all day long. She's sleeping when Jonna and I go to school. Then, when we come home from school, it looks like she hasn't left her bed. Something's wrong. It's a little scary."

"Well, your mother gets tired in the heat, you know."

"But you don't see her in the daytime like Jonna and I do," I pleaded. "She's not like the other mothers. After school, when I go down to the street to play, all the mothers, except Lila, are sitting outside talking to each other. And if you need her, like Jonna sometimes does, she grits her teeth and screams and scares her." I tried to make my voice a little stronger so that Arthur would finally listen, but he fidgeted with his shopping list and started to doodle on it.

"That's why it's good we're going to California!"

Listen, for once listen! Help all of us! My sister and me and our mother! I'm afraid something terrible will happen to Jonna because Lila doesn't watch her all the time. And I don't want to go to California, because I don't want to have to keep taking care of them. And anyway, I don't want to move away and leave all my friends because they make my life happier.

I didn't tell him any of this because he had resumed his conversation with the waitress.

Dejected, I said nothing more. I slowly sipped my egg cream through a straw, staring at the counter. I tried to think of a way to get his attention back. He turned away, this time to look out the front window of the candy store and focus on the traffic.

He doesn't know what Lila is like when he's gone. He doesn't pay attention to us or even wonder what goes on in the house all day. Someday, something really bad will happen and then he'll be very sorry.

The continuing silence made me squirm, so I told Arthur about the lake and memories of playing with my cousins and friends, going swimming in the plunge, and making breakfast for Jonna in the large kitchen provided for all the families. "Lila sleeps the whole day when

we're up at the lake. Even Aunt Hedy worries. And all the mothers who
are cooking in the kitchen look at me while I scramble eggs for Jonna and
me. They shake their heads and say, 'poor thing.' It embarrasses me."

"Mmhmm," Arthur mumbled. "You'll see, honey. California will
change everything. Now, come on, Kim. Finish that egg cream. We've
got some shopping to do."

Arthur led me through the aisles of Rapps Candy Store. I passed
my favorite rack filled with comic books, pencils, notebooks, combs,
yoyos and, the most treasured items for any Bronx kid, the baseball and
movie star trading cards and the "Spaldeen" ball.

Arthur picked up a coloring book, and a bright pink ball. "Do you
think Jonna would like this?" I knew Jonna would love the Spaldeen, the
nickname for the pink ball the size of a tennis ball which cost a quarter
and was made by the Spalding Company. On any given day on Bolton
Street, one could hear the thump-a-thump of Spaldeens, accompanied
by "A, my name is Alice and my husband's name is Alan. We live in
Alabama and we sell Apples." I looked at my father and realized for the
first time—even though I was not yet ten years old—that my father did
not want to know or hear about my concerns. I felt deflated and said,
"Oh, yes Arthur! She'll love it." Arthur thought that buying something
solved everything.

I didn't really like my father's false cheer. So many times, he just
glossed over problems as though they weren't happening. His cheerfulness
now only convinced me that I was absolutely right: he hadn't heard me
at all. I glumly followed him through the aisles as he picked out some
hard candies and coloring books. "Tomorrow, these will be fun when
you girls are riding in the car."

"Right, Arthur...they'll be lots of fun." I turned away from him to
wave to a friend who had just entered the candy store.

On the way home I trailed slightly behind him, thinking about
Jonna sitting by the window when we left. So often I was the only
one in charge of Jonna, and constantly cautioning her not to get hurt.
Jonna seemed to court dangerous situations, and I worried about her,

especially when she would lean too far out the big window that looked out over the courtyard to the apartments across the way, to wave at her friend Harry.

How can Jonni take it? She's alone here with Lila when I go to school. Maybe I shouldn't bug her about the window because it's her friend Harry who keeps her going. And she's not going to have Harry in California.

Just this morning I'd had to warn Jonna again about leaning too far out that window. "Jonna, stay away from the window!" I cried. "You're going to fall out, tumble all the way to the ground and smash your head! There's only concrete down there."

I often had nightmares about Jonna falling out the window, seeing her sprawled on the courtyard, her chalk white face staring up at me, her arms and legs a tangled mass wrapped around her body. I'd wake up screaming, calling for someone to help us. Strangely enough, it was Jonna, sleeping in the next bed, who would come and pat my arm. "Wake up, Kim. I'm right here. It's only a dream."

Jonna's response to my warning was to become more resistant and more playful. She'd say, "Kim, I'm only looking at Harry Landsman. He's eating his breakfast. He's looking at me, too. Hi, Harry!" Jonna yelled, excitedly waving her hand at her eight-year-old curly haired neighbor in his red plaid shirt and knickers. I could still hear Jonna's shrill, piping voice echo across the courtyard.

"Do you think he likes eating that terrible oatmeal, that same stuff Lila prepares for us, the goop that makes me want to gag?" Jonna glanced quickly at the closed door of our parents' bedroom located on the opposite side of the foyer of our small, two-bedroom apartment. A frightened look came over her face. "You won't tell Lila that I threw all the oatmeal behind the radiator this morning will you, Kim?"

I knew I would never say anything to Lila. My stomach would drop at the thought of Lila finding out that all of the food she resented making wound up behind the radiator. But I said, half-smiling and in a mock threatening tone, "If you don't move away from that window, I'll go wake Lila this very minute and tell her that you threw the oatmeal she made out the window this morning, and you even stuffed her dry hamburger patties behind the radiator the other night at dinner when she wasn't looking." I pointed to the long, creviced, standing radiator which ran the length of the window.

Jonna laughed, "Oh Kim, you'd never do that. She'd throw *me* out the window." Jonna laughed, and I wished I could have laughed with her. But I couldn't. I lived in a perpetual state of worry that some day, in a fit of rage, Lila *would* indeed do just that.

At least in California I won't have that big old window to worry about. Maybe our new house in California is different and only has one story so I won't have to be scared about Jonna.

My father and I entered the apartment as Jonna was going towards our bedroom. She looked right at me and saw my grim look. "Kim? Are you okay?" I put my arm around her and whispered that I was sad about leaving. Later I lay in my bed in the dark, my thoughts about leaving and California and my mother and sister swirling around in my head. The edge of my mattress gave a little as Jonna crept into my bed and said, in her small voice, "Kim, can you talk to me for a little while?"

"Yes, of course." I remembered that this morning she had said good-bye to Harry. I turned to comfort her, and we talked a lot about how much we loved our friends Stuey and Jimmy and, particularly, Harry and Rita Goldman.

"We'll never, ever have other friends like them, will we, Kim?"

"Who knows, Jonni, we could meet some great friends in California, too."

"I wish Lila were more like you and Harry. You both answer all my questions all the time. But Lila, she screams and stamps her foot at me.

She says, 'Enough questions, Jonna,' even though I've just asked her one. 'Just leave me alone!' she says. You and Harry never do that."

"Lila has a lot on her mind, Jonna. She doesn't have patience like Aunt Hedy. Sometimes, she doesn't answer my questions either." This was a little white lie to make Jonna feel better because Lila, no matter how distressed, always responded to me, even though I didn't always like her answers. But I didn't want Jonna to suspect what I felt to be true. For reasons I never understood, Lila did not like Jonna and treated her more harshly than she did me. I tried to be as gentle as possible. "Maybe California will make Lila listen more to your questions and treat you better. And about Harry, I know how much you like him," I said softly, to the dark mass of my sister's hair spread out just below my chin. "But like I said before, you'll make lots of new friends in California."

"I'm not so sure, Kim. Harry's the only one who makes me feel special. It's this thing that Arthur talks about sometimes. On Sundays when he got bagels and lox for our breakfast, he'd tell Lila that people have to feel they're important to another human bean. I didn't really understand. But whenever Harry takes my hand to cross the street, or he's playing stickball with the other kids and he looks at me and says, 'This home run is for you Jonni,' I feel so good in a way I never felt before. I feel I'm an important human bean."

I smiled, not bothering to correct "bean" and supply "being." "You know what I think, Jonni? I think you are a very special person and I also think you and Harry will always have a bond."

"You mean like Lila and Arthur bought during the war?"

I couldn't stifle my laugh. "No, Jonni, those are war bonds. The other kind of bond is a special kind of closeness that two people have with each other."

"Oh yeah," she said. But I suspected she really didn't grasp the idea. I felt so sorry for her. My sister's trust in Harry was touching. She told me many little stories about him. Each evening, Jonna would tell me about her visits to apartment 3C, when Harry's mother Jen would let her in so that the two could visit and play. Harry taught Jonna board games like Parcheesi, Monopoly, and chess. Harry had had a serious accident with a clothes hanger piercing his nose and cheek, so he had to stay in for two or three weeks until it healed. I thought I heard Lila tell a friend that Harry's mother, in a fit of temper, had thrown the hanger at him. Whatever it was, Harry looked forward to Jonna's knock every day, almost as much as she looked forward to seeing him.

That last night in the Bronx, Jonna and I talked for a long time. Then, she suddenly hopped out of my bed. "Guess what, Kim? Harry gave me a present today. Should I show it to you?"

"Show me." I switched on the little lamp next to my bed. Jonna returned and scrambled up beside me, carrying a box of Crayola crayons and a large writing pad. I watched as she tenderly turned to one of the pages of the large pad. Harry had written, "To Jonni, the best friend I've ever had. Draw me a picture of your trip on every page, then come back soon and give all of them to me. I'll miss you a lot…Harry."

I turned my face to the wall. I didn't want Jonna to see my tears. Harry was the only safe harbor Jonna had and she went every day to the window to seek him out. She hated to leave that harbor. What would happen to her, and to us, now?

Jonna's voice echoed in my mind. She had found the one person, across the courtyard, who made her feel important. Although the gaping window was wide and unprotected, by waiting like a sentinel every day to connect to her only friend, she had found a way to find protection and make her life bearable. Looking through the window had changed her life.

But then, I wondered, weren't Lila and Arthur seekers too? Wasn't this move not just to get away from people who could hurt Arthur— those people he often talked about, and Lila screamed about—who thought he was a bad person, and wanted to silence him, but to give all of us a different kind of life?

Suddenly, I was not as mad at Arthur and Lila as I had been. As I drifted into sleep, I could hear Lila's heavy steps as she moved from closet to closet checking to make sure that all of them were empty. Then,

I pictured Arthur and Lila in the foyer, examining all of the suitcases which lay open on the floor. They were whispering because they didn't want to wake us, and I could not hear exactly what they were saying. I imagined, though, that they were deciding what items to take and what they did not want to take. I could even see Lila hold up her thick black winter coat and tossing it on the little sofa in the foyer. I heard her say, "Well Arty, in California I'm certainly not going to need this thing any more."

Tomorrow morning, all our lives were about to change. I felt scared, and had the thought that maybe Lila and Arthur were also scared. Yet, on the other hand, scared as they might be, they had opened for us another kind of window. Their packing finished, Lila and Arthur had stopped whispering and had turned off their bedroom light. I fell asleep with the thought that maybe the big change Lila and Arthur were giving us was a new life in California.

Chapter 2

Deep in sleep, I felt a rocking motion and dreamt I was on a boat in the ocean. Gradually I realized there was someone's hand on my shoulder. "Kim, Jonna, time to wake up! We've got some traveling to do!" I had fallen asleep so late; it took me a while to open my eyes. Even then, I couldn't see very well. Through half-opened eyes, I peered up at my father.

"Arthur," I protested. "It's still dark outside."

"I know, but we have to get an early start to beat the heat. Your mother has breakfast ready, and Aunt Marion wants to say good-bye to you too."

Jonna and I sleepily got out of bed and stumbled into the kitchen, where we smelled bacon frying, almost burning to a crisp, typical Lila style. Lila was chatting animatedly with Marion, one of her oldest friends, who had become like an adoptive aunt to Jonna and me. We thought Marion was a very nice lady. She never came over without bringing us a little gift.

"Kim! Jonna!" Marion seemed so glad to see us, and held out packages for us to open.

"Thank you, Aunt Marion," Jonna and I said in a sleepy chorus. We sat down and unwrapped our presents. Mine was a new Nancy Drew book; Jonna's a large coloring book with a box of Crayolas. She always seemed to pick our favorites.

"Well," said Marion, "I guess I better let you all get to it. Have a wonderful, safe trip." She tearfully hugged Lila and then Arthur, who seemed to pull away from her slightly. I always thought that the way Marion and Arthur looked at each other was so funny. I didn't know how to explain it, it just felt strange.

As Jonna and I labored through our breakfast, Uncle Mort strode into the kitchen, tapping his wristwatch. "You know, Arthur, we need to get going—it will be getting hot out there on the highway pretty soon."

Lila swept our plates away from us, letting us know we didn't need to clean them. Jonna and I scurried off to cram the last few things into our suitcases. Then we did a lot of traipsing up and down the stairs to put things in Mort and Winnie's no-longer-roomy trunk.

It was 7:30 a.m. when we left Pelham Parkway. I felt sad as I stared out the window of the car. None of my friends had showed up to say good-bye. Was it too early? Or too hot?

It was July 8th, four days before my tenth birthday. Had I made a mistake telling my friends that Aunt Winnie's house in California had a swimming pool? Were they jealous? It never occurred to me that maybe my friends couldn't bear to see me leave.

Our car passed Bronx High School of Science, where many of my friends would go to school in a few years and I would not. We passed the Bronx Botanical Gardens and the Bronx Zoo and I knew it would be a long time before I saw these places again. I thought of the fun times I had at the zoo with Rita and Jimmy and the rest of my friends. I promised myself I would come back some day. I closed my eyes, trying not to cry, and dozed off.

Two hours later, I awoke with a start. Where were we? I didn't recognize any of the places we were passing.

"Aunt Winnie, can we please stop and get some drinks or something? I think I'm going to be sick."

"How many times can we stop, Kim? We've been on the road less than two hours and we've already stopped twice for Jonna. We can't stop every time you say you have to go to the bathroom, or need to stretch your legs, or say you're hungry. Isn't it enough that we let you girls sit by the windows?" Aunt Winnie asked sharply. "At this rate, we'll never get to California!"

Aunt Winnie glared at me through the tiny rear view mirror above her, then back to concentrating on the road ahead as well to the direction signs indicating "New Jersey Turnpike—13 miles" at the side of the road. When she saw me stick my head outside of the open car window, though, her tone quickly changed.

"If you're going to be sick," she said more kindly, "I'll stop immediately. Are you?"

I pulled my head back in. "No, I'll be all right. I'm just a little nervous." I fidgeted back and forth on the wide back seat of Aunt Winnie and Uncle Mort's 1947 four-door Dodge D24 Custom sedan. Arthur said it was "the deluxe car of the century." "Oww," I yelped, as my already sticky thigh came in contact with a new spot on the hot leather seat.

The week before, Aunt Winnie and Uncle Mort had arrived from Los Angeles, where they'd been living since they left New York five years ago. Aunt Winnie was Arthur's younger sister and Arthur told me she kept asking him to take a teaching job out on the west coast and buy a house not far from where she and my Uncle Mort lived in West Los Angeles. What Jonna and I didn't know was that when Arthur and Lila finally made the decision to move to California, Aunt Winnie and Uncle Mort drove to New York for a vacation with the idea that we'd leave with them on their return trip to California.

They had driven up to our apartment house on Bolton Street to show off their new tan car with green trim, the car we were going to use for the California trip. The car was beautiful. It was sleek and very long, with shiny chrome door handles. With its bulbous curves and elongated front end, it seemed as large as a truck. But I was discovering that riding in it and sharing the space with five other people was a different story. I felt so squashed that with each turn in the road, I bumped into Lila sitting next to me. Lila, in turn, bumped into Arthur on her right.

Jonna sat in the front next to the window and just to the right of

Aunt Winnie and Uncle Mort. She had her nose pressed so hard against the window I was convinced it would be flattened by the end of the trip. I wondered if Jonna felt like she was going to be sick as well.

I bit my nails and looked down at the packet of cards on my lap. Rita Hayworth smiled up at me from the stack of "Movie Stars of Hollywood." Glenn Ford, his wry smile set in his handsome face, had a friendly look. Then came my favorite, Margaret O'Brien. Mrs. Glaser, my third grade teacher, saw *Miracle on 34th Street* and told me I looked exactly like Margaret O'Brien, which made me feel very special.

Looking down at the twelve cards from Rita Goldman's precious collection, I began to feel weepy. Rita and I had been collecting movie star cards since we were seven. After the war, Fleers Double Bubble Gum issued a movie star card with each sheet of bubble gum. Whenever I could wrangle five cents from Arthur for the gum, I would rush to Rapps Candy Store, buy the gum and excitedly open the wrapper to see who the star of the week was. Sometimes, Arthur would treat Rita to a Fleers, making the rush to Rapps even better.

Every Saturday morning since we were five years old, Rita and I met at Rapps Candy Store. We'd share an egg salad sandwich on rye toast and a chocolate malt, and when we got older we'd go to the movies at the RKO Pelham across the street. When we were sipping the last malt we would ever sip together, Rita looked at me and said, "I hope you have a great trip, Kim. The day before you leave, I'm going to give you these cards and have you get them autographed by all of these stars and then bring them to me when you come back. That way, I know you'll be back. I wish I could come with you, and I hope you don't stay in California long cause I'll miss you a lot." She gave me a long hug, and told me that her mom had given her twenty-five cents to treat me to the movies and a box of Good 'N Plenty candies, my favorite, as a going away gift. I was so flustered, I could only mutter a faint "thank you" and hug her back. Then, since I knew I wasn't going to tell Rita that this was not just a vacation, I let her go on about how three months is such a long time to be away from a best friend.

The night before we were to leave, I wrote in my diary:

Today I saw the last movie I'm ever going to see at the RKO Pelham. When I come back here some day, I bet the RKO will be gone. And all of my friends will be too. I wish we weren't going. It's not exciting, even though Lila says it will be, and I don't care that it's not cold or snowy in California. Lila hates the cold. She says the tips of her fingers freeze. But how does she know that won't happen in California too? I don't want to leave here. And anyway, there's no snow in California so I had to give up my sled, my Rapid Flyer. They said it was too much to carry in the car, so I gave it to Jimmie Snyder's little sister, Lana. I didn't want to, but I did.

In four days, I'll be ten years old. I can't even go to Castle Heights Swimming Plunge with all my friends for my birthday like I have since I was six—except for the one year the polio epidemic came and they closed the Plunge—because on my birthday, we'll be on this road called "66." Whoever heard of a road named "66"? Arthur says it's famous. All the stars in my movie star card collection, he said, rode on it to California. Arthur always comes up with something like that so no one should feel sad. But I feel sad. And Jonni feels sad. We'll miss the Bronx. It's like a small village. Everyone knows each other and when Lila sleeps the morning away, especially in the summer, there are so many "play mothers" out in front of their stoops sitting in chairs and reading Ellery Queen. And during Lila's "blue periods," these other mothers fix me lunch, and let me use their bathroom when I have to go.

Today Rita and I saw a movie called Gentleman's Agreement. *It was all about this guy, Gregory Peck, and his friend John Garfield and this uptight-looking lady, Dorothy McGuire. Rita and I have movie cards of all of them, and so Gregory pretends to be Jewish because he's really a reporter and he wants to expose anti-*

semanticism. Rita's mother told us when she was walking us home from the RKO Pelham that anti-semanticism, I think that's how you pronounce it, meant people who don't like Jewish people. Rita and I were confused because we knew lots of them and we were Jewish too and we thought we're all okay people. So, her mother just shrugged her shoulders and said, "What people don't understand, they are afraid of and so they single certain people out and treat them badly."

I asked Arthur what anti-semanticism was, but he was writing an important letter about a job, he said, to some people in a university in Los Angeles and he couldn't be bothered. He said his letter had something to do with political beliefs and loyalty oaths and all that. I have to go to sleep now, diary, because tomorrow I have to stuff my suitcase before I leave. I can only take one suitcase on the trip, so I had to give lots of clothes away. We took all the giveaways over to Aunt Viola's, my Italian Catholic aunt, and she's taking them to her church, Santa Lucia, on Allerton Avenue, for the poor children. Arthur says in California they only wear bathing suits or shorts and a top, so I don't feel too bad that I had to give those winter clothes away. Goodnight, Diary.

We were completing our ride over the New Jersey Turnpike and nearing Harrisburg Pike on Highway 11 in Pennsylvania. We planned to go through West Virginia and then Ohio where, after a ten hour drive, we'd spend the night in something called a "motel."

"I wonder if a motel is like a hotel, only littler." I said to Jonna.

Arthur awakened from dozing in the back seat. "Good thinking, Kim, that's exactly right. There are many motels on Route 66. Some of them even have swimming pools!"

Jonna and I perked up immediately.

"Oh boy, does that mean we can get out of this hot box and go swimming?" I asked.

Aunt Winnie and Uncle Mort laughed. "Not only can you go swimming, they even have a gift shop in some of these motels and you two can start a collection of souvenir pins for the sailor hats that we bought you."

Jonna finally pulled her nose away from the closed window. I sat forward, waiting eagerly for Aunt Winnie to find the first motel so we could jump into the pool in our new bathing suits.

To pass the time, I read Burma Shave billboards to Jonna ("You can't help but win, with a Burma Shave smooth chin"), or played games with everyone in the car like License Plates and The Alphabet Game. For License Plates, we would pick out a car on the highway, then Aunt Winnie would try to pull close to the car and all of us would read its rear license plate. Whoever had guessed the highest number closest to the license plate number would win. In between West Virginia and Ohio, I won five out of six games. For The Alphabet Game, someone would start with a letter, and then have to think of an animal, vegetable or mineral that went with that letter. Arthur won almost every Alphabet game because of his amazing vocabulary.

When we finally arrived at the Cozycuzzin Inn, an hour out of Cleveland, Ohio, I was already fast asleep again in the back seat. Jonna, nestled on Uncle Mort's chest, was also out like a light. The four hour drive from West Virginia had been grueling. The Dodge wheezed and pinged. The burlap sack of water draped across the front of the car's radiator, and intended to act as an air conditioner, had turned from cold to warm to hot within an hour. It hadn't provided much relief.

The rotund proprietor of the Cozycuzzin had a stomach so large that Jonna whispered to me, "Do you think his belly will blow up? It's so huge!"

"No," I laughed and whispered back, "Jonni, that isn't nice. Anyway, he's smiling at us and he seems kind of friendly."

His belly preceded him by what seemed to me like a full city block, but Mr. Portman looked like Santa Claus and greeted us warmly. "Well, well, and what do we have here? Two little pretties, I must say. Well, are you ready for the pool?"

Jonna and I beamed.

"Everyone that comes through here, and I must say there have been many folks crossing over this highway since early morn, can't wait to get into that pool—but beware, we keep it plenty freezing!"

Our beams froze.

"How freezing?" I asked.

Mr. Portman guffawed heartily. "It will be a heck of a lot cooler than the car you just came from." He glanced at the car, covered with dust from radiator grille to back fender. "Looks like you folks poured out of a hot box. So, maybe it don't matter if it's freezing or not, you gotta go now and take a dip."

Lila fished around in the back of the Dodge for a suitcase filled with clothes and towels. She had heard rumors that motels on Route 66 provided very few amenities and that large towels were a rarity.

Arthur ran over to the office of the motel to buy a newspaper. Soon after he opened the paper, I could see him shaking his head back and forth. He turned to Uncle Mort, who had just finished registering for the room.

"Can you believe this, Mort? They succeeded in making HUAC a standing committee. Congress really has some gall to take this committee seriously." Arthur had an angry look on his face.

"I thought HUAC was started to investigate the Ku Klux Klan and other organizations in America like it," Mort said.

"It was started for that purpose," said Arthur, "but in these hysterical times where everyone is terrified of being called anti-American, they had the audacity to say something like, 'the Klan has become an American institution. We have more to fear from Reds in our midst.'" With that, Arthur thrust the front page of the newspaper at Uncle Mort while pointing to a large black and white photograph of John Parnell Thomas, HUAC's chairman, smiling at the press.

"This is only the beginning," Uncle Mort said. "I'm glad you're getting out of New York when you are, Arty. You don't need them hounding you."

Mr. Portman stood listening. His smiling face became a frowning one. Silently, but politely, he showed us to our room, Cozycuzzin Number Three, located very close to the highway and right next door to Aunt Winnie and Uncle Mort's room, Cozycuzzin Number Two. I heard him whisper something to the bell boy who was helping with the luggage. It sounded like, "I think we've got some 'Commies' among us." I reminded myself to ask Arthur what Commies were.

After we were in the tiny motel room, Lila opened the suitcase she had retrieved from the car and took out two large orange towels, and Jonna's and my brand new bathing suits.

"All right kids, here's your suits and towels and for goodness sake, try not to drown."

"Stop that, Lila," Arthur cautioned my mother. "You'll scare them."

"Arthur, I'm just warning them. This is a strange swimming pool and anything could happen."

Jonna and I didn't wait to hear the end of our parents' discussion. We were in and out of the tiny bathroom and on our way to the pool behind the motel in a flash. We arrived to find the pool crammed with children of all ages, accompanied by one or both of their parents.

"This reminds me of being in the crowded car we just came from," I complained to Jonna. We put our towels on nearby chaise lounges and walked to the side of the pool. We stood there until we heard a voice calling to us from the middle of the pool.

"Hey there you guys, I done saw yew on the road—cummin in?"

We looked out over the sea of bodies and spotted a tow-headed boy, about Jonna's age, beckoning us with both hands. We smiled and I walked down the steps of the pool into the water. Mr. Portman was right. The water was freezing!

I swam out to the boy. He smiled and extended his right hand to shake mine. "Howdy. I'm Ezra Lyons. From *Caintucky*. We're on our way to Hollywood. And you? Are you guys going west too?"

As I took his hand, I was surprised at his friendliness. "I'm Kim and that's my sister Jonna and yes, we're going to Los Angeles. I guess that's like Hollywood." I suddenly realized Jonna was not by my side. I got concerned because she was afraid of the water. I turned around. Jonna stood shivering on the step. "C'mon, Jonni, swim out here," I called. I held up both of my arms to show her the water wasn't too deep.

Jonna shook her head and lingered on the pool step. "Not yet, Kim, it's too cold."

"It sure am cold Jonna," Ezra said, in his Kentucky mountain accent, "but you'll see how warm it gets once you get in. Come meet my older brother Willard. We'll all swim together."

Jonna kept her hands crossed over her chest, but smiled and hesitantly walked down the remaining step into the pool. In less than a minute, the two brothers became our friends and we were comparing notes about our Route 66 drive. Jonna and I introduced Ezra and Willard to our new game, counting numbers on license plates.

Two hours later, as the sun was setting, we got out of the Cozycuzzin swimming pool with our new friends. Our lips were blue and we felt chilled to the bone. We had already agreed to try to eat at each other's table in the motel's family style restaurant. We heard from others at the pool that Mr. Portman's wife, Edith, cooked a mean southern style fried chicken.

When Jonna and I got back to the room, Lila and Arthur, heads close together, were poring over maps, underlining in red pencils the sights and cities we'd see the next day. How rare and wonderful to not hear them bickering and yelling at each other, I thought. They seemed so relaxed. Lila's face looked flushed, and Arthur looked a little rumpled. I guessed that while Jonna and I were swimming, they both had time for a much needed nap.

After a filling dinner of delicious fried chicken, we sleepily stumbled back to our room. Lila unpacked her own nightgown, as well as two wrinkled pairs of cotton pajamas for us. As we readied ourselves for bed in the cramped motel room, I turned to Arthur, "You know, this isn't going to be as bad as I thought. This road number 66 might be fun."

Arthur smiled. "That's what they say, Kim. You get your kicks on Route 66. You never know who or what you're going to run into. And tomorrow we're going to enter Indiana and then Illinois, and visit Springfield where Abraham Lincoln lived."

The cramped motel room had three beds: a double bed for Arthur and Lila, and two cot-like single beds for me and Jonna. I lay in bed excited about tomorrow's prospects, and hoped that Jonna and I and Ezra and Willard wound up in the same motel in Springfield, Illinois. Within moments, the dim yellow lights of the motel room were turned off and all of us fell asleep instantly.

Left to right: Hollywood actors Gene Kelly, Humphrey Bogart, Paul Henreid and Richard Conte embarking for Washington, D.C. in October of 1947. As members of the Committee for the First Amendment (CFA), they and other actors, including Marsha Hunt, traveled to Washington, D.C. to witness the proceedings of the House Unamerican Activities Committee, chaired by J. Parnell Thomas (R-NJ).

"I had been on that chartered plane in 1947 that...close to 30 of us—filmmakers, actors, directors and even Ira Gershwin— took to protest what was happening at the HUAC hearings in Washington...I didn't know or care about Communism. I was terribly worried about what we were doing to democracy."

—Marsha Hunt, actress and a member of the CFA, speaking at the 60th anniversary of the Writers Guild of America restoring screen credits to formerly blacklisted writers. The event, "Hollywood Strikes Back...Again," was co-sponsored by the ACLU Foundation of Southern California and PEN USA in October of 2007. Photo courtesy of Miriam Harriss.

Chapter 3

"I could answer the question exactly the way you want, but if I did, I would hate myself in the morning."

—Ring Lardner, Jr. replying to J. Parnell Thomas, Chairman of HUAC, 1947

A horn was blaring. I awakened, looked over at my brand-new Benson alarm clock, and saw that it was nine o'clock, pretty early on a Sunday for such loud noise. Stumbling over to the window of the bedroom I shared with Jonna, I peered out beyond the five neatly planted oleander bushes fanned out across the lawn. There was my father doing the impossible. He was driving down our street in a huge 1941 green Chevrolet. Lila, in her bathrobe, was out on the front lawn of our new tract house clapping her hands like a child, applauding her "conquering hero."

Things had gone so fast since we left the Bronx. It didn't seem that long since we'd been driving in Aunt Winnie's car to get to California. But now, with my father behind the wheel of his own car, the Bronx seemed very far away. It was an interesting chain of events that led my father to purchase a car. Just a week ago, I had overheard the early morning telephone call he got from Don Carleton, his friend and fellow faculty member at LACC. Both of them were also guest lecturers at UCLA and Don would drive Arthur each Thursday to the university.

"Don, I can't believe what you're telling me," Arthur said. "I'm flabbergasted. How could they do that to you? You've made such a great contribution to the department. On what grounds are they dismissing you?"

Still in my pajamas, I came into the kitchen and watched Arthur pace, clenching and unclenching his fists. He often did that when he was worried. "That's awful. So, you think it's because of the salary board business with LACC? Is that why? Or is it your political affiliations?"

Don Carleton and his wife Till lived only three blocks away. They often came to dinner at our house. Don was a very tall, stocky guy with a razor edge wit and a blustery, openly expressive way. He and Arthur would sit for hours discussing HUAC becoming a standing committee, the "Red Scare tide" at LACC and UCLA, the politics of Los Angeles, and the up and coming 1948 presidential elections. They both intended to campaign for Henry Wallace. Don was also an officer in the newly founded Independent Progressive Party and very involved in its political scene. Till was one of Lila's mah jongg buddies. I could tell by Arthur's tone that he seemed frightened by Don's dismissal. "Don, how can we help? Is there anything we can do for you and Till?"

Phone in hand, Arthur looked around the room for a place to sit down. I was sitting on the chair in the kitchen closest to the phone, so I jumped up and leaned against the kitchen wall to make room for my father.

"Yeah, Don, I'll hold." Arthur cupped his hand over the phone. "Where's your mother, Kim?"

"I don't know Dad; I think she's over at Agnes's planning next week's mah jongg game schedule."

"I don't want her to hear any of this. It might set her off. Please don't repeat any of it."

I got nervous. Whenever I had to keep one of my parents' secrets, I felt like a traitor, like I was being forced to ally with one against the other. It happened a lot. One of my parents would confide in me and ask me to keep it from the other. It made me feel terribly guilty. I also felt like a human ping-pong ball.

"I won't say anything, Dad, but won't she hear it from Till when they play mah jongg next week?"

"Probably, but I'd rather have some time to talk to her about it and explain it, and…" Just then Don must have come back to the phone because Arthur turned away from me.

"I can't believe you're going to have to move. Is the position they've offered you at Reed guaranteed? Of course I will, Don. I'd be glad to buy your car. You name the price. I'll make an appointment at the new DMV to get my driver's license."

Back in the Bronx, I never thought I'd ever be living in a house, let alone see my father driving. Apartments in New York were a way of life. I had seen Don Carleton's car when he came to pick up Arthur. It seemed two times bigger than Aunt Winnie's new Dodge that we brought to California. I could hardly imagine my father behind the wheel of a giant car.

But sure enough, Don brought the car over later that week, and even drove Arthur down to the DMV so he could get his license. Now I felt we were real Californians.

I was brought back from my reverie by Arthur, who was continuing to blow the horn, as if to announce to the world that with his new found mobility, he was, indeed, conquering the new West. Taking my mother's cue, I decided it would be all right to go outside in our bathrobes. Excited, I said, "C'mon, Jonna, let's go see what Arthur's doing with our new car."

As Jonna and I came out the front door, John McVey, our neighbor, stuck his head out his window and shouted: "Hey Art, where did you get that smashing hot rod?"

McVey's friendly greeting diverted Arthur's attention just enough so that he failed to realize that he was now careening onto our front lawn. He narrowly missed Lila who grabbed us, dashing into the garage for safety.

Gritting his teeth, his eyes agape, Arthur looked horrified as he tried to control the huge machine. It crashed into the five newly-planted oleanders which were supposed to act as a protective hedge on the front lawn.

John McVey and Phil Coulter, dressed in suits and ready for church, came running across their lawns shouting and waving their hands. "Arty, just step on the brake. Step on the brake! Not the gas, the brake!"

Arthur seemed to emerge from his trance and succeeded in bringing the car to a stop, narrowly avoiding the side of the garage. The loud squeal of the brakes was followed by the engine dying.

"For God's sake, Arty, you almost killed us like you killed our trees." Lila had a knack for stating the obvious.

By this time, all of the neighbors were awake on Oakwood Avenue, standing in their doorways or out on their lawns, shaking their heads from side to side. Ian McDonald, his four-year-old daughter Mattie on his shoulders, called out, "Arty, next stop Indianapolis!"

Arthur, still gripping the steering wheel, had turned ashen. He looked terrified. I was mortified. *I can hardly wait to write Rita and have her tell all the kids back in the Bronx about this!*

"Boy, you New Yorkers have an interesting way of learning to drive!" said John McVey good-naturedly. He helped Arthur out of the car, and urged him to set and then double-check the parking brake. I took Jonna's hand and went back into the house. I looked over my shoulder to see John put his hand reassuringly on Arthur's shoulder, giving him more advice.

Lila was already preparing a typical Lebow Sunday breakfast. The eggs were over-fried, the bacon wilted and listless. I was thankful for the only saving grace of Sunday mornings: fresh bagels from Brown's Bakery that Arthur brought home after his now-infamous foray as a California driver.

We forged our way through breakfast in complete silence. No one said a word about what John McVey called "Smarty Arty's Chevy Party," and no one ever would. That's the way things were handled in our household. Arthur didn't like to be confronted with anything negative. Maybe he'd had enough of that from Lila. Jonna and I learned to avoid talking about anything that would upset him. I often wondered if Jonna's frequent stomach aches were a combination of Lila's cooking and not talking enough about things that troubled her.

I learned to focus my attention on what I enjoyed. I loved to look at the bright, yellow flowered wallpaper in our tiny kitchen. It was my favorite room in our new house. I did everything there. I talked on the phone to the few friends I had been able to make. I sat at the kitchen table every day and did my homework that I brought home from the newly built Coldwater Canyon elementary school several blocks from my house. I sat for hours on weekend mornings and listened to Lila, after her fourth cup of coffee, reminisce about her family and friends in the Bronx. Lila seemed so much softer when she talked about her world back east. The small yellow kitchen was cozy and comforting.

On our trip west, Lila explained to Jonna and me that the new housing development we were moving into in the Valley was like an interracial experiment on the order of Levittown—a novel, post-war housing community—and was built in 1946 by a steel czar named Henry Kaiser. So far, I didn't notice any people of different races in my walks around the neighborhood. Back in the Bronx, I always thought the whole world was composed of Jews and Chinese people, because that's who I saw every day: thousands of Jewish families and a laundry run by a very industrious immigrant Chinese family. I was very puzzled if anyone went to school or work on Yom Kippur. Why, I wondered, would anyone go to school on a national holiday?

The Valley, the people in it, and our house were a whole new world. Everything was brand new in our little tract house, and it was much roomier than our apartment in the Bronx. We weren't piled on top of each other. We had two bedrooms, a living room, dining area, kitchen, one bathroom, outdoor patio and backyard. My parents told us they put everything they owned into the house. One-bedroom homes in our part of North Hollywood sold for $6,480, but ours was $8,500. Ours cost more because of the extra bedroom, the patio, and the size of our backyard, which was a little larger than most, although still very small.

In the summer, we barbequed in our backyard. I often sat in the sunshine on the patio adjacent to the house and played games with Jonna or read. I loved my Nancy Drew mystery books and had read no less than five of them since we arrived in California.

Even though I still worried about Lila's up and down moods, she seemed to have more energy for fixing up the house and settling into the new tract life. She had already met a group of friends through a New York acquaintance. Several were émigrés from New York, and several others were from Chicago and Detroit. Soon, Lila had a foursome for bridge and was playing mah jongg once a week.

Both Jonna and I had a lot of trouble making friends because everything in the Valley was so spread out. So, I took up my role as big sister and tried to keep her occupied. When we finally made a few friends, we would all play "potsy"—which my new friends called hopscotch—on the patio or jump rope.

Arthur was either teaching at LACC or away at the many faculty meetings he was expected to attend. He promised me I could go with him on the Red Car to LACC for one of his classes when I got a little older. He had to get up at 6:00 a.m. to make the 7:00 a.m. Red Car to Hollywood, then switch to another Red Car going east on Santa Monica Boulevard to Vermont Boulevard where he would then get off and take the bus to the college. Despite this difficult morning commute, Arthur was pleased with the number of friends he had made and particularly pleased with the history and political science courses he was teaching. On his days off, he often accompanied Lila, Jonna, and me to the El Portal, North Hollywood's only movie theater. Jonna and I saw our first movie in California at that theater: *The Wistful Widow of Wagon Gap* with Bud Abbott and Lou Costello. All of us laughed a lot and it felt good, because laughing together was rare in our family.

Thanks to Arthur's job, he and Lila were making a few friends. Discovering that Don and Till lived only three blocks away was "a bonus," said Arthur, and the two couples become close friends right away. Usually, when Don and Till came for dinner, there was a lot of fun and joking around. But on this evening, the week Arthur got Don's car, the foursome talked in a more serious tone about Arthur and Don's faculty positions and the political climate at the college.

Till's voice sounded worried. "I've been hearing that the House Un-American Activities Committee is starting to make inquiries at the College. Is this true? I've also heard that two faculty members in your department have been threatened with dismissal. What is this all about?"

Instantly I saw Lila go pale, and turn toward Arthur. For once, Arthur did not try to minimize or lighten the subject for my mother's benefit.

"It's not just here in California at UCLA or LACC; I really think this country is experiencing such a Red Scare that it's affecting not only teachers and university faculty, but is touching everyone. Even us. There's been talk that faculty at the University of California and other state systems will be forced to sign a loyalty oath. Already several have spoken up, saying that as Americans their allegiance should not be questioned. They're very outspoken about it. I hope their colleagues support them. I certainly would."

Lila pressed her lips together, like she always did when she was really angry. I tried to understand what everyone was so upset about, and shuddered inwardly, because I knew what was coming. And, sure enough, it came: Lila exploded.

"You certainly *would*? Don't you care what happens to your job, or to us?" As the Carletons looked on, Lila did not bother to hide her fear. She turned toward Don. "I'm terrified and furious that some day you and Arthur might be called up before that HUAC committee," she said. "Your progressive politics and your loud way of talking about your views will bring trouble to all of us." Lila began to cry, and Till put her hand on her shoulder to comfort her.

I couldn't wait to get away from the dinner table. Jonna, too, began to look frightened. In the past, whenever these discussions took place, I would excuse myself, go to my room and write in my diary. This was my way of trying to sort out what was happening and make sense of my world and my parents.

Jonna and I looked like we were at a tennis match, our heads turning left as Lila spoke, then right as Don and Arthur responded. Till handed Lila a tissue and Lila wiped her tears away. Then, she threw her napkin on the table: "Nothing will change you, Arthur. Do what you have to do. Don't think about anyone else." Lila angrily pushed herself back from the table, and ran out of the room into her bedroom, slamming the door behind her.

Don got up, and put on his jacket. "We'd better go, Art. Till and I will keep you posted. I'm due at Reed in Oregon for my hiring interview by the end of the week, and I'll let you know what they say. And by the way, thanks a lot about the car. It was a great relief with all our other worries."

Till got up, came around the table, and bent down to hug Jonna and me, still seated at the kitchen table. "I know you kids must find it hard to understand what you're hearing, it must seem so senseless," she said, her voice gentle and tender as always. "But someday, when you're older, Arthur can explain to you how important all this is, and what it will mean for your future." Till went over to Arthur, put her hand on his shoulder, and leaned down. We heard her whisper: "Stick to your guns!"

I felt so sad. By the way Jonna was looking down at the table, it looked like she felt sad too. We both went to our bedroom after Don and Till left. I lay on my bed continuing a letter to my friend Rita in New York that I had begun months ago on our trip. I'd been avoiding writing the letter because what I had to write, I knew, would make Rita unhappy.

Dear Rita,

This is so hard for me to tell you but I think I'm going to have to return the movie star cards you gave me that I was supposed to keep until I returned from California. Well, it's turned out that we're not just going to be here for a vacation. Arthur and Lila bought this tract house in North Hollywood. They told us about all this after we stayed with Aunt Winnie for a few weeks, while we waited for our house in North Hollywood to be ready. They also told us we should all be very excited about moving into it in at the end of July. Well, we weren't all that excited. That's how Arthur and Lila do things. They make all the arrangements and then dump it on Jonna and me. It's like we have no say in the matter. Bip, we're not going back to New York. Bip, we're moving into a new house. Bip, you're gonna like it or lump it. I'm very sad, because l miss you and our gang terribly. I had no idea this was a forever move. Even though I love the climate, and the people are very friendly, and it's like living in the country, because all you see around our new house are avocado and orange groves, and lots of open washes. It's just very different than the Bronx, and I'll never have another friend like you. One of the things I've thought about is either I could return your cards that you gave me and I love, or I could wait to meet movie stars and have them sign them and send them back to you. It's the least I can do since I'm the one that's leaving you forever. Yes, that's what I'll do, I'm going to see if I can get all of your cards autographed. But I hope you'll write to me anyways because I haven't met many kids and I don't have a lot of people to talk to. Please write cuz I really miss you and our gang a lot and I'm lonely.

Love, your dearest friend forever more, Kim

I folded up the letter and put it in an envelope. It felt like another good-bye to my beloved Bronx neighborhood. Not that all the reminders from the Bronx were gone, though. The next day, after school, as we did at least once a week, Jonna and I walked down to the only local market, Thatcher's, to buy milk and eggs or other sundries that Lila had forgotten to buy. The first time we returned home from one of our grocery trips on a hot summer afternoon, we had entered our house and heard familiar sounds: "one bam," "two crak," "three dot." I had turned to Jonna. "It's like we're back in the Bronx again!"

We knew immediately that the mah jongg sounds meant we weren't to disturb Lila, who sat in our living room at a bridge table, surrounded by three other women, all very intent on the game they were playing. When we entered, no one looked up.

"I'm kinda glad Lila found some friends," Jonna said, as we put away the groceries and tiptoed to our bedroom, hearing the bams, craks, and dots again and again.

The mah jongg sounds took me back to my old neighborhood in the Bronx. As far back as I could remember, I had often fallen asleep to the rhythms and strains of mah jongg calls. Every woman in the section of the Bronx where I lived played mah jongg. It was their passport to friendship. It was their quilting bee.

The game transformed Lila and brought her out of her lethargy. She became the bright, vivid and charismatic Lila Cooper she often described to me during some of our morning coffee discussions. She was transported back to the days before her marriage. Being with the other women not only quelled her loneliness, it brought out the best in her. For a short time, her softness came back.

"One Bam"
"Two Crak"
"Three Dot"
"Flower"

I smiled, recalling the mah jongg days in New York, and remembering many nights when Jonna and I, unable to sleep in our tiny bedroom in our apartment on Bolton Street, listened to the same chant hour after hour, long into the night. Once a week, the same chant—"one bam, two crak, three dot, flower"—would be followed by a lot of shared reminiscences, catty comments about those women who were absent that evening, and endless amounts of talking.

"So, I told her, 'Letty, you've got to leave him. He's playing around. I know he's playing around.'" Three heads bobbed up and down in agreement, not one losing sight of the mah jongg tile rack in front of them.

"Let me ask all of you. What would you do with my son? He's only interested in playing his trumpet and going out with that girlfriend of his. He never does any homework, and tells me he gets all As, which I know is not true. I wonder if his teachers at Bronx High School of Science think he'll ever get to college."

Again, three heads bobbing up and down, interrupted by:

"Two Bam"

"Three Crak"

"Flower"

I would look through the alcove between our bedroom and the foyer where the women played, and see my mother mixing multitudes of ivory tiles, smiling and humming "Symphony," her favorite song from the year before, while racking her tiles.

I turned to Jonna in the twin bed next to mine. "Lila's never blue when her friends come. She only gets that way when she's alone with us, or when Arthur comes home, so you have to be quiet, Jonna. She'll be mad if you ruin her game. And then she'll be in one of those moods you hate."

I watched my mother, her shining auburn curls swept back with ivory combs, her wide smiling face radiant when surrounded by her friends.

As I listened to the same chants and calls I remembered from the Bronx, I thought to myself that often it was during her mah jongg gatherings that my mother's secrets were revealed. It was at one of the mah jongg games that I overheard her talking about being on the verge of a very big move. I could hear her voice clearly from the other room and as I listened, I grew more dismayed and upset as she said to the group, "So, I told Arthur, if LACC in Los Angeles would give you as nice a salary as you got at CCNY, I wouldn't mind going to California. The college has given you great recommendations, even though they've told you to pipe down about your politics, and I think LACC would be lucky to have you." Then, after a moment's silence. "And anyway, I think it's so important that you get away from this HUAC threat."

Lila's announcement was greeted by the sound of tiles smacking into each other and being moved about in the middle of the bridge table, along with the bobbing heads I could see through the hallway.

I could remember feeling the heat rush to my face when I heard my mother's friend Ruth Moore say, "Lila, we're really going to miss you. Who will we get to take your hand when you leave for 'Califawnia?'"

"Ruthie," I heard Lila say, "Not so loud. I haven't told the girls yet. And anyway, we're not certain Arthur will get the job."

I could barely suppress a cry. My parents never explained anything to us. Jonna and I were never told about decisions that were made until the event was actually happening—even when it would change my entire life. I remember that I couldn't keep it in anymore. "Lila," I called, "come here! I need to talk to you. I need to talk to you, now!"

There was Lila, with a look of suppressed irritation, in the doorway. "Kim," she said between her teeth, "I told you not to interrupt me while I'm playing," and I knew she was toning down her anger a lot for the benefit of her friends. Always persistent, I pressed her: "Where is this Califawnia? Why are we going there? Is it for a vacation?" Lila, half-turned toward me, but with her attention on the three friends awaiting her in the foyer, responded impatiently: "Yes, we're going to visit Aunt Winnie in Los Angeles—it's only for a short time. It'll be like a vacation. She'll take us to movie studios, and we'll all have a good time. Now go to sleep!" I remember the expression on Lila's face when she turned away from the door. I can still see her, looking back with a kind of awkward and uncomfortable look.

Lying on my bed in our little house in North Hollywood, I began to bite my nails as I remembered how anxious I was about whether to confront my mother again. I remember Jonna crying, "I won't go, I don't wanna go. I wanna stay here with my friends." I knew that despite our protests neither Jonna nor I would have any say whatsoever. My parents were going to Aunt Winnie's in California and that was that. My parents made it sound like it was a wonderful vacation, and kept saying they had no idea how long the vacation would be.

On the day we all left for our long journey across the country, I was really mad, because what had become more clear with time was that the vacation was not a vacation, it was a permanent move. Even though Lila and Arthur insisted at first that the family was only going on a vacation like they had every summer, I was distressed when I saw that my parents were selling all their furniture. Each day, some neighbor would come and take a piece of furniture. I watched as Mrs. Kahn from apartment 3F took our beautiful red velvet sofa, and Ruthie Koff from downstairs came with her two sons and carried away the wonderful large gray velvet chair with the huge armrests, where on so many evenings Arthur would sit with Jonna and me and talk or read us stories. I became so mad and actually began stamping my foot when Lila gave away mounds of clothing, most of them Jonna's and my favorite snow clothes. It finally dawned on me that Arthur and Lila planned to live in Aunt Winnie and Uncle Mort's house in Los Angeles until they bought their own home. But not once until the day before our departure did they say out loud to us that this move was forever–that we would not be returning at the end of the summer.

My anger grew as the weeks went by. I hoped it would pass, but when my mother forced me to leave the boxes of movie-star postcards I'd saved since I was six years old, and my baseball hero cards which I bought at all the major league baseball games I attended with my father, I had visions of breaking her mah jongg tiles one by one.

"It took me years to save them, now you're making me give them away," I cried, kicking the shoebox full of cards across the room and watching them splatter. "You have no feelings. You only care about you, not about me or Jonna or what's really important to us." At that point, I had run from the room, tears streaming down my face, out the door and down the three floors and out onto the crowded Bronx street. By the time I reached the bottom floor and got to the lobby of my apartment building, I'd decided to distribute all my card treasures among my friends. Maybe that way they wouldn't be angry with me for going away. I also vowed to get even with Lila and Arthur some day.

The day we left the Bronx, Lila had tucked under her arm her precious mah-jongg set in its leathered covered case. I was dumbfounded. Lila had taken my treasures from me. How come, I thought, she can carry something that reminds her of the Bronx, but I can't?

"One Bam"

"Two Crak"

"Three Dot"

Now, as the sun set over our new tract house in North Hollywood, Jonna and I, trying to read and do our homework in our small bedroom, were overhearing a different group of women reminisce, gossip about the women who weren't there, and discuss their daily lives.

"One Bam."

"Two Crak"

"Three Dot"

"Flower"

Thelma Fine, intent on her mah jongg tiles, talked loudly and gossiped freely. When she saw me as I was making my way to the bathroom, she shouted: "Kim, you've got to come to our house and meet my daughter, Andrea. I'll even force her to take her nose out of her books if you come over. Maybe you'll show her how to have some fun."

I smiled, and hurriedly made a dash for the bathroom. I heard Thelma say to Lila, "They'd like each other, and maybe Andrea wouldn't spend another Valley summer with nothing to do."

Lila smiled, "That would be nice, Thelma. Maybe they'll become good friends." Thelma and the mah jongg group began to chatter, and Lila, focused on her tiles, half listening to them, bobbed her head up and down as if she were.

"Mah Jongg!"

Chapter 4

1950

"**D**o you know what verisimilitude is?" My question punctured
the afternoon silence as I sat with my friend Andrea on the
huge flood-control pipe.

"Verisimiwhat?" said Andrea, somewhat startled by my unexpected
outburst.

You know," I said with obvious impatience, "it's like truth or
something like truth."

"I don't know what you're talking about—and who cares, anyway?"
Andrea obviously did not share my chronic fascination with words.

"I care, that's who! My dad uses that word all the time. Like this
morning he was talking to Lionel, his buddy at LACC, and I heard him
say, 'Who would believe college professors like us would have to deal
with this lack of verisimilitude?' So it stayed in my mind, and if you
don't know, then I'll look it up when I get home."

"Why don't you just ask *him* what it means? Wouldn't that be
simpler?"

I looked away. "He doesn't have time to talk to me any more."

"Why not?"

"Something at work, about Reds or the Loyalty Oath. I don't

completely understand it. He's always on the phone with the other professors, or sitting in the living room and writing something or he doesn't come home at all."

"What about your mom?"

"My mom? She's a basket case. If he even mentions his troubles at work, she slaps her hands to her face and starts yelling at him. Then, he disappears for hours, and sometimes he doesn't come home until midnight. It's not a great scene."

"At least up here it's peaceful," said Andrea.

As we sat perched forty feet above the concrete below, Andrea and I dangled our feet freely and dangerously in the air, regretting as we became increasingly sticky in the blazing August San Fernando Valley sun that we were in our dungarees and blouses rather than our halter tops and shorts. Ever since its completion the year before, we had adopted "the Pipe" as our private meeting place. Every Saturday when school was out, Andrea and I walked the five blocks from our houses across the huge expanse of the wash, a dry, desert-like flood plain, and parked ourselves on top of the concrete monument. Not once did it ever occur to us that we could forever maim ourselves by falling from the huge round pipe to the concrete floor of the flood control channel below.

Most of our future planning and philosophical discussions began and ended on the Pipe. From this vantage point, we could see heat waves shimmering on the sands of the wash, giving rise to fantasies of *Lawrence of Arabia* appearing on a barren desert. Tumbleweeds gently bobbed up and down like dancing sylphs, colliding lightly, and then gracefully bouncing away from one another.

The first time I spied one, I turned to Andrea, surprised. "Andy, what are those things that look like bundles of dry sticks?"

"What is this, Kim—*The $64,000 Question*? Or am I the *Encyclopedia Britannica*?" Andrea teased. She often called me "a stupid genius," since I was able to tackle almost any kind of academic exercise, but had so little grasp of the physical or mechanical world around me. When it came to the day-to-day practicalities of life, I didn't have a clue.

"Haven't you ever noticed them before, Kim?" Andrea continued. "I saw some of those for the first time when my family came out to California. They're called 'tumbleweeds.'"

"Tumbleweeds…hmm," I mused, thinking of the Roy Rogers song, "Drifting along with the Tumbling Tumbleweeds." I used to sing that song and all my friends back in the Bronx used to sing along, but I was sure none of them had any idea what "a tumbling tumbleweed" was.

Today, I barely noticed the tumbleweeds because I was distracted by my father's conversation this morning. Finally, seeing that my friend was in no mood for a discourse on word usage, I said, "Do you want to go to Thatcher's Grocery Store?"

Andrea nodded. Walking the length of the channel which formed the border between North Hollywood and Van Nuys was one of our favorite activities in the boredom of the Valley summers. Going to Thatcher's was another. Of course, at night there was the drive-in movie. We weren't old enough to drive yet, but we would often go with our families to the drive-in, or occasionally crowd into the trunk of a car driven by a sixteen- or seventeen-year-old friend. That way we could get in without having to pay. Another meeting place was the El Portal Theater where we met all of our friends. We weren't in that "popular" crowd, like the older high school girls who spent their time shopping at Rathbun's, one of the "trendy" stores on Lankershim Boulevard. They focused solely on cashmere sweaters, cars, school clubs and preening for male attention at Bob's Big Boy, home of the famous "Big Boy" hamburger, on Riverside Drive every Friday night.

Andrea and I didn't care, though, because we had bigger ambitions. Andrea wanted to be an opera star, like Renata Tebaldi. She even tried to do her jet black curly hair like Tebaldi's, often spending hours winding curls across her forehead. She used bright red rouge on her cheeks to look more like Tebaldi in *Tosca*, until I told her she looked more like Olive Oyl from the *Popeye* cartoons.

While Andrea wanted to sing opera, I had always wanted to be a writer. Andrea would sing with the New York Opera, and I would marry and have four boys. Their names would be Lance, Thor, Keith, and Kevin. After raising them, I would retire to Greenwich Village where I would write the novel of the century.

Phil Fine, Andrea's dad, often took Andrea to the Shrine Auditorium downtown near Jefferson Boulevard to see the New York Opera when the touring company came to town. Every now and then I was invited to go. We paid fifty cents for each ticket and after the opera was underway, we would move down to the elegant and expensive empty box seats of the auditorium. There were so few people in Los Angeles interested in opera that we rarely had trouble finding plush seating.

"Hey, Kim, why don't we see if Thatcher's has any Good 'N Plenty? I'll treat you to some. My dad gave me fifteen cents before I left the house. 'Don't spend it all in one place!' he said."

"Can't, Andrea. Have to save my babysitting money if we want to go to the El Portal on Saturday."

"It's on me, Kim; I said I could treat you if you wanted."

Andrea's dark eyes fairly danced as she spoke. It was one of the things about her that I noticed when we first met about three years ago. I could still hear Andrea's cheerful voice as she introduced herself on the telephone.

"Hi, is this Kim?" she chirped. "My mom was at your house playing mah jongg the other night and said we should meet. She told me something like, you seemed like a nice girl and I was spending too much time indoors reading books."

While I was surprised by the call, her voice perked me up. Finally, I might have a close friend like the one I had left back in the Bronx. I still missed Rita a lot.

"Yes, that would be great. I'd like to meet you. I don't like many of the kids I've met at school too much."

"How come?"

"They're only interested in clothes and guys and sneaking a puff on a cig…I guess I get bored. The only thing I really like to do is play tennis and read."

"Wow," Andrea replied, "you sound just like me, without the tennis. I could care less about Rathbun's and hanging out in a clique. When can we meet?"

We decided to meet at Ludlow's Coffee Shop which had just opened on Coldwater and Victory. So we would recognize each other, I would wear my New York Giants baseball cap, while Andrea would pin a little piece of a bougainvillea blossom on her shirt. I remember being excited as I walked the short distance from my house to the coffee shop-café nestled at the end of a sloping driveway off of Victory Boulevard. As I walked towards Ludlow's that day, I noticed the increasing number of bougainvillea bushes and trees already adding a little bit of lush color to the bland Valley.

Ludlow's had a warm, convivial atmosphere. Most of the waitresses were residents of the new tract homes surrounding the restaurant. Their welcoming nature and friendliness defined the aura of the restaurant. It also reflected the open spirit of the newly developing Kaiser Tract in North Hollywood.

I spotted Andrea immediately. She was nestled in a corner of the restaurant, focused intently on the book in front of her, the largest piece of startlingly red bougainvillea I had ever seen pinned across her blouse pocket. Two hours whizzed by during our first meeting, each of us trying to out-talk the other. Who we were. Where we came from. Who we liked. Who we disliked. How much we enjoyed the movies and how thrilled we were that Bette Davis won the Academy Award.

After two hours, we were tired of talking and we decided to take our first walk along the flood control channel. The hot autumn midday sun, unimpeded by any trees or vegetation, beat down on us. Our fascination with the new flood control channel distracted our attention from the beads of perspiration which began to appear on our foreheads. Finally, we decided it would be much cooler at Thatcher's, the only grocery store within miles of our houses. We set out along Victory Boulevard until we reached Thatcher's on the corner of Victory and Whitsett Avenue.

Today, when we reached the store, we planted ourselves between three fans working vigorously to cool the interior of the darkened grocery store, and noticed three other girls from the high school junior class browsing around the store. Both Andrea and I flinched; this was our turf. Why were those girls here? Shouldn't they be shopping at Rathbun's? We felt awkward, almost intruded upon, neither of us really wanting to deal with them. Andrea looked nervous. She used to complain to me that these girls belonged to a clique at school which had its own little area for "hanging out." It was easier to avoid them there; here, at Thatcher's, we felt almost cornered.

Andrea and I turned away and focused our attention on a flickering eight-inch television in the corner which showed President Harry Truman shaking the hand of the Nobel Peace Prize winner for 1950, Dr. Ralph Bunche. We were transfixed by the handsome, smiling man being lauded by our President.

"I'm glad he's Negro," I said. "My father says everyone stereotypes Negroes as dumb."

"Well, they can't do that to him. No Nobel Prize winner is dumb!"

"Right, he is far from dumb. Arthur says that Ralph Bunche would be a wonderful president. He's intelligent, knows how to negotiate and would be very kind to the less privileged because he knows what it's like to struggle."

Andrea became quiet, as if pondering Arthur's statement. Finally, she said, "I hate to say it, but this country has too many prejudiced people to ever elect a Negro president."

I remained silent. I didn't like what Andrea said, because I didn't like to think of my country—which I loved—as having so many prejudiced people. Somewhere inside of me, I planted a hope that it wasn't true and finally said, "Let's drop it, Andrea. It makes me feel sad."

When we turned our attention back to the "trio," all three of them were totally involved with a group of boys who were trying to pick them up. I recognized Alec Brown, one of the popular "hunks" from the 7th grade. The older guy he was with looked sixteen or seventeen. I had seen him driving around school in his brand new 1950 Willys, called a "Woodie Jeep."

I found myself making mental notes about the colors of produce to distract myself from the trio. It always surprised me to see green grapes, bright red strawberries and huge avocados—such a variety that I'd never seen back in the Bronx. Now that my family was more settled, and it looked like I finally had a close friend, life in the Valley just might become a little bit more comfortable.

It seemed that Andrea and I agreed on many things. For instance, everything in the world that was creative or worthwhile, according to us, emanated from Paris or New York. We idealized those two cities. Someday, we wanted to live in Greenwich Village, where Andrea would take opera lessons and I would join a writers' group. We would share our goals and our dreams of fulfilling them, while living in a first story walk-up with Bohemian neighbors. We saw the Valley as a boring wasteland, and decided if we couldn't manage to get to New York or Paris, at least we would wind up "over the hill," as migrating to West Los Angeles was called.

We might have been considered an unlikely duo. I was five foot seven; Andrea five foot two. I was thirteen; she was fourteen and a half. My dark olive complexion (from my father's side) was in contrast to Andrea's very fair skin. But our striking physical differences were minor compared to the bond we'd formed. We were both émigrés from the streets of New York. Andrea came from Brooklyn, and we would spend a lot of time comparing our lives in New York to that in the Valley.

"Remember how close together everything was in New York?" asked Andrea, as we started to head back from Thatcher's.

"What do you mean?" I asked.

"In my neighborhood back in Brooklyn, I didn't have to go two miles to the market! I could take the El anywhere I wanted to go. I could walk to Coney Island, it was so close."

"Yeah, that's right—and in the Bronx, we didn't have smelly septic tanks. We had front steps and underground plumbing and no lawns to take care of!"

Because of the new semester coming up, I found myself thinking how lucky it was that I met Andrea. Last year, as a seventh grade "scrub," I had had a very difficult time. I felt isolated, was ridiculed because of my height, and at the brand new Van Nuys Jr. High School, I felt awkward and alone. Because I was far ahead of some of the kids in academic subjects, the school skipped me one year past the eighth grade and I was very nervous about the idea of going into the ninth grade. Andrea, a full year ahead of me, was entering North Hollywood High School as a sophomore. So that would help some. At least my good friend could introduce me around.

But for right now, I could put my school worries behind. As we ambled down the near-empty dirt road that was Victory Boulevard, we heard in the distance the clang-kaboom-swat of the trolley, followed by three resounding bell blasts warning anyone in its path.

Andrea, hearing the trolley sounds, became excited. "Let's see if our folks will give us money to go to the movies tomorrow. It's Sunday, and we could take the Red Car into Hollywood."

"That sounds great! What do you want to see, Andrea?"

"My dad said that Judy Holliday is playing in *Born Yesterday* at the Grauman's Chinese. He loves Judy Holliday. He says she only plays a brainless bombshell, but actually she has an I.Q. of 172."

"No kidding? That's okay with me. Let's plan on seeing it."

"I don't know, Kim, the more I think about it, my dad was complaining the other night that my brother and I spend too much on movies. You know it went up to twenty-five cents. And then, there's the fifteen cents for the trolley. It's a lot."

"Andrea, we've got to get more babysitting jobs. What about that lady whose husband works at night at Barone's restaurant? You know, the one who lives across the street from you with the three screaming kids? You told me that she told your mom if she doesn't get out more, her brain is going to crack. Maybe, we could ask her if she wants both of us to sit for her, and if she goes out for three hours, we'll have seventy-five cents. Then, we can go to Hollywood in two weeks."

"Well, it wouldn't hurt to ask, Kim."

As we strolled along in the still-sweltering sun, we noticed the open doors of the houses along the way. Protected only by their screen doors, housewives bustled around in their living rooms, roaring vacuums in front of them. As we passed one house, we could hear a loud radio and the voice of Patti Page singing "The Tennessee Waltz," while in another small house nearby, Nat "King" Cole sang "Mona Lisa."

"That's one of Lila's favorites, 'The Tennessee Waltz.' She sings it all the time, when she's not moping around and feeling sad."

"Wow, sometimes these days just seem so long, don't they Kim?"

"Yeah, I guess, but you know what? I heard about something we could do to fill in the time, if you want to hear about it."

"Really? What's that, Kim?"

"If you can come back to my house, I'll show you." Andrea looked at me quizzically, but I just smiled and motioned her on. I had heard about an inspiring woman candidate running for the U.S. Senate, and I had been talking with both Lila and Arthur about working on the campaign. Today seemed like the perfect time to bring up my plans. I was almost prancing with excitement about telling Andrea, and there was a real plus: my parents were all for it.

At first, I carefully considered whether I should even broach this with Lila, given her fear of any openness of political thought in the current climate, but I could not suppress it. "I think I'm going to work for Helen Gahagan-Douglas this summer and I'm going to ask Andrea to work with me."

We were in the sunny yellow kitchen, and Lila was on her third cup of coffee. She said nothing for a few minutes. Then, to my surprise, she said, "That might be a stimulating way to spend the rest of your summer. From all I read, Douglas is for the common man and has a good chance of winning."

I was elated. I never expected such a response from her. It was one of those rare moments when Lila encouraged me.

"For all we know," Lila said, "she might be a boon to the IPP and support diverse opinions."

"That's what Arthur told me he was talking about in class," I said.

"Campaigning for a Democratic candidate is one thing," Lila said. "Your father sometimes goes overboard with his radicalism, although I must admit he, too, is excited about Douglas."

I knew I needed to broach the subject carefully with Andrea, and had been biding my time. In the past couple of weeks, I turned to my scrapbook, neatly cutting out from the *Los Angeles Times* and *Daily News* articles about Nixon and Gahagan-Douglas, and planned to present this to Andrea and convince her to join my plan to go into politics.

When we got to my house, I didn't see the car in the driveway. Arthur, Lila and Jonna seemed to be gone. The front door was unlocked. It was always left that way. Lila would say, "We live in the Valley and it's a safe place, we have nothing to worry about." Once in the house, I drew Andrea into my room. "I have the perfect idea for what we can do for the rest of this summer until school starts. We won't be bored for one minute."

"Tell me, what's your perfect idea?" Andrea smiled.

"We're going to get our feet wet in the political arena."

"I don't know if that's for me, Kim. My father and brother blather about it enough. And you certainly hear enough about politics with your parents screaming about it all the time. Let's do something different. Why don't we think more about going to the beach, taking in some movies and having some fun before we go to Yosemite?"

I pulled my scrapbook down from the closet. "You must look at this. This is all about Helen Gahagan-Douglas. She won the election in 1946 for a seat in Congress and again in 1948. She's a congressman, I mean *woman,* from California. She could really make a difference. Look what these articles say about her."

Andrea took the scrapbook from me, her attention caught by an article from the *Washington Post*: "Helen Gahagan-Douglas, surely one of the most beautiful women in America, is a tall, blonde, Barnard

College graduate. Washington had prepared for her stately, gracious beauty, but they weren't prepared for her brilliance…"

"I don't understand. Why are you giving this to me to read?"

"Andrea, read this article from the *New York Times* about her, then I'll tell you."

Underneath a picture of a tall, willowy blond, the article read:

"Douglas is a riveting, charismatic speaker in her advocacy of liberal causes, particularly civil rights. She has great sympathy for the plight of the Negro, and is profoundly aggrieved by the state of the Okies. Mary McLeon Bethune called her 'the voice of American Democracy.'"

Andrea continued to hesitate, but I was not going to give up. For some reason that I did not understand, Helen Gahagan-Douglas inspired me. I became more determined to convince my friend. Andrea sensed it and began to waver a bit.

"We *have* to support her, Andrea. She's going to run for the Senate against Richard Nixon. We can do lots of things: pass out leaflets, make calls, deliver papers, and get things printed. And, if we're lucky, maybe some day we can meet her."

I could see that Andrea still wasn't sold on the plan, but I was prepared for her hesitation. "I've saved the best for last." I handed her a recent article from the *New York Times*:

"Not only has Helen Gahagan-Douglas established herself as a success in writing, but in dancing, theater and opera as well. She had her debut in the title role of *Tosca* in Prague and toured Europe for two years in several operas."

That did it! Andrea agreed to campaign for Douglas, who was a model for both of us: I wanted to emulate her successful career as a woman writer and politician, and Andrea saw her as a model for a woman politician who was also involved in the arts—and opera, no less! We both agreed with the *Los Angeles Times* journalist, Jack Smith, who called Gahagan-Douglas "the renaissance woman of the century."

The next day I telephoned two UCLA seniors, whom Arthur told me headed the Valley Youth Drive for Douglas, and arranged for Andrea and me to meet them for an interview. That afternoon we went to the North Hollywood campaign headquarters which was located in a small office on Victory Boulevard and Coldwater Canyon.

People were bustling everywhere busily sealing envelopes or diligently working the mimeograph machine, their arms purple to their elbows. The two campaign coordinators, Arnold and Ted, welcomed us and let us know that anything we could do would be greatly appreciated. Douglas needed all the help she could get.

"I know you guys will be terrific," Arnold said. "Ted gets scared that if the polls show that Gahagan-Douglas isn't doing as well as he'd like, all of our helpers will abandon our cause. But I sense you two are committed." We nodded our heads vigorously. We couldn't wait to tell our parents that we were recruited.

Every weekday at 10 a.m. during August of 1950, I'd walk the few blocks to Andrea's house to pick her up. Together, we'd make our way to the newly erected Democratic Headquarters where we picked up campaign materials: buttons, bumper stickers and leaflets. We'd ring doorbells, speak to residents who were unfamiliar with Gahagan-Douglas, and tack leaflets on telephone poles all over the Valley.

We visited only those houses where families were said to be voting Republican, relieved that very few verbally attacked us. We'd heard from other precinct workers, that due to intense feelings about the coming election, some homeowners shouted at the campaign workers. But most of the Republican "Valleyites" welcomed us and a few even offered water or iced tea.

In all, we visited seventy homes. Only once did an elderly gentleman, whose breath smelled like he was three sheets to the wind, call us "dirty, rotten, Commie Pinkos."

There was a rumor that Douglas herself would come to visit the office.

"Of course she'll come," Andrea said. "My dad says the mood of the Douglas campaign is dismal and deflated and she knows she needs to buoy us up."

Andrea's prediction came true. During the last week of August, right before school started, Helen Gahagan-Douglas showed up one day surrounded by other political luminaries. When Andrea and I reported for duty, Ted led both of us, his hand on each of our shoulders, to the front of the campaign headquarters. "Mrs. Douglas, may I present to you two of our most tireless workers, Kim Lebow and Andrea Fine."

The tall, stately women whom Nixon had labeled "The Pink Lady" was, in fact, quite elegant. Douglas smiled at us in a most personal way. She was gracious, soft spoken, and kind. "I don't know what my campaign would do without people like you. I do appreciate all you have done." As the other workers looked on, Douglas gave each of us a hug and our own special campaign buttons with her photograph on it.

That Sunday, to our surprise, neither of our dads had a moment's hesitation about giving us permission and the money for the movies and the ride to Hollywood on the Red Car. "Say, girls, we wanted to give you a treat because you've both been working so hard for what you believe in," said Arthur. Phil Fine nodded in agreement. They didn't have the slightest concern about the two of us going off alone. Our parents were relieved that we had something to do to help us pass the time in the otherwise quiet Valley. And anyway, the Red Car was safe because there were always adults riding the car who could give assistance if we needed it.

We met at 9:00 a.m. on Sunday morning at the corner of Coldwater and Victory and began our hike to Chandler Boulevard to catch the 9:30 a.m. trolley to Hollywood and Highland. We decided that once we were there, we would stop at Coffee Dan's on Hollywood Boulevard, get a hamburger and coke, then go on to the Grauman's Chinese Theater. We were so excited about our journey—the challenge of going to unknown places thrilled us—and we never knew when we would encounter something new on our adventures into town.

The new red plush seats on the Red Car felt cool and soothing. Every window in the long trolley car was open. Andrea and I enjoyed the cross breezes as the car whizzed down Chandler Boulevard and threaded through the Cahuenga Pass to take us to Hollywood. Every now and then, we would rest our heads on the window sill, the brisk, cool air brushing back our hair. As we felt the trolley crest the top of the pass and begin its rapid descent southward, our excitement grew, knowing that in moments we would be strolling along Hollywood Boulevard.

On the trolley, across the aisle, a young student in his early twenties, his brown hair cut finely in a buzz cut, was reading *Catcher in the Rye*, oblivious to the hum of conversation and the clickety-clack of the car on the tracks. Sitting next to him, a lady in her 40s, eyes closed, smiled as her rapidly moving hands skillfully negotiated two knitting needles. At the rear of the car, four teenage boys in white tee shirts caroused and laughed, their sleeves rolled up almost to their shoulders showing their muscles, and their hair done in the frontal wave of James Dean, the teenage idol who had just done his first Pepsi commercial.

"Isn't this great, Andrea? I feel so free!"

"Me, too, and I hope next time we can go to the beach, not just the movies. Let's get a schedule and find out which Red Car we can take to get to Santa Monica."

The air felt fresh and clean, and the Red Car seemed brand new. I mischievously toyed with the idea of pulling the long cord that stretched from one end of the car to the other. I knew, however, that that would bring the car to a screeching halt and that was something I did not want. I couldn't wait to get to Hollywood and after the movies end the day with a chocolate marshmallow sundae at C. C. Brown's.

"You know, Andrea, we're very lucky."

"How come?"

"Well, look what we have. We have our friendship, we're working in politics for a terrific candidate, we can go lots of places together, and we have this trolley that will just about take us anywhere. Freedom and friendship, that's what it is. No matter how bad things get at home, when I'm on this trolley and we're going someplace, life is good!"

Chapter 5

It was 7:30 a.m. Monday morning, my first day of high school. I was standing at the bus stop, trying to ignore my thumping heartbeat as I saw the large yellow and gold school bus rounding the corner. Despite Andrea's reassurance that she'd already be on the bus, I was terrified and could barely look at the kids around me who were clumping together as the bus roared toward us. Finally, I took a deep breath, straightened my shoulders and stepped up into the bus. The noise was deafening, as I wended my way down the long aisle searching out my friend. Stepping gingerly between the books, gym bags, tennis rackets, and jackets in the middle of the aisle, I spied Andrea patting the saved seat beside her. I breathed a sigh of relief, grateful to be out of the aisle and beyond the kids staring at me like they were thinking "she's the new kid," as I slid into the seat.

"Comment allez-vous?" asked Andrea, smiling at me. I shot her a look, as if to say, "What in the world are you doing?" Andrea nodded toward the kids across the aisle, who were listening intently. They seemed impressed, so I joined in. We began reciting the first few pages from our beginning French Primer.

"Bonjour, mes élèves."

"Bonjour, mon professeur, comment allez-vous?"

"Je vais très bien, et vous?"

We went on talking that way for another ten minutes, and I found that getting into the joke was helping me to forget my first-day jitters.

"Hi, I'm Abby. Where did you two learn French?" asked the girl sitting across from us.

"Boy, you two sure talk fast. That's neat," said a boy sitting nearby.

With a wry smile, Andrea casually replied: "We learned it in Paris, of course! We were there last summer, and we're going back this summer."

By now we had the attention of everyone around us. The bus driver, a good-natured, portly man, smiled at us through his long rear view mirror. Catching my attention, he gave me a wink. Feeling he and I shared a secret, I smiled back and wondered if I should say "good-bye" or "*au revoir*" to him when I left the bus.

The bus rounded the corner on Magnolia Avenue and stopped in front of North Hollywood High School. Andrea and I, along with all the students, stood up and filed out of the bus. As I passed the bus driver, he said: "*Au revoir, mes pretties.*" I smiled again as Andrea whispered to me, "I think he has our number."

We all walked briskly up the concrete walk and through high arched doors opening to a large foyer inside. We had until eight o'clock to make it to our classrooms.

Following my classmates through the foyer and out onto small pockets of green lawn, I saw a huge quad surrounded on all four sides by buildings. The campus had a distinctively institutional look, and except for the elm trees lining the walk, I thought it looked quite regimented. It made me feel claustrophobic, like I was being hemmed in.

"I have this eerie feeling of being watched Andrea, like Big Brother is up there in one of those windows looking down on me."

"He is." Andrea said. "He's looking down at us and wondering if you're going to make trouble on your first day of school with your big mouth!"

"Now, why would I do that?"

"You'll find some reason, I'm sure."

I was getting my first glimpse of my high school. A concrete path bisected the length of the large quad. Rows upon rows of long oak tables lined the pathway with attached benches on either side. The entire quad area was empty. Andrea said that in two hours the multitude of tables would be filled with students who would meet for recess, then two hours later for lunch. The long path separating the quad ended at the steps of the Administration building. A pair of tall wooden doors sat in the center of the building through which one could get to the boys' and girls' gymnasiums, located a fair distance away across a wide grass field. The entire field was surrounded by an eight-foot tall chain link fence. My "hemmed-in" feeling came back again.

I hurried to my first morning class, Mr. Gilmore's English IA class. He had a kind and easy manner. I felt relieved to be in school. Even though I hated to be hemmed in, the calmness, organization, and structure satisfied me. It was a direct contrast to my unpredictable and chaotic home life.

I went from Mr. Gilmore's English class, to Madame Aronson's French class, finishing the morning with what I later told Andrea was my absolutely favorite class, Mr. Samuel's Social Studies class. He was not only the most welcoming of the teachers, but his reflections on the world around him really interested me. Even his appearance was welcoming. He was tall and lanky, had graying, longish hair and a rumpled look, different from many of the other "buttoned-down" teachers I had seen. He had a knack for making each one of his students feel important. Greeting each member of the class with a smile and a handshake, he asked that each of us introduce ourselves and state what we expected from him as a teacher. Then, he clearly outlined his expectations for the semester; most notably that he wanted to challenge the thinking and stretch the minds of each and every one of us. He let all of us know right away that he liked lively discussion, and welcomed many different opinions on any subject being discussed. I was in heaven.

When Mr. Samuel's class broke for lunch, I followed everyone back to the quad, looking around anxiously for Andrea. Strangely enough, the quad, with its various blocs, reminded me of my neighborhood in the Bronx with its Italian section, its Irish section, and its Jewish section. Each bench was occupied by a group of kids who all belonged to a club, and who all wore the same color sweaters or tee shirts to designate which club they belonged to.

The girls gathered around tables on one side of the quad, the boys on the other side. One group of the chattering girls wore powder blue sweaters emblazoned on the front with PUFS, and another group wore bright red sweaters with the name SONGBIRDS on their fronts. Some of the PUFS and the SONGBIRDS were yelling across the aisle to their male counterparts, the WILDCATS and the JETS.

I finally found Andrea, and followed her as she moved in between the tables.

"We're going to a bench where there's a group I like." Andrea took my arm and led me to the furthest end of the quad, quite a distance from all of the other tables.

"Are we going to our own Clubbie's Table?" I asked, trying to keep up with her.

"No, silly. We don't call it a "Clubby Table" because we don't want to be dressed like everyone else. We're unique individuals." With that, she led me to a table where instantly I could see the difference. These kids wore no matching clothing or sweaters and they seemed more down to earth, less like Sandra Dee and Frankie Avalon. Also, boys and girls were sitting together.

"This is Kim, guys," Andrea beckoned me to take a seat.

All the kids greeted me. I immediately felt comfortable and less alone.

After lunch I hurried to my first afternoon class, History IA, taught by Mrs. Fielding. After a brisk introduction about class expectations and an equally brisk taking of the roll, Mrs. Fielding told the class to get out their notebooks. She pointed to the outline she had already written on the chalkboard with Roman numerals and alphabetized sub-categories.

"Now class, we're going to have an overview of the history of the current Cold War. Copy down these topic headings and fill them in as I lecture." *Wow, this teacher really means business.* I glanced at the underlined topics, saw that one of them was "Communist Infiltration of American Institutions," and started to squirm in my seat. What would Arthur think of this?

As if he were reading my thoughts, the student next to me raised his hand. "Yes, young man?" Mrs. Fielding said stiffly. It was perfectly clear she did not want anyone to interrupt the flow of her lecture, but it was the first day of school, so she waited for him to speak.

"Umm, isn't it true that the notion of communist infiltration is a matter of opinion, and has not been proven?"

Was it my imagination or did the classroom go utterly still? I saw Mrs. Fielding press her lips together and her cheeks blanched. "Young man, your job is to copy down this outline and listen to my lecture."

I couldn't believe what I was hearing. All he had done was to ask a question. I stole a glance at this boy across the aisle. He looked very surprised at our teacher's response and started studiously copying down the chalkboard outline. *I guess I better just start writing and mind my own business. If he can't question, maybe I can't either.* Mrs. Fielding cleared her throat to resume her lecture.

There wasn't a sound in the classroom as she droned on and on about the Red Scare and the Soviet Union. Her voice became more piercing. In reverent tones she began to praise Richard Nixon for what she called his "valiant fight against the Red menace, and the treacherous Communists... He has the determination to weed out the vultures with Red sympathies from our midst." In conclusion, she folded her hands together as if in prayer, saying "Lord help us and save us from those who seek to destroy us."

The same student who had spoken out had a grim look on his face, and I had a battle going on inside of me. One side told me to keep quiet: *don't mess up your first day of school.* The other side couldn't stand it any more. *Richard Nixon as the champion against the Red Menace?* It went against everything I had heard at home. Arthur told us that Nixon's tactics were ruthless and that he kept an enemies list. The student who had questioned Mrs. Fielding before immediately raised his hand. Apparently he and I were on the same track.

"Yes, young man?" she asked irritably.

"Don't the people who oppose Mr. Nixon have as much right to their political beliefs as he does?"

Mrs. Fielding stopped in her tracks.

"Yes," I joined in, having decided to take the side of my fellow student. "And isn't it a violation of the separation of church and state to invoke the name of the Lord in a public school classroom?"

The rest of the class initially tittered nervously at our questions, and then fell quickly into another ominous silence. Mrs. Fielding was clearly angry now. By the long silence and the look on her face, it became clear to me that the cold war she spoke of was not just with the Soviet Union.

She walked slowly toward us down the aisle and stopped at my desk. First, she glared at him, then at me. She was tall, much like a beanstalk, and wore a tight black dress with huge white camellias all over it. Her tense, reddened face reminded me of squished tomatoes. "I think you two have said enough. You're both impertinent. I am the speaker; you are the listeners." With that she handed each of us a pink slip and instructed us to go straight to the principal's office.

As we shuffled down to the principal's office, walking as slowly as we possibly could, the young man said, "I'm Jared Connelly. Thanks for your support."

"Hi. I'm Kim Lebow, and I think everyone in the class should have stood by you. We did nothing wrong. You had a right to question," I said with bravado. But my insides were roiling. *Oh no, what have I done now? Andrea was right. I just had to shoot off my mouth, didn't I? And on my first day of school!*

"My folks and I discuss politics all the time, and we go back and forth. My dad's a radio announcer and he encourages me to question all the time, so I really didn't expect that from a teacher," Jared said. "And you?"

"I know just what you mean. My dad and I always get into discussions about things happening here in America, and I ask him hundreds of questions. In fact, he encourages me to buy the daily newspaper and circle it with any questions I have, and then bring them to him. That's why I was so upset when you were told to just listen and not question. I decided right there and then to question her too, so she couldn't just lay blame on you."

"Well, it really made a difference, Kim. It's harder for her to point a finger at one 'impertinent' kid if there are actually two," Jared said, mimicking Mrs. Fielding's tone as he said "impertinent."

When we finally found Mr. Firth's office, thanks to the help of the school janitor, I was struck by the size of the larger outer office, and how all the walls were paneled in shiny oak wood. A very businesslike secretary looked up.

"Yes, how can I help the two of you?"

"We've been told to come to the principal's office," Jared said, handing her his pink slip. I handed her mine. She looked down at the slips, frowned at us for what seemed forever, and then got up from her chair. She approached the large rolled plate glass door behind her on which, painted in large black block letters was the name: Henry Firth, Principal. She knocked gently, and I heard a mumbled, 'Cmmin.' She entered and, after a minute, the door reopened.

Mr. Firth was huge. He looked down at us and requested we follow him into his office. He waved us to two seats in front of the largest oak desk I'd ever seen, and then seated himself in his swivel chair, hands linked together and lying gently on his stomach. Above him was a picture of General Eisenhower, smiling down benignly on us.

What a kind face Ike has, I thought, and almost forgot why we were there.

My heart thumped so loudly I didn't hear everything Mr. Firth was saying. In his gruff voice, he was saying things like "students knowing their place," the "penalties for disrupting class," and "parents being called to school." I thought my heart would fall to the floor with a loud plop. *Oh geez, not my parents, especially Lila. It will set her off like a firecracker. What can I do?*

Jared spoke very clearly about his right to voice his questions and opinions. He seemed to approach Mr. Firth like an equal. "I didn't see myself as disruptive, Mr. Firth. I saw myself doing just what I would do with my parents when we discuss things."

"And you, young lady, what was the reason for your pink slip?" Mr. Firth asked.

At that moment, I was unable to speak. I had a vision of falling to my knees, pleading, and saying in my most earnest voice, "I promise you Mr. Firth, it won't ever happen again. Never again…never!" just to avoid facing Lila's wrath. But when I looked over at Jared, I found my voice. "Mr. Firth, I'm here because I feel Jared and I have a right to question in class. I believe our parents would want us to do just that." *Parents! Lila will have a cow. But I have to support Jared.*

After a considerable silence, Mr. Firth said: "Okay, I hear you two. I am going to ask that perhaps you can consider not embarrassing your teacher by asking disruptive questions. Perhaps you can talk to her after class, or at the beginning of the school day, since I see you are both assigned to her homeroom. Since this is a first-time infraction, and it is your first day of school, I will not give either of you detention, or call your parents to school. But, you can be sure we'll keep an eye on both of you if Mrs. Fielding complains of any more disruptive incidents. And keep all provocative questions to yourselves; I don't want to have either of you brought before the Academic Council. Return to your classroom now, and tell Mrs. Fielding I will talk to her later."

Jared had a grave look on his face. The unspoken awareness between us was that nothing had been accomplished by our protest. I opened my mouth to speak to Mr. Firth, and just as I was about to do that unacceptable thing and question again, Jared quickly put his hand on my shoulder. His message seemed to be, "Don't bother. We'll have to find other ways to question."

When I met Andrea at the bus that afternoon, after my long ordeal, I felt drained. My first day of school, and I'd been introduced to Mrs. Fielding's view of teaching and learning. During the bus ride, I complained bitterly about it as I told Andrea every detail of what had happened, even what had gone on in my head about swearing to Mr. Firth…never, ever.

"You didn't actually say that?" Andrea began to laugh hysterically. "I can't imagine you sounding like that!"

"It's not funny, Andrea. I had to give in. I really wanted to support

Jared more, but my mother would have a cow if she heard I was spouting off my views in class. And never mind that, if she got wind of my being called into the principal's office, she would lose it completely. My father would probably be proud. He thinks questions are golden."

"So, it's great then that Mr. Firth gave you another chance."

"Yeah, he said that since it's the first day of school, he'd excuse us…but at the end of our meeting he said something about Jared and me shaping up, whatever that means, or he'd need to recommend we go before the Academic Council. I don't know what in the world an Academic Council is, but I felt so relieved, I ran out of his office. What is the Academic Council, Andrea?"

"I think it's a group of students that meet to judge infractions. Then, they decide on penalties and all that. Getting on the Academic Council is like a popularity contest."

"Well, I don't care about the Council; I'm just relieved that we have another chance so Lila, Arthur, and Jared's parents don't have to come to school."

"You know Kim," cautioned Andrea, "you better go slow, and play it safe. I think what you're seeing is that not everyone is as open as Arthur. I mean you and he can sit around your kitchen table spouting off your views, but not in class. It's not the same. And from what I've heard about the Council, they can be pretty tough."

At dinner that night, we were all seated around the table. Arthur smiled and patted his mouth with his dinner napkin. "Well, Kim, how were things at the big high school?"

One of the few things I liked about my family was that they became excited on special occasions and seemed to forget their usual troubles. One such occasion was the first day of school. These were the rare times when I could be lulled into thinking it might be possible for my family to be normal.

I glanced nervously at Lila. "I guess I learned today that I have to be more careful about asking questions and stating my views."

Arthur looked at me quizzically. "What do you mean?"

"Well, my history teacher starts talking about how great Richard Nixon is, and then right in class she says a prayer for people fighting the Communists. And I wondered, are teachers allowed to talk this way? Aren't they supposed to ask our opinions, but not get into theirs? So, this guy in class Jared and I got upset and started to question her. We also asked her about people's freedom to have different political views. Then she got really mad and lectured us about her being the teacher and us being the students." I was aware that I was carefully editing the situation, not wanting to unduly upset my mother.

"I guess my teacher isn't very open to discussion or exchange of ideas."

Arthur's face was grim, his lips in a straight line. Lila jumped up from her chair. She ran around to where I was sitting and put her face close to mine. "You didn't say anything, did you? Tell me you didn't argue with her."

"Of course not. She's a nut case and it wouldn't even be worth it." I looked over at Arthur, who seemed disappointed that I didn't argue more with Mrs. Fielding. I felt conflicted. I couldn't win.

With an annoyed glance at Lila, Arthur sighed. "Well, you've got to learn, Kim, there will always be people who can't accept views different from their own."

Lila's chair clattered to the floor and she abruptly left the room. She had three ways of dealing with her nerves: hysterics, throwing things, or storming out of the room. When she returned, her lips were pressed in a painful grimace, and the family spent the rest of the evening in a glum silence.

Back to same old, same old.

Okay mom, calm down, the FBI is not going to come and take Dad away just because his citizenship papers got lost somewhere. Arthur says this country is trapped by the hysterical irrationality of the HUAC. Meanwhile, I'm caught inside the same kind of trap at home.

The next day at school, I was surprised when, after my Social Studies class, Mr. Samuels cornered me as soon as the bell rang. "Can you stay a few minutes, Kim?" I was puzzled, but said I could.

Mr. Samuels looked concerned, but said in his gentle voice, "Kim, I understand you and Jared had a little run-in with my colleague, Mrs. Fielding."

"I guess you could call it that, Mr. Samuels." I related the whole interchange I had with Mrs. Fielding. I was both surprised and pleased that Mr. Samuels was not at all critical of me. In fact, he seemed very sympathetic.

"You know, Kim, differences in views should be more tolerated in a school setting. It is unfortunate that sometimes they are not, particularly during this time in history when our freedom of speech is often threatened. You might consider, though, that a confrontational stance is not always the most effective way. You and Jared may have embarrassed Mrs. Fielding in front of her class. But, you must not, under any circumstances, give up your valuable ideas or ever forget that you have a right to have them or to express them."

I was shocked. I looked at this man, so large in stature, with salt and pepper hair, smiling eyes, and a warmth and kindness I had not experienced with any of the other teachers in the school.

"Why don't you put the thoughts you were confronting Mrs. Fielding with, into words…put them into writing instead of jeopardizing yourself by angrily confronting your teacher? Could you do that?"

"I guess I could, Mr. Samuels. It's a great idea."

"Well, I'd like you to do that and even more. If your writing is satisfactory, I will make sure you are given a position on the editorial staff of *The Daily Husky*. I'd like you to come to our meetings. I'm in charge of organizing the paper, and I would really value your contribution there."

Hearing his words, I felt elated. It was as if I had been in an overheated, suffocating room, and someone had just opened a huge door for me and let the fresh, cool air in.

"Thank you, Mr. Samuels, this means a lot to me, and I'll really look forward to working with you on the newspaper. Will Jared be working there as well?"

"I'm afraid that, after yesterday's fracas, Jared's parents have removed him from our school. They are enrolling him in a private school more to their liking."

"Well, I really like your offer, Mr. Samuels—and I'm glad there are teachers like you here at North Hollywood."

Barely knowing Jared, I couldn't say I would miss him terribly, but I did feel like I was manning the Fielding Fort alone. As hard as I tried, by the end of October, Mrs. Fielding and I continued to have a serious problem. Once again, it began with one of those pointed political diatribes she was in the habit of showering upon us. This time, it was worse. She spouted her support for Joseph McCarthy and his "religious crusade to rid America of the Reds."

Here we go again! I may be digging my own grave, I thought, while my knees started shaking. I drew myself up straight and said, "I disagree with the content of your lecture, Mrs. Fielding, and I do not agree with your characterization of events. Joseph McCarthy's methods are a threat to all Americans."

"Miss Lebow," said Mrs. Fielding, the disdain mirrored on her pinched face, "I am not conducting a class in debate, nor am I asking for your opinion on what I am saying."

"But Mrs. Fielding, you are not presenting the other side of the picture. There are many people who don't feel the way you do and you seem to impose your opinions on us without our having a chance to tell you how we think."

Mrs. Fielding was furious. She looked as if she wanted to hit me but instead turned and went to her desk and scribbled a note, jabbing it into my chest.

I glanced at the pink piece of paper I was carrying to the principal's office, and saw that Mrs. Fielding had underlined the reason for the pink slip: "Miss Lebow continues to attack me. She is disrespectful and refuses to take in anything I am trying to teach!"

This time, seated opposite Mr. Firth, I felt a certain kind of bravado and very little remorse. I kept thinking that I was my father's daughter and even though I was scared, I felt proud. And anyway, I had tried my best to get along with Mrs. Fielding and just couldn't.

Mr. Firth looked at Mrs. Fielding's complaint note. "Well, young lady, I guess our conversation about appropriate behavior in the classroom was to no avail. I'm afraid I shall have to suggest you be brought up before the Academic Council, with the possibility of some sort of disciplinary action."

The elation of my action was wearing off. I was mostly nervous about Lila and I decided I'd wait a little while to tell her.

It was the policy of the high school that when a student was to be brought before the Academic Council, a courier was sent to the homeroom class with that announcement. I sat in homeroom the next morning dreading the moment the summons from the Academic Council would be delivered.

To my surprise, it was Mr. Firth himself who came to the classroom. He was accompanied by the assistant principal who, he said, would take over the class because Mrs. Fielding needed to attend an important meeting. He whispered something to Mrs. Fielding. Annoyed, she took her purse from the bottom drawer of her desk and quickly put on her suit jacket. Mr. Firth pointed at me and waved his finger in the direction of the door. Mrs. Fielding, Mr. Firth and I silently walked down the long hall.

Entering Mr. Firth's office, I was surprised to see Mr. Samuels already seated in front of Mr. Firth's desk.

Mrs. Fielding seemed embarrassed and somewhat agitated by Mr. Samuel's presence, and chose a seat far across the room from him. "May I ask what you are doing here, Harold?"

"Yes, of course, Pauline," Mr. Samuels smiled. "When Mr. Firth shared his concerns about Kim and Jared and their difficulties in your class, I asked to be given the opportunity of giving a statement written by myself and the editorial board of *The Daily Husky.*"

"But," she said, looking directly at Mr. Firth's face, "it is my understanding that Mr. Firth recommended that Miss Lebow be called before the Academic Council for so vigorously stating her opinions in my class."

"Exactly, Pauline. But many of those who are on the Academic Council are also on the editorial staff. We decided to voice our concerns on Kim's behalf."

Mrs. Fielding, her eyes wide and her mouth set in a silent scream, said, "What in the world do you and your staff have to do with a student of mine being impudent?"

Mr. Samuels, his tone gentle but firm, said, "Pauline, this goes way beyond Miss Lebow. And questions or verbal protests do not constitute impudence. She does not stand alone. She represents those who are chastised because of their differing views or because they dare to question or speak out. She came to the defense of and joined with a fellow student who was making inquiries. That is all he was doing. Instead of silencing their inquiries, we wish to urge you and all other faculty members of this institution to permit an openness of discussion—of differences and of conflicting points of view. In this crucial time in our history, this is not the place—here at our high school—for you or other faculty to engage in censorship."

"Harold," Mrs. Fielding now pounded the desk in front of her, "you go too far!"

"Maybe not far enough, Pauline. After all, we are merely asking you to do your part in teaching your students the importance of preserving the First Amendment to our Constitution."

I can't believe this man. He's like a rescuing angel. I wish Jared were here to appreciate him as I do. I wish Arthur could be sitting here now.

Mrs. Fielding asked for a glass of water. Her face was flushed, and I thought her cheeks would burst. "Harold, you are supporting a very rebellious person, who doesn't allow herself to be taught. Nor did her friend whose parents removed him from our school."

"Pauline," Mr. Samuels said, his voice betraying his impatience, "I do not see what you are describing as rebellion. I see it as the responsibility of teachers to rise to the challenge that piercing questions and new ideas bring. If I were to recommend anything, it would be that Miss Lebow be moved to a class environment that does not retreat into the simplicity of 'ostrich thinking' and imperious ideas. I do not see her as rebellious, although that wouldn't be the worst thing either!"

Mr. Firth, who, up to this time had remained silent, looked at Mrs. Fielding. "It's interesting that what comes to my mind are the words of Thomas Jefferson: 'A little rebellion, now and then, is a good thing…It is a medicine necessary for the sound health of government…' I'm beginning to wonder, with all of the censorship going on in the country at this time, if that same kind of medicine, as long as it's verbal, may be good for our high school as well. We all might benefit by questions and verbal rebellions which may cause us to ponder our own systems and rethink our ideas. And speaking of rethinking our ideas," Mr. Firth said, looking straight at Mrs. Fielding, "I have listened very carefully to what was said here today, and I have decided against my prior recommendation that Miss Lebow be brought before the Academic Council. I think as an accommodation to both of you, I will, however, recommend that Miss Lebow be moved to another homeroom and History IA class."

I was nearly in tears as I looked at Mr. Samuels.

I don't know what to say, but I will never forget what you have done here today. I will treasure this moment as I will treasure you! I'm getting a taste of the workings of democracy in America. There are Americans who are like the Fieldings of the world, and Americans who are like the Samuelses of the world. And I have been supported by the latter. I can't wait to tell Arthur and Andrea. I wish I could memorize everything Mr. Samuels and Mr. Firth said, word for word.

Mrs. Fielding started to sputter something and got red in the face. She turned to Mr. Firth: "Is this meeting over?" she asked. "I must get back to my class." Mr. Firth concluded the meeting and Mrs. Fielding abruptly left the room.

Later, riding home in the bus with Andrea, I was bursting with excitement as I told her what had happened.

"Wow," Andrea said. "Wow, that's all I can say! This is so great. Now you can tell Lila."

I nodded in agreement. I couldn't wait to get home and share all this with Lila and Arthur. That night at dinner, I related the whole meeting minute by minute. Arthur beamed and Lila, uncharacteristically, had tears in her eyes.

"What did you say that teacher's name was?" she asked. "I'd like to give him a call."

"He's great, his name is Harold Samuels, and he encouraged me to be on the editorial board and start writing my own ideas in a column for the school newspaper."

"Really? Does he need help with that project, or any of his projects?" Lila asked.

I had never heard Lila sound this way, so interested, so intelligent. "You know, he might like that. Why don't you go to see him?"

Lila made an appointment with him the very next day. She thanked him on behalf of the whole family, and then volunteered to help with the school newspaper, filling in to do mimeographing and distributing copies of the finished paper to classrooms. She was always returning home with purple ink residue all over her hands, but never complained about the work she so obviously enjoyed. Lila and Mr. Samuels formed an easy relationship, often discussing my future and my wish to be a writer. When I saw them together, my mother had a youthful attractiveness that I hadn't noticed before. Lila always seemed so relaxed and outgoing around him. I harbored a secret wish that Lila and Harold Samuels could be more than friends.

Mr. Samuels continued to encourage me to pursue my writing.

He read my piece in *The Daily Husky* protesting the club system at the high school as being "elitist" and not serving any meaningful purpose. I suggested that all clubs be devoted to some worthwhile community charity or help for the poor. Mr. Samuels championed this cause.

Throughout September and October, Andrea and I still made time to volunteer with the Gahagan-Douglas Campaign, scaling back to Fridays when school let out early. As the November elections drew closer, we noticed that the usually upbeat atmosphere at the campaign headquarters had turned somber. I pointed this out to Andrea one Friday on our way back home after working in the office. "Wow, Andrea, it seems like everyone in the headquarters office is reflecting a feeling of 'gloom and doom.' Even the Valley campaign manager, who used to be so glad to see us, doesn't look up any more."

"Kim, Election Day is around the corner and everyone is getting worried. My dad says Nixon is playing dirty, portraying Douglas as a 'Commie Pinko.' He doesn't think she has a chance."

On Friday, as we approached the building, we were startled by a cloud of pink papers wafting over the storefront. An airplane was dropping them all over the Valley. We watched the pink papers floating through the air.

"It's like a sea of flapping flamingoes!" I exclaimed. The flimsy papers looked eerie as they floated like ballerinas to the ground. I stooped to pick up one of the flyers and read what it said. "Andrea, look at this!" With a sinking heart I read the bold white letters on the pink background: *Helen Gahagan-Douglas, Soft on Communism*. It accused Douglas of supporting "Red Organizations" like the IPP and Henry Wallace for president in 1948. And in bold script it called her "A Closet Red"!

"Horrible." I started to rip it up, but Andrea snatched it from me.

"We need to save this," she said. "Other people need to see how low Tricky Dick will stoop to win an election!"

We numbly walked into campaign headquarters holding the scandalous flyers. "What can we do?" sighed Ted Rosier. His outrage seemed sucked into a vacuum of despair. "There is such a thing as freedom of speech, and anyway, we don't have the campaign funds to make them retract their vicious remarks."

"But couldn't Helen go on television and protest?" I asked.

Ted seemed evasive; perhaps, he didn't know how to say that Douglas and everyone around her, including himself, was unprepared for the virulence of Nixon's attacks. Our shoulders slumped as we all succumbed to a kind of hopelessness.

The next week, as we sat around *The Daily Husky* office discussing our next issue, I brought up the viciousness of the Nixon campaign against Gahagan-Douglas. "I just don't think it's fair," I complained, "when somebody uses smear tactics to gain an advantage." Mr. Samuels thought for a moment, and then said: "Sounds like the beginnings of an editorial column to me, Kim." The other staffers nodded in agreement. "Yeah," said one kid, "maybe we could have pro-con viewpoints on whether this violates free speech." We were off and running, my fellow staffers and I. Writing that editorial gave some added purpose to my feelings about the situation.

On election night, 1950, we went down to the headquarters to be with our coworkers and watch the results come in. As CBS News came on the tiny, eight-inch screen, we knew this evening was not going to be the uplifting experience we had hoped for. The longer we watched, the quieter everyone became. Around midnight, the chairperson gathered our staff together. "Congresswoman Gahagan-Douglas just telephoned me. She wishes to thank all of you who worked on her behalf. She has conceded to Nixon. She also regrets to announce that after her defeat in this election, she will be leaving the political scene and taking up other pursuits. She decided that her family, particularly her husband, Melvin Douglas who was Jewish and had experienced anti-semitic attacks, had suffered enough."

I thought, though we did not say it to each other aloud, that it would be many years before Andrea and I would engage in another political campaign. Having left politics, we had no recourse but to return to our old fantasies—Andrea would sing at the New York Met and I would have to be satisfied with the Pulitzer Prize.

When Arthur came to drive us home, he found us crestfallen. "You know, girls, this is your first election. You must not give up. The time is ripe to be more vigorous in your efforts."

"Dad, we don't feel like talking."

Arthur seemed not to have heard me. "Seriously, Kim, your mother and I are proud of the work you and Andrea have done this summer. You did a great job. A lot of other students would have been content to just laze around all summer, and use going back to school as an excuse to quit."

Why doesn't he just leave us to our doldrums? You'd think he'd be worried; didn't he say if Douglas lost there would be trouble? Now that the 'commie bashing' Nixon is in power, what's going to happen to my dad?

Andrea put her arm around my shoulder. "Hey, Kim, I have an idea. Let's wear our Gahagan-Douglas buttons to school tomorrow. It'll be our own personal salute to such a great lady."

I nodded; it seemed a fitting tribute. So the next day, we both pinned our buttons on our sweaters and walked, with heads held high, in the hallways.

During fifth period, I was given a hall pass and told to follow the monitor to Mr. Lewis' office. At first I didn't know why, but then I remembered: *Oh heck, that's right. I was told last week that I'm supposed to meet with Mr. Lewis to start my college prep planning.* I followed the hall monitor to the Administration building and was ushered into the counselor's office.

Mr. Lewis was working on a file folder when I walked in. He did not look up. My greeting was a bald spot shining up at me from his desk. When Mr. Lewis finally looked up, I saw a middle-aged man, meticulously dressed, his shirt and tie looking like he had just had them pressed. He had thin lips and a very pinched face. I shuddered inwardly. He reminded me of Mrs. Fielding.

"Well, Miss Lebow: At last we have a chance to meet and discuss your plans," he began. At this point, he looked at me and I could see his eyes flicker to my Gahagan-Douglas button. He bristled visibly and cleared his throat.

"Ahem; I see that you indicate on your forms that you would like to attend the University of California at Berkeley."

I nodded.

"Are you sure, Miss Lebow? You know they have a reputation for breeding anti-establishment types there. I don't know how good that would be for any future career plans."

What was he getting at? Wasn't he just supposed to advise me about the proper classes and credits to qualify?

I was a little stumped. "Well, uh," I stammered. "I just need to know what the requirements of the UC System are so that I can take all the proper classes now," I explained.

Mr. Lewis' tone was critical. "Yes," he said, "I can advise you about the requirements, but I would further advise you to be careful about your actions and, particularly, your affiliations."

What? What is going on here? This is beginning to sound like the kind of stuff Arthur told me he goes through! Who does Mr. Lewis think he is, anyway? My guardian?

I began to take some notes in my notebook, and realized that what I really needed to do was to get away from his needling eyes and nasally voice as quickly as possible. Mr. Lewis gave me a slip indicating we'd need to talk each fall to discuss my plans. I quickly slid out the door of his office.

Only a few minutes of my last period remained when I got back to class, and I was so angry I couldn't even pay attention. When I got to *The Daily Husky* office, I slammed down my notebook in a rage.

Mr. Samuels looked up in surprise. "Kim! What's the matter?"

"Oh, Mr. Samuels," I began, and then my frustration and rage came pouring out: how unjust some authority figures were; how dare they try to run our lives; this was a totalitarian setup!

Calmly, Mr. Samuels handed me some tissues, and waited until I caught my breath. "Sounds to me like another editorial, Kim. But you'll have to be careful to mask the real names and identities, and make sure you do your research."

I nodded, pleased to have some outlet for my feelings, and got right to work.

I was so grateful to have someone like Mr. Samuels in my life. As frustrating and as maddening as it was to deal with the Fieldings and Lewises, I was lucky, I knew, to have a way to balance those experiences by working on my writing and having a vehicle through which I could express my views.

After that afternoon, *The Daily Husky* editorial office became my second home. I thrived within the expansive atmosphere of the editorial room. And I received another gift. Mr. Samuels assured me that when I was ready, he would write a letter of recommendation to whatever university I pursued.

Chapter 6

1953

The weather was unpredictable and the radio suggested that it might rain. It was hot and very humid. On my way to the bus stop, I wished for one of those new round swimming pools that many families in the Valley were setting up in their back yards. As I stepped up into the bus, I was having a daydream of doing the breaststroke in my own pool. I felt out of sorts, even a little weepy, but my period wasn't coming for two weeks. I spotted Andrea in the back of the bus.

"What's up?" she asked.

"I feel rotten," I said, and plopped down in the seat Andrea had saved for me. "All this heat and so many sweaty kids on this bus don't help my mood. Maybe I'm just bored. It's the end of my sophomore year and nothing is new. You think?"

"No, I don't think so. What's happening at home?"

"My parents are acting stupid again. They fight all the time. Maybe it's because it's Monday morning. Who knows?"

"And your dad—did he finally come home? Were they fighting because your mom didn't know where he was?"

"Yeah," I said, now near tears. "He came back twice over the weekend. One day he's home, and flies away the next. I really miss

him. He seems tired all the time and then he gets impatient with Lila
and she goes bananas."

"Then what happens?"

"He leaves in a huff, doesn't say where he's going. Something's going
on with him, but none of us know what it is."

"That's so mysterious," Andrea said. "Did you ever think of following
him?"

"Funny you should say that. One night a few weeks ago, I did. I
watched him board the Red Car, the one with "Hollywood" on its front.
As the trolley rolled away, he was staring out the window. He looked so
sad, I felt like crying. I didn't dare tell him I followed him. He would
have been furious."

The bus rolled up to the front of the school and Andrea and I got
out. As we headed for the quad, we noticed our classmates were gathered
in clusters, whispering. They looked glum and were looking at the clock
high up on the front wall of the Administration building. It had globs
of red paint splashed all over it. Spidery red trails ran down the wall.

I turned to Andrea: "Wow, what's going on here?"

Andrea looked up at the hideous red paint on the school clock.
"Gosh, yes! It's freaky. It's really weird. I've never seen it like this. Who
did that to the clock?"

Every kid on the quad continued to look upward at the words on
the clock erratically painted in bright red: *Samuels Is a Red! Get Red of
Samuels! Down with Communism!*

Everything started to vibrate before my eyes. I knew that Mr.
Samuels was not everyone's favorite teacher. Sometimes, when I stood
talking with him in the hallway, I could see the snickers on some of the
students' faces as they passed by. But why would someone do such an
outrageous thing? I wondered where Mr. Samuels was. Maybe he was
in his room, preparing something to lecture about. I could envision him
shaking his head at what he would call kids' "knee-jerk patriotism."

I looked around and saw no trace of any teachers at all. It was the
strangest feeling, as if we were all suspended in space, just staring up at

that awful, hateful sloppy red lettering. Then, all of a sudden, I realized: The hysterical world I had been living in at home, Lila's terror of Arthur's being labeled Red and losing his faculty position, now seemed as real as the concrete I was standing on. The world of my home came to life as I stared at the tendrils of red paint above me. Maybe, Lila isn't so off the wall after all. This Red-baiting thing that she's always so terrified about—It's actually happening right here on my own school campus!

"I have no idea," Andrea said, "but whoever it was is angry, crazy, or both."

On one bench, I saw six girls, wearing light blue cashmere sweaters with the name PUFS in loud pink letters. I spotted my friend Mollie Kerrigan. She was talking with a group of girls gathered around her, a serious look on her face. I shouted across the quad: "Hey Mollie, what happened? This place looks like the night after Halloween!"

Mollie beckoned me over. We'd become good friends since we both wound up at the nurse's office with poison ivy after the school's field trip to Griffith Park, and after I saved her from being dismissed from the Academic Council by tutoring her in algebra when she was on the verge of failing the class.

"Kim, you can't believe what happened," Mollie began, her normally sweet voice cracking. "Mr. Samuels, well, he, like, he…" She stopped mid-sentence, eyes like a deer in the headlights, as Mr. Firth walked down the middle aisle of the quad. An ominous silence fell over the quad as five hundred pairs of eyes immediately locked onto him advancing down the walkway, looking tall and elegant in his gray pinstriped suit.

Mr. Firth climbed the three steps leading to the landing in front of the administration building, where two teachers were struggling to hook up an outside microphone. He approached the microphone, turned on the sound system, and an antiquated speaker system began crackling as his secretary turned it on from inside the office.

His solemn voice echoed the mood of the quad. "Please be advised that all students are required to attend a special assembly at 10:30 this morning for a very important announcement. No one will be excused from this assembly. Please report to your homerooms, immediately!"

The students quickly began to file out of the quad. Andrea and I followed Mollie and the PUFS. Mollie whispered, "I don't know how to tell you this." Once again, she stopped talking and looked away. "Mr. Samuels harmed himself...I mean...he...what do they call it? He..."

"Mollie, what's wrong? Is he sick? Was he in an accident? Did somebody hurt him?

She shook her head.

"What? Tell me!" By now I was feeling very frantic.

"Mr. Samuels harmed himself...I mean...he...what do they call it? He..." She broke off her sentence and clutched her throat.

"What?" I couldn't believe what I now realized she was trying to tell me. Harmed himself? But that could only mean one thing.

"Mollie, you can't mean he committed suicide?" She nodded.

"No!" I heard myself shouting, as if my voice was coming from inside a tunnel. "I don't believe what you're saying. Not Mr. Samuels!" My thoughts were racing, my stomach turned over, and I felt dizzy. I reached for Andrea to steady myself. I was vaguely aware of other kids staring at me.

It couldn't be! He couldn't have done that! I just saw him Friday at the editorial meeting. He didn't look the least bit upset. He was so warm to me. Why, he even complimented me on my latest piece. I just can't believe it. It must be a mistake.

Maybe I have missed something. That is entirely possible. With Arthur not around much, I'm always preoccupied with the thought that something bad is going to happen to Lila or Jonna. I even had a nightmare last week that I'd taken the Red Car to Hollywood to escape. In my dream, my mother had killed herself after killing Jonna, and I was trying to run away from it all. Maybe Mr. Samuels was sad and worried and I missed it. I remember now that Lila said he told her last week he was upset with the school administration over something. She said that he told her Firth offered his support and wanted to back him, but the forces downtown were adamant. What they were adamant about, she didn't know. Maybe I should have helped him the way he always helped me. I bet I could have talked to him the way he talked to me, like telling me after the Fielding incident that everything would work out, he would be there for me. Could I have been there more for him?

"Kim, do you believe this?" Mitch Kerrigan, Mollie's twin brother, was suddenly at my side, his hand gently touching my shoulder.

"It's unbelievable, Mitch. It's not just that he was accused. They're accusing everyone in America these days. Now, it's John Garfield, yesterday it was Dalton Trumbo, tomorrow it may be another teacher somewhere being cited. No, it's not only that he was accused; it's that I can't understand his reaction to the accusation. He had to feel desperate to do this. But how could he, after telling so many of us to hold onto our ideas, and fight for what we believed in? How could he not fight? How could he let them get to him?"

"Of course," said Mitch. "But who knows what they threatened him with. Maybe he was afraid if there was too much publicity it would not only hurt him but would destroy his family. Maybe he did this to protect them."

A hot feeling started in my head and traveled down to my toes. I suddenly began to feel a creeping bodily sensation, like a raging fever.

We numbly walked down the long hallway to our classrooms. "I knew that Mr. Samuels was having a lot of trouble," Mollie said. "Someone on the Council told me Friday that some teachers had accused Mr. Samuels of being a Red, so he got fired and wasn't even given a chance to defend himself."

"What about Mr. Firth? Did he agree with Mr. Samuels being fired?" Andrea asked.

"I heard Mr. Firth went downtown to the L.A. Unified School

Board to protest Mr. Samuels' dismissal, saying that they needed proof to accuse him. They said that he belonged to some suspicious subversive organization—the IPP, or something like that. Speaking of which, wasn't that the same organization your dad was in, Kim?"

"Where did you hear such a thing, Mollie?" I tried to hide the old fear that gripped my stomach.

Why am I so afraid…and what am I afraid of? I'm beginning to sound just like my mother. I almost feel guilty for being afraid, like I'm letting Mr. Samuels down. But he let me down. Why would he do this? Why wouldn't he stand up against those terrible people and their irrational accusations? That's what he taught me to do.

I suddenly froze, shaking my head from side to side. "No, you're mistaken; he was never in that kind of organization, Mollie."

Walking closely behind me, Andrea almost tripped on the gleaming waxed floor. She told me later she couldn't believe what I said. I often told her how proud I was of Arthur's leadership role in the newly formed California Independent Progressive Party and his determination to help elect Henry Wallace for President. Andrea told me she was totally unprepared for my reply to Mollie. I must say, I was too.

"I didn't mean anything bad, Kim," Mollie went on. "What is the IPP anyway?"

I was saved an explanation by three loud rings of the bell echoing down the long corridor. We broke away from each other to rush to our respective homerooms. In another five minutes, anyone not in their homeroom seat would be given detention.

Mr. Gilmore was my new homeroom teacher. He seemed quite somber, so I assumed he had heard about Mr. Samuels. I felt like crying. I was so immersed in my feelings, I barely heard Mr. Gilmore take the roll…

"Baker, Barnap, Culligan, Cullins, DiMetrio, Farmer, Frank, Lebow…"

"Uh, yes, here," I heard my voice answer, but it didn't seem to be coming from me. I was trembling; my lips felt numb; I was barely able to open my notebook.

Why do I feel I could've helped him? What could I have done anyway? After Lila told me about his concern with the administration, I should have talked to him at least and seen if there was anything I could do to help him, like he helped me.

The memory of Mr. Samuels' openness and warm smile caused tears to roll down my face. Images of him started popping into my brain. Months ago, when Andrea and I boarded the Red Car, we had run smack into Mr. Samuels, his wife and a few of their friends. When he introduced me to his friends as a promising journalist on the newspaper, I felt so proud. As the Red Car streamed over the Cahuenga Pass to Hollywood and Highland, the Samuelses and their friends chatted with us. We talked about the recent earthquake in California which had killed more than eleven people, and the new Negro leader, Malcolm X, whom Mr. Samuels liked because of his willingness to publicly speak his views. I recalled Mr. Samuels' openness and warm smile, and the tears began to roll down my face.

I put my head on my desk. It just felt too heavy to hold up, and I was swimming in tears. I could feel the eyes of other kids on me, but I didn't care. Someone slipped me a tissue, and I tried to sop up some of my tears.

After what seemed like years, Mr. Gilmore quietly said, "All right, students, it's time to proceed to the assembly."

The mood in the auditorium was solemn. The curtains were drawn across the few large bay windows in the auditorium, and the lights were dimmed. It took a while for my eyes to adjust. I found my way to a seat and sank into its plush depth, feeling so heavy, like I had lead in my pockets. I looked to the front of the auditorium, and saw that Mr. Firth was surrounded by the faculty who sat in two rows of chairs which spanned the length of the stage. All of them were wearing black. A few were crying. Many hung their heads, looking down at the floor as the principal began to speak; others gazed in the direction of the large covered bay windows.

Mr. Firth cleared his throat and began to speak. "It is with great sadness and distress that I announce the passing of one of our finest and most inspired teachers, and a dear friend, Mr. Harold Samuels, who died this past Saturday of unknown causes."

A buzz from the audience grew louder and louder. Questions flew back and forth among the students.

"What causes?" someone yelled from the back of the auditorium.

"How did he die?" another cried.

"Did somebody hurt him?" a third yelled.

Several cried out, "Did the red paint on the clock have anything to do with his death?"

Mr. Firth raised his hand for silence. He flattened his thick gray hair and pulled down on his suit jacket, which now looked wrinkled and less elegant than it had earlier. "At this time, in deference to the family, we'll have to wait until they make an official announcement concerning the cause of his death."

I don't get it. He seemed so strong, as though he could handle just about anything. What happened? How could he leave his wife in that way? Arthur never stops talking about David Saxon. Maybe Lila isn't so crazy after all. Are any of us safe?

I felt a creeping dread, almost as if the red paint was seeping into my life too.

My shoulders began to heave and I sobbed uncontrollably. Andrea put her hand on one shoulder and Mollie put her hand on the other. That settled me for the moment.

When the assembly was over, Mr. Firth announced that students were free for the next hour to stay out on the quad, or talk with teachers if they needed to. When we got back outside, the glaring sunshine and heat made me feel woozy. Andrea and Mollie steered me over to a shade tree on the lawn where we sat with some friends. Our efforts to comfort each other were clumsy: a touch here, a hug there, an uncomfortable look, then a move away.

"Pretty tough, huh?" Jimmy Walker said to me.

"Can't believe that guy would do something like that," said Phil Larson.

"How could anyone get up that high, to the very top of the clock? How could they climb so high up?"

"You can do that easy. I have an uncle who learned how to do that in Korea; he could scale right up a straight wall."

"Big deal about your uncle! Whoever did this was pretty damned determined."

Phil's and Jimmy's voices seemed to get very faint. I felt myself gulping for air, and the trees above me started to spin…a while later, I was staring straight up at a ceiling fan. Where was I? I could see faces leaning over mine and realized I was lying down on a cot. I heard a voice calling my name. It was the school nurse. "Kim? Are you all right? Can you hear me?"

I moaned and tried to move my head, but now had a giant headache.

"Do you want me to call your mother?" asked the nurse.

All of a sudden my head cleared. Call Lila? "No! I'll be okay, really I will," I said, faintly. "Can I can just lie here for a while?"

The nurse nodded and let Andrea, who had been hovering in the doorway, come to sit beside me. I clutched her hand and whispered: "Andrea, don't let them call her, okay? She would flip her lid!"

Andrea nodded, and then passed me a cup of water to sip. After a while I was able to sit up. Andrea hugged me, as warm tears slid down my face.

Later, as we returned from school on the bus, to avoid thinking of Mr. Samuels, I ticked off the names of the North Hollywood streets in my head: Colfax, Magnolia, Victory Boulevard and our stop: Coldwater Canyon Avenue. I practiced in my head over and over again how to break the news to Lila. *Lila's going to freak out,* I thought.

My god, it suddenly dawns on me. I wonder if Arthur is going through the same thing that Mr. Samuels went through. Maybe Arthur feels as desperate as Mr. Samuels must have felt. Maybe he's evasive about his actions because he's protecting us. Is he in the same fix as Mr. Samuels because he's a teacher? Is the College going to dump him the way they dumped David Saxon at UCLA? Maybe it's not just Cold War paranoia, but an actual threat to our family. I'm facing it at school with Mr. Samuel's suicide, and at home with worry that something could happen to Arthur, and that my mother could have a breakdown. Could Arthur ever do what Mr. Samuels did?

Unsteadily, I got off the bus, and just to put off going right home, I went straight to the newspaper stand at the corner of Victory and Coldwater Canyon. Every morning, Arthur gave me ten cents to buy *The Valley News.* I was more interested in reading Mr. Samuel's obituary than the continuing coverage of the HUAC hearings which I cut out of the paper and added daily to my scrapbook.

I found his notice, a nondescript obit, giving his age, date of death, and burial at Paradise Valley Memorial Park. No cause of death, and no funeral time listed.

I took a deep breath and turned toward home, mentally preparing, as I walked, to face my mother. When I got there, the house was very dark. Lila had drawn the curtains and was still in her bathrobe when I walked in the door. My heart sank. I wished that this was one of the days when Lila was with her friends playing mah jongg. She seemed so buoyed up on those days, so much more chipper, and they'd all be there to support her after I broke the news.

But Lila sat alone at the kitchen table, a cigarette between two fingers, reading an Ellery Queen mystery. When Lila needed to escape, she read Ellery Queen or Erle Stanley Gardner pocket book mysteries. Jonna and I knew we were not to bother her. When she was reading her mysteries, it was depression time.

Lila barely noticed me come in the back door. When she saw me standing there instead of going directly to my room, she sounded alarmed. "What is it?" she asked.

"Mr. Samuels…well he…I don't know how to tell you this."

"Tell me what?" Lila began to become agitated.

As I began to relate the news——not just Mr. Samuel's death, but how he died—Lila began to tremble. She pressed her lips together and started moaning. She looked like a mad hatter. I hated that look–it always preceded a hysterical outbreak. "Oh God, you can't mean that… Oh no! Not Harold Samuels too!" She began to sway while hugging her body. "Now you know why I'm a nervous wreck. Now you see what your father's outspoken political diatribes could do to all of us. If HUAC ever investigates him, he'll wind up like Trumbo and Hellman. They'll blacklist him out of the college! Poor Harold." Lila began to cry, and then started banging the Ellery Queen pocket book on the table. "Poor us."

It was the first time I saw my mother's fears as plausible. After all, wasn't Arthur in the IPP like Harold Samuels?

Just as I feared, Lila began to scream. Jonna, who had just come to the kitchen for a snack, quickly retreated to a corner of the room. I could only stare as Lila charged around the room, then began to pace from one side of the kitchen to the other, turning chairs over, picking up a dish on the kitchen table and throwing it against the wall. Jonna, still crouching in the corner, let out a loud cry and raced into our bedroom. I continued to stare at my mother.

> *She's so crazy. I feel like I'm in the eye of a hurricane. She's never here for us when bad things happen. Doesn't she know that Mr. Samuels was one of the most important people in my life? She goes on about herself, like we're invisible to her.*

I tried to move quickly past Lila to get to my bedroom, and narrowly avoided being hit by a plate.

Someday, she's going to injure Jonna or me and she'll be sorry.

The strange thing was, I could not remain angry with my mother for long. She was like a caged animal trying to escape. When Jonna would tell me how much she hated Lila, I tried to explain that Lila was ill. "She can't help it, Jonna. She needs a doctor. Sometimes, I feel sorry for her." Jonna would look at me in disbelief. Her hatred towards Lila was out in the open. Mine was buried deep inside.

I bet none of the other kids at North Hollywood go through this. It's safer out on the street, certainly less crazy than in my own house! Maybe that's why I resent those Clubbies. I'm envious. All they have to think about is their next date, their next party, their next cashmere sweater, and the car soon to be in their future. All I have to think about is my mother's next bout of hysteria, and my father storming out of the house to somewhere! We'll soon be like some of our neighbors who have lost their jobs, have no money and not enough to eat because of the Blacklist. Arthur will lose his job and they'll be no one to support us! It's going to be terrible tonight when Arthur comes home, if he does come home. I don't know if I wish he would, or if things would be calmer if he didn't.

Arthur did come home that night, and found no dinner waiting. "How was your day, Lila?"

Lila snapped at him. "What kind of day would you have if you just heard that one of our daughter's teachers committed suicide over Red-baiting?"

Disbelief in his tone, Arthur said: "How could that be? I just helped Kim with an editorial Mr. Samuels asked her to write."

"You don't believe me? Call Kim out here; she'll tell you."

Arthur stuck his head into our bedroom, where I had retreated, carrying the telephone with me.

"Kim?" he said, a worried look on his face. "What happened to Mr.

Samuels?" As I began to explain, the tears again welling up in my eyes, we could hear the sounds of closet doors slamming and a plate being dropped in the kitchen. "Kim, I'll come back to talk to you; I have to go to your mother," Arthur said, and rushed into the kitchen to calm Lila.

What I really wanted was for both Arthur and Lila to take me in their arms, to encircle me, comfort me, and assure me that we would be okay. Instead, I nodded when he closed the door, and called Andrea, knowing her family would be finished with their dinner.

"Hi. What did Lila say about Mr. Samuels?" Andrea asked.

"What do you think? More of the same! I'm telling you, Andrea, I can't stand another minute of this! When my dad got home, they both started screaming. They're still at it. Can you hear them in the background?" I stared up at the ceiling where I'd taped a huge photograph of Jean Paul Sartre with his arm around Simone de Beauvoir.

"Kim," Andrea offered, "if it gets too bad, come over to my house. You could have dinner with us and we'll watch Milton Berle or *The Show of Shows* on the television."

I smiled at Andrea's pride about her family's eight-inch Emerson television, which expanded to twelve full inches by using a huge magnifying glass. On Tuesday evenings, the Fine living room was packed with people of all ages sitting in front of the new device, straining to see the flickering images of Uncle Miltie, Sid Caesar, and Imogene Coca.

"Sure, Andrea, that's a great idea. I'll come over tomorrow after I finish my chores. Then, maybe Saturday we'll take the Red Car and go to the movies." It was great having a friend like Andrea. Just knowing she was there helped me.

Jonna stirred. "Kim, sit on the bed with me."

"It'll be okay, Jonna. It's just another one of their fights. They'll get over it soon."

Jonna pulled the blanket over her head, and I could hear her muffled voice saying, "It's scary, Kim. I always think they'll really hurt one another."

"No, it's like I said: just another fight that will pass." I patted Jonna's head through the blanket and quietly tiptoed to the tiny bathroom to the left of our bedroom. I didn't want Arthur or Lila to see me. It was best to stay out of their way during their torrential battles, so as not to become a target. In the comfort of the bathroom, I sat on the closed toilet seat, arms crossed and head perched on my arms which were resting on the porcelain sink. I began to cry all over again thinking about Mr. Samuels. How would I be able to cope at school without him? The editorial office of *The Daily Husky* had become my new home. The class I had with him and the newspaper project were my islands of safe refuge. Now he was gone.

I tried to concentrate on my next chapter for History. It was no use, though. I couldn't dial down the cacophony outside the door. Lila's voice rose and fell, "You idiot! You moron! You thought you were God. You thought no one could touch you. You thought your so-called friends could save you! Where are they now? They are lounging in their backyards, while we worry endlessly about what that HUAC Committee will do next. What happened to Harold Samuels could easily happen to you!" I could picture my mother circling the huge, black leather sofa, tossing her thick auburn colored hair, her face contorted, her eyes ablaze, aiming her words like sharpened spears at Arthur's long lanky figure on the couch. She knew he could not silence his opinions when he saw an injustice, and this drove her mad.

Trying to focus on the chapter about the Korean War, I played a game of mental ping pong whenever they argued. First, I'd take my mother's side, and then try to mediate for my father. He's so out of touch with Lila's terror. For once, it would be nice if he'd show some compassion. He leaves me to pick up the pieces because Lila feels she only has me to turn to. Like the time she told me that Arthur never got his citizenship papers, and she was terrified he would be deported. What am I supposed to do with that information? But then, I thought, why was he so irresponsible about those papers? According to Lila, he just accepted the fact that his original birth certificate burned when the shtetl in Russia went up in flames. He *could* be deported. Yet, he always seems so calm and just lets Lila do all the worrying. My face felt warm from all the crying. I put my cheek on the porcelain sink to cool it. But the cold surface, instead of soothing me, made me feel cold inside too. Why can't my parents be more comforting, especially when my favorite teacher has committed suicide?

It was no use, I decided. I wasn't going to be able to get any homework done tonight. Well, at least I could complete the work in my scrapbook, and maybe add the obit about Mr. Samuels. I tiptoed back to my room, opened the book, and flipped through the pages. I stopped at one of my favorite articles, about a plane filled with movie stars Humphrey Bogart, Richard Conte, Lauren Bacall, Jane Wyatt, Gene Kelley, and Marsha Hunt. They had all flown to Washington to support the Hollywood Ten, the blacklisted writers who were called to appear before HUAC. The article chronicled that momentous event of 1947 and spoke of the punishment actors and actresses such as Marsha Hunt, Jane Wyatt and Richard Conte received for going on this mission. Even though no evidence was ever provided that they were Communists, their careers were threatened. Again, I realized that maybe that's what would happen to Arthur. His career too would be threatened! I closed the book, full of sadness.

On a whim, as I began to get ready for bed, I sat down at my desk and reached for my writing pad and the Parker pen with my initials on it that Arthur had given me the day I was appointed to the staff of *The Daily Husky*. I had been thinking about writing a novel for quite a while. What better time than this, one of the saddest days in my life? I had to let out my feelings somewhere.

I lay back, thought a while, then it all came to me and I began to write,

Storm Warnings
By Kim Lebow

The splattered paint, its tendrils branching out in every direction, almost covered the clock which was set high above the quad in North Hollywood High School. For all who saw it or remembered

it, these markings would conjure images of mean-spirited people with small minds who would indirectly become responsible for taking the life of a man whose integrity and commitment to human values were unquestionable. A man who believed in freedom of ideas and the right to promote them.

If I ever finish this novel, I told myself, I will dedicate it to Mr. Samuels, who had given me such a sense of freedom and purpose in my life. As I wrote, I was crying. My face felt swollen, and the words were not coming easily. At times, my grief felt overwhelming and I would get up from the desk, walk to the window and look into the darkness outside. I would honor him by trying to follow in his footsteps. I would become a teacher and a writer.

Years later, when I found this notebook in a cardboard box, its pages were wrinkled from the tears they had absorbed. It was unfinished, an attempt by a young writer to pay tribute to her beloved teacher and mentor. I had fallen asleep before I could write the second paragraph.

Chapter 7

I awakened feeling puffy and stuffy from all the crying the day before. I had overslept. As I became more fully awake, I realized I hadn't heard my alarm clock. And then it hit me about Mr. Samuels, his suicide, and my fainting the day before.

In a daze, I stumbled into the kitchen, where I found Arthur engrossed in the newspaper, but no Lila. Arthur looked at me as if nothing had happened the night before.

"Good morning, Kim!" he said brightly. *How could he be so cheerful? Doesn't anything ever get to him?* He pushed a plate with toast towards me and poured me a glass of orange juice.

"I was thinking, Kim—you've been wanting to come to my weekly class lecture at UCLA for some time now. Would today be a good day?"

My mind drew a blank. I was way too late to catch the bus to school, and after yesterday, I just didn't feel like dragging myself there. As I mulled his invitation, Arthur repeated it:

"Well, Kim. What do you say? Come to my class with me this morning?" Arthur peered at her over his coffee cup, as we lingered over breakfast.

"Sure, Arthur, I guess so, that might be nice," I said.

I was reluctant at first to go anywhere with my father that morning, particularly after the argument he and my mother had the night before. I was extremely tired after losing sleep listening to them fighting late into the night. But neither did I feel like walking back into that quad at school so soon after Mr. Samuels' suicide. I still felt bruised and battered by the loss. I had to admit it might be nice to have a break from the many reminders those halls and classrooms would dredge up of Mr. Samuels.

Arthur said that Lila had awakened feeling ill, as she often did after their fights. She had "unexplainable pains" and had to go to Westwood to see Dr. McDonald. So Arthur suggested I come with him to his class and Lila could pick me up after her medical visit. Jonna was going to visit a friend after school and would stay there for dinner.

Arthur started clearing the dishes and said gently, "Kim, although I want you to join me so you can see what the college is like, please listen and do not talk. The class is for the college students, and you're to be an observer."

"All right, Arthur. I promise I won't say a word."

It was nine-thirty in the morning and the drive over Beverly Glen took less than half an hour. Most of the Valley students who used the Glen to get to UCLA had already crossed it hours before. While Arthur concentrated on the narrow and curving road, I looked out the window at the little houses clustered in the Glen. "You know, Arthur, I feel so sad about Mr. Samuels. Will anyone on your faculty be fired the way he was?"

"It's a dangerous time, Kim. It's been continuing to get more dangerous ever since Nixon defeated Gahagan-Douglas and the right wing has gathered an even bigger head of steam. I've only had this lecture job here at UCLA returned to me since last year. They fired a bunch of us lecturers too when we supported David Saxon for refusing to sign that Loyalty Oath, remember?"

I thought about the sense of mission Andrea and I had had when we worked for the Gahagan-Douglas campaign that summer almost three years ago. I had actually thought that if she were elected she would have been able do something about HUAC and the Red Scare, and that way I could help save my father from worrying about losing his faculty position. Of course, that dream went up in smoke with her terrible defeat. I felt that nameless sense of doom start to creep into my mind, like when I had seen that awful scrawled red paint yesterday on the school's bell tower.

"But, you'd never want to do what Mr. Samuels did, would you?"

"No, Kim, never, but I can see how he got so torn apart by the hysteria."

"Why do you say that, Dad?"

"Well, people are very frightened now, Kim. They believe Communists are a threat to the United States and they are afraid of people who think a certain way, so they make scapegoats of them. In this climate of censorship people are afraid to speak their minds. Since Nixon was elected, there has been even more censorship. I think even more innocent people will be persecuted for their beliefs."

"I see. I put some articles like that in my scrapbook about the election that said Nixon wanted to find Reds in the closet. He thinks this is the right direction for the country, doesn't he?"

"Well put, Kim. There are two things you don't want to happen if Nixon becomes President—and it looks like he is trying to leverage his Senate seat into running—one is to be on his enemy list; the other is to be a progressive liberal. It's a frightening time and politicians like Nixon are playing into that fear."

"But Lila thinks you might lose your job."

"Lila overreacts. My job seems fine, so don't worry." He looked away and seemed very uncomfortable when he said this.

As we approached the UCLA parking lot, I started to feel a little bit better—but only a little. Political discussions with my dad made me feel more like a part of his world. I had two feelings, though, about our talk. One was that he seemed to be a little bit more forthcoming and was treating me almost like his equal, even though I knew I wasn't. The other was that he seems to gloss over the real danger. He's so logical. His words did not erase my creeping feeling of dread that something might happen to him and, as a result, to our family. Somehow, Arthur rarely made me feel safe.

Last year, Arthur had taken Lila, Jonna and me to a faculty party at UCLA. Arthur chaired the History Department at LACC, but, by invitation, taught two classes at UCLA for their History-Political Science department every Tuesday.

Now, as I looked around me—just as when I saw UCLA for the first time—I loved the stately buildings on the campus. Their imposing brick and stone structures instilled in me a sense of awe, even inspiration to learn. I couldn't wait to become a student here. Of course, my other "first choice" was Berkeley, so it would be a hard decision when the time came. In the distance, across the crowded dirt parking lot, I could see building cranes in every direction. "Why is there so much construction, Dad?"

"UCLA is putting up new buildings to accommodate the increasing numbers of GIs returning to college and now applying under the GI Bill."

We continued to chat as we strolled up the tree-lined walk and entered Haines Hall, the center for history and political science studies at UCLA. We were greeted by a group of students seated on the floor on either side of Arthur's classroom door. Arthur briefly introduced me as his daughter, "who someday wishes to teach here."

He smiled, "You eager beavers look like you spent the night here."

I followed Arthur into the classroom, and took a seat in the back of the large room, while Arthur arranged his papers up front. The *Los Angeles Times* newspapers he'd ordered the day before had been delivered and placed in two neat stacks on his podium. He handed out the eighty copies of the paper. Before he began his morning lecture, he tacked a copy of the front page of the newspaper on the bulletin board which covered the front of the large, crowded lecture hall. His thin, lanky frame looked Lincolnesque as he paced from one side of the room to the other. His steps were measured with deliberateness. I was awestruck at his facility with words, as well as his ability to captivate his audience.

Each student sat in a wooden desk with armrests, notebooks opened and pens in hand, prepared for Dr. Lebow's weekly course, American Political Thought: Historical Perspectives.

Arthur pointed to the large posters on each side of the newly placed newspaper clipping. I recognized his "Gallery of Independent Thinkers" that he told me about.

"Look at these photographs carefully, class. Who do we see here? We see Aristotle, Galileo, Thomas Jefferson, John Brown, Sigmund Freud, Helen Gahagan-Douglas and Edward R. Murrow. I have selected these individuals because each one of them dared to think independently, act on his or her ideas, and contribute to society in a meaningful way. They were not afraid to stand up for those ideas. Now, look at this newspaper clipping from this morning's *Los Angeles Times.*"

"Are you preaching or teaching, Dr. Lebow?" asked a young man, whose haircut made him look like James Dean. I admired the ease and openness with which my father's students could talk to him.

Arthur smiled, then in a more serious vein said, "The focus is defining your own feelings and values and staying true to them. The essence of this whole course is the importance that is placed on diversity of opinions. I encourage you not to defer to authority—mine or anyone else's. Always think for yourselves."

A young coed, her pretty face intent, her eyes wide and innocent, spoke up. "You're telling us to stand up for what we believe, but can't that also be dangerous?"

"And what would the danger be?" Arthur asked.

"My uncle works for Universal Studios as a writer. He says that it's better in this climate to keep your political views to yourself or you'll wind up appearing before a committee."

"But if we keep quiet, it may only get worse," Arthur said. "There are no easy answers, but inciting fear about "Reds in our backyards," and silencing opposition is a form of oppression. You may disagree and debate this with me any time. After all, this is America!"

You could have heard a pin drop in the classroom. Every face, thoughtful and concerned, was focused on their teacher. *That's my father.* I was so impressed with him in his role as a professor at the University that I wanted to leap up and claim ownership of him. I looked around at the college men with their duck tail haircuts and the young women with curly hair piled on their heads. *This brilliant thinker that you're all admiring is my father!* Swept away by the aura he was creating in a college classroom, it was easy to forget that this was the same father who so often disappointed me at home.

Arthur pointed to the front page of the *Los Angeles Times* which showed a photograph of a large red trolley, filled with beach-attired riders. On the blackboard my father had written: Red Car Subject of Controversy: Board of Supervisors Consider Dismantling It for other Forms of Transportation! He said to the class, "Let's have a discussion on the possible connections between the call for the demise of the Red Car, and the House on Un-American Activities Committee, better known as HUAC."

A tall, dark-haired, serious-looking young man in the back of the room raised his hand. "Dr. Lebow, are you saying the Red Car might have something to do with civil rights? I can understand what you mean by HUAC, but what is the connection to the trolley?"

"Good question." Arthur smiled, obviously pleased that the student was beginning to get it. "The Red Car provides mobility to the people living on the other side of the hill, in that far-off place popularly known as The Valley. It has come to represent a source of freedom for that group of people. It provides them access to the vast resources of this huge city."

I saw many of the students nodding. They must be Valleyites.

"Why do the Board of Supervisors and our Mayor want to dismantle the trolley?" asked a young woman seated in the first row.

"Another good question. Let me follow this question with another. The Board of Supervisors is the governing body for the people of Los Angeles. Why, then, would they want to limit the mobility of their Valley residents, without providing an alternative? Doesn't this seem rather paradoxical?"

The students thoughtfully pondered his question. Finally, the same student in the back of the room, his black wavy hair glistening with pomade, raised his hand. "Are you suggesting that the Board of Supervisors and the Mayor are connected to interests who might benefit from the demise of the trolley? I mean, wouldn't this be an illegal act or a conspiracy of sorts?"

Arthur picked up a piece of chalk, moved to the blackboard at the front of the room, and drew a rectangle. In each corner of the rectangle he wrote a name and drew arrows connecting each of the names to each other.

Standard Oil	Firestone
General Motors	City Hall

"As we look at these names, who stands to benefit most from the Red Car's removal? Is it privately or publicly owned? How do the folks behind HUAC tie into this picture?"

He moved to his desk, sat on its front edge, and waited. I was so excited I completely forgot my promise to my father. I couldn't contain myself. "Those companies want cars to be the major form of transportation, so they're influencing the politicians to get rid of the trolley and support those companies who want autos."

Every eye in the classroom turned toward me and I heard the blonde girl in the front row whispering, "Who's she? Why is she here? She looks too young to be in college!"

My father, at first shocked, quickly regained his composure and spoke to me in that tone which everyone in our family recognized as his almost-beginning-to-fume tone. "All right, young lady, let's ask the rest of the class what *they* think, and if they think that those companies might be paying off the politicians."

Aware that I had annoyed my father, I avoided any eye contact with him and focused my attention on the same young man, who had a thick accent and joined in the discussion as if he was on a par with my father. Arthur seemed to enjoy sparring with him. The rest of the class enjoyed what easily became a stimulating debate between them. I could not forget his face and so admired his openness. My father later told me that his name was Lucien Rahbar, an émigré from Iran and the youngest and most brilliant member of his class. "Isn't it fairly obvious, Professor Lebow, that there is not only a demand for more cars in Los Angeles, but also companies who seek to benefit from the demise of the Red Car?"

"You and I think it is obvious, but that still is an assumption unless we carefully establish how we arrived at our thinking."

"Professor Lebow, the answer to 'why' is an easy one. Each company—Standard Oil, Firestone, and General Motors—stands to gain if the trolley disappears. Then we will need more cars, and cars need tires, and gallons and gallons of gas, not tracks."

"Exactly right, but we have another question to ponder. Who allows such a thing to happen? And where is the public's voice?"

Lucien Rahbar spoke clearly and forcefully. "It would go something like this: with the intense focus on the Cold War with Russia, everyone is in a state of perpetual fear. We fear the atom bomb and potential destruction. So few protest the HUAC because the public becomes convinced that we have dangerous Communists in our midst and they must be weeded out. People are afraid to protest anyway, because of the repressive climate and their concern about official reprisal. And nobody speaks up about the possible dismantling of the Red Car because we are all led to believe that 'futurism' means moving ahead and being in front of all countries, including Russia. In this scenario, the trolley is an archaic symbol of the past, an outmoded method of transportation."

Arthur's smile indicated his admiration for his student's observation. "I appreciate your comments, Mr. Rahbar, and agree that flashy new cars with fins and exotic silver grilles are the wave of the future. It's not just the Board of Supervisors and the Mayor who support these large business interests. Nixon has amassed the support of millionaires and the industrial complex."

Again, I could not keep quiet. "That's why we should all have worked for Gahagan-Douglas and not Nixon!" I blurted out. Realizing too late what I'd done, I quickly looked down. When my eyes finally met my father's, to my surprise, this time he was nodding his head in agreement.

I didn't realize that I'd been staring intently at the tall, dark-skinned young man with dancing almond colored eyes who had spoken so eloquently. After my spontaneous outburst, he looked across at me and gave me a dazzling smile. I smiled back.

The class continued. The students were extremely involved and asked more questions. As the discussion became livelier, Arthur began to encourage differing points of view. The students became increasingly engaged with each other. "Our society is a capitalist society," said Ryan Folger, whose father, Arthur later told me, was the head of the North Hollywood Chamber of Commerce. Ryan had recently been elected President of the Senior Class at UCLA.

He turned away from Arthur, and addressed his fellow students. "Capitalism is based on free competition and independent action of the business classes. So, perhaps developing other forms of transportation by increasing the numbers of cars and busses, for example, would be more helpful to the public than riding on a rickety trolley which can only handle fifty people or so at a time. Politicians who support progress are not necessarily schemers who are not serving the public interest."

I wonder if you worked for Nixon! The loud ringing of the bell announced that the class was over. I picked up my jacket and waved good-bye to my father, who was surrounded by a horde of students, then raced out of the room and down the steps to the parking lot to greet my mother. Lila had learned how to drive the year after Arthur. Despite her being as nervous as she was most of the time, she turned out to be a much better driver. Her driving was slow, but relaxed. Arthur's was fast and "lurchy."

Lila looked a bit tired, but she seemed more at ease. "How did you like Arthur's class?" she asked.

"It was exciting. Arthur's a great teacher. His students seem to really like and appreciate him. Lila, what did Dr. McDonald say?"

Lila talked as she looked ahead, maneuvering the car onto Sunset Boulevard and turning right to Beverly Glen. "He's going to try a medication that's brand new and he hopes it will calm my nerves. He calls it the state of the art antidepressant."

I didn't ask her more about the antidepressant, but I silently wished there would be some ray of hope that she would be less anxious and sad around the house.

As we rode back through the Glen, I thought about the discussion in Arthur's classroom. I couldn't chase the worry from my mind.

Now that the 'Commie bashing' Nixon is in power, what's going to happen to my dad? And now that the bashing has invaded my school, how will I be able to stand going there? Not that I have a choice.

All of a sudden, the awful realization of Mr. Samuels' absence came crashing back to me. When my dad wouldn't answer my concerns, I could always count on Mr. Samuels. Now he's gone, forever! I felt so sad and so dejected again that the little bit of brightness from Arthur's classroom seemed to just fade away.

As we pulled into our driveway, though, there was another reason to be hopeful. There sat Andrea, excitedly waving to me to welcome me home.

"Hey Kim! Where were you? We missed you at school today!"

Lila smiled at Andrea. "Would you girls like some iced tea in the backyard?"

I could see that Lila was in a better mood. I guess her doctor saying he would help her to get over her depression made her feel better. She brought us out a tray of iced tea, the ice cubes clinking cheerfully in the glasses, and put it down on our patio table. She had opened a package of chocolate cookies for us too. I could see that she was trying to do whatever she could to make us feel better.

As the afternoon shadows lengthened, Andrea and I sat and softly talked. She filled me in on the day's events and then, almost at once, we started planning our next jaunt on the Red Car. I quickly forgot Arthur's ominous predictions and instead took comfort in knowing that on the weekend we could get away. The two of us could escape these Valley doldrums and create the world the way we wished it to be.

Chapter 8

I cannot and will not cut my conscience to fit this year's fashions.

—Lillian Hellman, appearing before HUAC, 1952

The Emerson television set, Lila's pride and joy, was turned up loud so that it could be heard throughout the house. We were all rushing around getting ready for the day. The twelve-inch set, encased in an elegant maple console, had six Colonial-style decorative brass handles on the cabinet doors. Lila pleaded with Arthur for over a year before he finally relented and purchased the set. She promised she'd get a job to help with the payments.

It was six-thirty in the morning on May 21, l953, and Edward R. Murrow was hosting a broadcast focusing on Hollywood's blacklisted writers and featuring footage from Lillian Hellman's appearance before HUAC the year before.

It seemed that Murrow, cigarette dangling from the side of his mouth, his cheeks perpetually darkened by his five o'clock shadow, had almost become a part of our family. He began his introduction in the retrospective telecast, "And so, my fellow Americans, it is important to reiterate that dissent is not unpatriotic…it is the voice of an informed and caring electorate. The more we care about something and cherish it, the more we want to become involved in changing its ills and expressing our concerns."

Arthur, after many futile attempts to fix his bowtie and prepare to leave for the university, glared at the television. "You're so right, Ed. Look at those ghouls. They seem to really relish attacking creative writers and Hollywood stars, maybe because it gets them more attention. It was infuriating when they called up Lillian Hellman. She's one of the finest writers who ever lived! There isn't one among them who can hold a candle to her brilliance."

Lila, who was rarely up at this time, left the dining room and began puttering around the kitchen, after readying herself to go for a job interview at the local library. Agnes Learner, her new friend across the street, told her about the opening. Hurriedly attempting to scramble a few eggs for all of us, Lila kept leaving the stove to glance at the television in the living room. Cooking was not her forte: she'd burned her hand twice on the thick iron skillet.

Lila's new internist, Dr. Lipton, advised that she should seek some meaningful work, get out of the house more, and occupy herself with something productive. As soon as Agnes told her about the job opening, she sent in her application. She also had to keep her bargain with Arthur and help pay for the new television set. Jonna and I were skeptical. We'd heard her many pipe dreams in the past about what she wanted to do with herself, but none ever materialized. We often watched her retreat to the bedroom and sleep away many a day. Now, she was at least willing to try to get a job. As was usual for his pattern, Arthur was so intensely involved at the college, he barely noticed.

Lila cheered as she stuck her head out from the kitchen door and watched the camera refocus on Murrow, who was reminding his audience of other famous writers who had been called before the committee. "Remember Lillian Hellman's response, when asked by the committee to name names of friends or associates who were Communists: 'I cannot and will not cut my conscience to fit this year's fashions.'" Lila, Arthur and I remembered her courageous stance the year before and when Murrow repeated it, we began to applaud.

"You better believe it; good for you for reminding your audience of Lillian!" Arthur exclaimed. "Not one of them has her smarts, and I bet not one of them has read *The Children's Hour* or *The Little Foxes.* The ones who profess to weed out un-American activities are so un-American themselves." With that, Lila abruptly raced back to the stove where the scrambled eggs crackled their protest as they sat in the frying pan a few seconds away from being burnt.

I frantically brushed my hair, pausing to put the last two answers to my calculus problems into my homework notebook which was propped up against the cabinet of the television set. I overheard Murrow's speech as I hurriedly wrote answers in my notebook and took in what Lila and Arthur were commenting about in relation to the hearings. *Isn't it amazing that the only thing which brings those two together is something political? They only agree when they feel attacked by an outside enemy.*

Even though it was tempting to get caught up in my parents' fervor about the "Committee," I had another major worry this morning: I was scheduled to meet with my school academic counselor, Mr. Lewis. Ever since my first meeting with him, we had clashed and he had been unfriendly to me. He never missed an opportunity to criticize my involvement in politics. All my friends saw Mr. Lewis as a narrow-minded person too. He made disparaging remarks whenever he could about our "leftist" newspaper staff and about the few Negro students at the school. But their agreement with me about him might not help me when I was alone with him in his office. I hoped that my plans to go to UCLA or Berkeley wouldn't get sidetracked by him.

Funny, Lillian Hellman's enemy was HUAC and mine is Mr. Lewis. What if he tells me I can't go to UCLA or Berkeley? I'll petition, that's what. I'll go to Mr. Firth, and tell him that Mr. Lewis is an academic counselor who not only has a bias against Negroes and homosexuals, but also against bright and outspoken women.

Lila's agitated voice startled me out of my private musings.

"Kim! Call Jonna and tell her to get out of bed! If she wants to have breakfast, she should be at the table in two minutes!"

The sound of a banging frying pan against the porcelain sink followed me as I opened the door to our small bedroom.

"Jonni, time to get up. The eggs are still hot."

Jonna whispered, her head still under the covers, "I hate her breakfasts. They make me sick!"

"Don't start trouble, Jonni. At least she's trying. When was the last time she cooked us breakfast?"

I walked through the narrow space between our beds and opened the curtains. The two single beds, with a dresser in between, were covered in bright yellow and green bedspreads which also served as extra blankets when it was cold. The beds rested against the walls, with a window a few inches above each one. Both windows looked out to the far reaches of the backyard where two large oleander bushes hid our brick incinerator.

The 1947 vintage incinerator came with every house in the Kaiser Tract. Every day, bits of trash, garbage, and unwanted odds and ends went into the incinerator. In the summer it enjoyed a miraculous change and doubled as a barbeque. Jonna and I had friends over and enjoyed making s'mores on its grill. At night, the smell of assorted garbage, trash, and food scraps wafted over the entire tract. This, combined with the pungent odor of the cesspools, which functioned as sewers, caused many complaints from Valleyites. Many a summer night we wished for a ride on the Red Car to Hollywood just to get away.

Now it was Arthur's turn to become impatient: "Lila, isn't that breakfast done? I'm going to be late for my eight o'clock class. If you're not ready, I can't drive you over to the station to catch the Red Car!"

Finally, we were all gathered and sat eating our breakfast in the dining room, all of us watching the last of the CBS Morning News. Lila and Arthur reminisced about Lillian Hellman's courage in not naming names. I thought about *Watch on the Rhine*, my favorite Hellman book. Arthur bolted down his food, and then reached for his pipe and the stack of new history books he was bringing to class. With a quick peck on everyone's bowed heads, he ran through the living room and out the front door. "Lila, I'll start the car. Please hurry."

Lila jumped up, not making eye contact with either of Jonna or me. We both knew what was missing, and I was the one to say it.

"Good luck today, Lila."

Lila attempted a smile, but couldn't quite make it, unable to mask her hurt and disappointment with Arthur. She turned from the table, grabbed her coat and ran out to meet him.

Soon we heard the Chevy, which Arthur never had time to take in for repair, take off with a loud, sputtering sound. We sat in silence, glumly finishing the last of our bacon and overdone eggs.

"He could have said something to her. Just a little something."

"Well, you did, Kim."

"Jonni, it's just not the same. He treats her like she's not there."

"Well, most of the time, she isn't." Jonna looked down and forked her remaining strip of bacon. "She's in her own world, like we're not there either."

"Jonni, you've got to get over this resentment of her. Both Dr. McDonald and Dr. Lipton say she's depressed. Depressed people often walk around in a daze like Lila does."

"You're always defending her. I don't care if she's depressed or not. She makes my life miserable. My friends don't go through what you and I do."

"Well, you and I have a way out. We can go to school. I have an appointment today with Mr. Lewis about UCLA or Berkeley. I'm scared though."

"Why, what are you scared of?"

"He's made it hard on students like me who say what they think. He hates me for writing an article in *The Daily Husky* which he thinks is about him. I have this terrible feeling he'll use anything he can to stop me from going to the university."

Jonna's fork stopped in mid-air. "He can't do that, can he, Kim?"

I put my hand over Jonna's free hand on the table. "Don't worry, if he makes it hard on me, I'll go to Mr. Firth. He'll make it right. C'mon, we'll both miss our bus if we don't get out of here."

On the way to school, I confided in Andrea about how worried I was about my meeting with Mr. Lewis.

"Kim, he's just an advisor," Andrea said. "How much influence can he really have?"

"That's just it—too much. Last year, some kids were advised to go to technical school, when they really belonged in an academic university. He's just plain arbitrary."

"Is it because of the article you wrote in the *Husky*…you know, the one that I told you was stepping over the line?"

I knew exactly what Andrea was referring to, and that was the problem. I was sure Mr. Lewis had a plan to get even with me. The article I'd written for *The Daily Husky* observed that power was often vested in those who could do damage to innocent people. I used HUAC and McCarthy as examples. I wrote that the Hollywood Ten were courageous to stand up to the power mongers of the HUAC Empire and its little Napoleon, McCarthy, who used the committee for his own political ends. I referred also to "certain others" in our school who were given too much power to decide the fate of graduating seniors. *What was I thinking? I'm so much like Arthur. I can't keep my views to myself. I wish Mr. Samuels was here.*

"Well, even though that article was a little over the top, I think you're worried for nothing," Andrea said. "Your grades are good, and you've done great work for the school newspaper. All your teachers, except Mrs. Fielding, value you. Why are you so worried?"

"I just know Mr. Lewis has too many biases. And one of them is openness and outspokenness, that kind of thing."

Before lunch, as I sat in English class, Mr. Lewis' secretary, Miss Pemble, walked in. It was too soon for her to be coming for me, so I turned back to the poem we were discussing, but noticed out of the corner of my eye that she was fixing her humorless look on me. I scrunched down in my desk, trying not to look at her. I gazed out the window where I saw some friends from French class, smoking at the Husky Café across the street. I wished I was with them.

In my peripheral vision, the yellow and white roses of Miss Pemble's dress moved closer and my nasal passages swelled with her nasty body odor. Her bony hand touched my shoulder. *Not me, not now, I'm not ready.*

"Mr. Lewis needs to see you right now. You are to come with me immediately."

I couldn't believe it! I'd planned to have lunch with Andrea and my other friends before my two o'clock appointment, but he wasn't even allowing me that comfort. As I walked between the rows of desks, Roger Willoughby whispered, "Give 'em what for, Kim!" Roger and I had a shared dislike for Mr. Lewis. Roger's major disagreement with him was over whether Dalton Trumbo's book, *Johnny Got His Gun*, should be allowed in the school library. Mr. Lewis said it was an unfavorable description of war and "a nasty bid to discourage all young men from joining the R.O.T.C. by depicting a quadriplegic war victim." He said Trumbo's "unpatriotic" views were "questionable."

Roger's father was fighting in Korea and wrote scathing letters about the "rotten war" he was forced to fight. Roger stuck to his guns, and I stuck up for Roger. "And since when is any war favorable or unfavorable?" Roger cried out. "You don't know what war does to people."

To Mr. Lewis' chagrin, I jumped in to support Roger. "If every person saw what war does to people like in *Johnny Got His Gun*, maybe we wouldn't have any more wars. And would you think if Roger's dad gets shot or something that that's favorable or unfavorable, Mr. Lewis?"

Mr. Lewis' face began to look like the color of a beet. His eyes narrowed, and in a state of contained rage he told Roger that he would not assign him to detention that day out of respect for his father, but his rude manner would not be forgotten. Mr. Lewis then turned to me wagging his finger, "And you, Miss, always have too much to say!"

Roger never made the varsity basketball team, even though he was the best player in the school. He didn't get the recommendation he needed to go to Stanford either. We were convinced that the cruel hand and heart of Mr. Lewis was responsible for both.

And now it's my turn, I gulped, as I walked behind Miss Pemble and listened to the clickety click of her high heels on the solid oak floors and stared at the perfectly straight seams of her nylon stockings. As we walked through the wood doors to Mr. Lewis' office, I couldn't shake the bad feeling I had.

Mr. Lewis waved me in, and pointed to a chair in front of an extra long, imposing desk. There I sat facing pictures of Mr. Lewis sitting on a sofa with two boys, about five and seven. The taller of the two had a sort of pinched look like his father. The other, rather cute, with a much more pleasant face and looking somewhat impish, was shorter and blonder.

Mr. Lewis put his fingertips together in the precise way I hated. "Well, Miss Lebow, I have reviewed your entire record here at North Hollywood and will come directly to the point. Despite the fact that you are an A student, your public demeanor and unnecessary rebelliousness strike me as a reflection of an immature character."

My heart began to pound. I needed to keep my cool, but I was seething. I felt something wet on my cheek and understood what "tears of rage" meant. I also felt desperate. "I apologize, Mr. Lewis, if you feel I have been outspoken and immature, but I wasn't trying to be rebellious. I don't think you realize that you're contradicting everything my father taught me. He says if your rights are abridged, you protest; if there's something that seems unjust, you fight it. I have been trying to listen to him, as well as Mr. Samuels, who urged us to speak out against any abridgment of rights."

"Miss Lebow, every student has a story. Now you tell me that at your father's and Mr. Samuels' urging, you found just cause to write incendiary pieces in the daily high school newspaper?" he said snidely.

I tried another direction. "Mr. Lewis, I know you didn't like my piece in the *Husky,* and the person I was describing with pomaded hair sounded a little like you, but I assure you it wasn't you. It was Roy Cohn, Joe McCarthy's right hand man. He had pomaded hair, too–a little bit like yours. And the whole thing was a metaphor, and…"

"Enough, Miss Lebow! I think some of the faculty here misjudged your overly-aggressive openness for innate intelligence. My records indicate that the best place for you is a little college somewhere out in the Midwest where you can learn decent values. Therefore, I can't write a recommendation for UCLA or any institution of its caliber!"

The picture of Mr. Lewis and his sons blurred. I began to feel dizzy. I had to marshal my resources. My mind raced, and I thought of Mr. Samuels, wishing that his spirit was in the room with me now. Just as I was ready to confront Mr. Lewis and possibly shoot myself in the foot, I remembered watching Edward R. Murrow talking about Lillian Hellman and the courage she showed as she went up before HUAC, and reflected how important it was to speak up. I tried to remember what Arthur said. Something like, "Not only did she not give names, but she spoke out against the whole vile process. She insisted on preserving her integrity. She knew this was not a time to remain silent."

"Mr. Lewis," I began, my knees shaking, my voice soft and even, "This is not a time for me to remain silent. After five semesters of all straight As, I deserve to go to UCLA or Berkeley. I question your objectivity as a counselor, and will appeal your decision to higher authorities."

Mr. Lewis picked up the file with Lebow on the front. "You are not the authority here, Miss Lebow, nor are you in a position to evaluate me as a counselor. What I say goes."

"My future is at stake. I have a right to question your decisions, Mr. Lewis. I also have the right to go to Mr. Firth and defend my case."

"Oh, so now you are a lawyer or a litigator, Miss Lebow?" Was it my imagination, or did he squirm when I mentioned going to Mr. Firth?

"Thank you, Mr. Lewis. At least you recognize that I have a mind, and can speak up for myself and for what I think is right."

"Miss Lebow, you go too far!" Mr. Lewis' temples bulged, his face reddened in anger.

Just as Mr. Lewis readied to dismiss me, his telephone rang. He angrily picked up the receiver, then immediately softened his tone: "Yes, Mr. Firth; no, Mr. Firth; no she didn't tell me that, Mr. Firth. I had no idea you had received a…" Then I couldn't hear because he rolled his chair around and turned away.

After some time, Mr. Lewis carefully returned the receiver to its cradle. I could see his hand was shaking ever so slightly as he turned to me. "Well, Miss Lebow, I gather you've received some sort of award for your reporting. Our principal just informed me that you are to be nominated for an honorary position on the Academic Council."

I felt surprised and jubilant at the same time. "I didn't know that, Mr. Lewis, and I'm really pleased. Does this mean you'll consider writing the recommendation to UCLA or Berkeley for me?"

Mr. Lewis, his look as somber as his tone, said, "The matter has been taken out of my hands. Mr. Firth just informed me that he and the entire *Daily Husky* staff have all signed a letter of recommendation to any university of your choice."

"Oh…my," I stammered. I was speechless.

"You didn't ask me who wrote the letter of recommendation, did you?" Mr. Lewis said sternly.

"No, Mr. Lewis. Who wrote it?"

Mr. Lewis pressed a button on his desk, and seconds later Miss Pemble entered the room and handed him a manila folder, the front of which read "University Recommendation—Kim Lebow."

Mr. Lewis opened the folder and took out the single sheet of paper inside. As he handed me the paper, I immediately recognized the long, extended flourishes I'd grown accustomed to receiving when commentary was being given to an editorial piece I'd written. At the bottom of the page, the entire *Husky* editorial staff, as well as Mr. Firth, supported the writer of the letter by adding their own signatures.

I noted the date on the letter. It was written by Mr. Samuels and dated two weeks before his death.

Chapter 9

1954

When my bedside alarm rang at 7:00 a.m., I was awakened out of an intense dream where I was hurtling through space, not sure where I was going to land or how hard the fall would be. The terror of falling into an abyss with nothing to stop my speeding form from destruction took quite a few moments to get over. I sat at the side of my bed, finally leapt up and briskly ran for the bathroom. The hum of Jonna's nasal breathing and the familiar sound of Arthur's low pitched guttural snoring, coming from the other side of the paper thin walls, brought me back to reality. I returned to our bedroom and looked at the calendar above my bed. July 12, 1954: the date was circled in red because it was my seventeenth birthday.

Humming quietly to myself, I rummaged through the closet deciding what to wear, unable to contain my excitement about my birthday plans. Andrea, Ruthie, and Robin would meet me at the Circle M Market. I had invited Ruthie and Robin at the last minute. They were on the editorial staff with me at North Hollywood and were going to UCLA in the fall. UCLA was so huge it would be comforting to have some friends on campus.

We planned to ride the Red Car into Hollywood over the Cahuenga

Pass, and get off at Hollywood and Highland. First, we'd go to the Egyptian Theater to see Marlon Brando in *On the Waterfront*, then to Coffee Dan's for dinner, or we might go straight to C. C. Brown's for ice cream sodas or sundaes.

I tried to forget the damper my father had thrown on our plans the night before when he said, "I cannot believe that my daughter would pay money to support a film directed by Elia Kazan." Every day for the past two weeks, Arthur had been glued to the television watching the recent events of HUAC and the attacks on the newly blacklisted writer, Arthur Miller. He muttered to himself and cursed at the television screen when any witness friendly to HUAC appeared. Elia Kazan, a former close friend of Miller's, had been asked and agreed to be one of the witnesses to testify against Miller.

"Leave her alone," Lila said, in one of her more collected states and in a rare moment of support for me. "She has a right to see what she wants to see." Arthur quickly shot back at Lila. "Everyone, including my daughter, should stand up for what they believe in."

"Does that mean we stop listening to Beethoven because he was German or Wagner because he was anti-semitic?" Lila knew that the two composers were Arthur's favorites. "She can tell the difference between an individual's talent and his political beliefs. Even though we think Elia Kazan's actions are unconscionable, he's still a great director who makes great films."

Too bad Lila didn't have more moments like this, I thought wistfully.

Arthur finally capitulated, shrugged his shoulders and affectionately hugged me. "It's your birthday tomorrow. You can do anything you want."

I was grateful Arthur had relented. The tension between my parents had escalated since my father was summoned to the chancellor's office at the university two weeks ago and asked to explain his political activities. Jonna and I listened to them fighting nightly over this. Lila was in hysterics, and Arthur, of course, down-played the seriousness of his situation. Late into the night, I could hear Lila pacing back and forth, the heels of her slippers making loud noises on the linoleum floor in the kitchen. Following these "fight nights," the morning after brought a cold silence accompanied by a wooden stillness in the household. This would continue until both of them left the house for the day, neither looking behind them, nor saying good-bye.

For the moment, I was grateful that things had quieted down. Now that I knew I would be going to UCLA to pursue a major in history, I had quite a bit of preparation to do. The History Department suggested that for extra credit, incoming freshman bring in an ongoing research project. It so happened that several students from our French class had been able to convince the teacher to meet with us over the summer in a French History Study Group. This fit in really well with my UCLA requirements and my own interests, so I had begun an essay about the Dreyfus Affair for the study group. The Dreyfus Affair had always fascinated me. And with what my family and the country were going through, the similarities between that time period and the current Red hysteria, HUAC and McCarthyism intrigued me. I was hoping to tie together the events of the 1890s, when Alfred Dreyfus, a Jewish officer in the French Army, was falsely accused and convicted of treason, to our present situation. Dreyfus, just like Aaron Copland, Robert Oppenheimer, the Blacklisted Ten and so many others, had been falsely accused. Dreyfus had a champion, Émile Zola, who in January, 1898 in an open letter to a Paris newspaper wrote *"J'accuse."* The letter aroused vehement public protest and exposed the severe anti-semitism and corruption in the French Army, Legislature, and Judiciary which had led to the assault on Dreyfus' civil rights. The intense political and judicial scandal that ensued after Zola's letter divided French society between Dreyfusards and Anti-Dreyfusards. Dreyfus' case was reopened and all accusations against him were demonstrated to be baseless.

The schisms over the Dreyfus Affair reminded me of the division between liberals, conservatives and reactionaries in my own country. Mostly, it reminded me of all those unfortunate people being accused in this era of McCarthy, and how baseless so many of the accusations were.

I was eager to get a little work done on my paper before the rest of the family got up. I went to the kitchen and turned on the little Philco radio on the counter near the toaster. I combed my hair by running my fingers through my thick, brownish-black curls, twirling a few of them onto my forehead. I pushed my chair back, rushed into the tiny bathroom to the left of the bedroom and jumped in the shower. Returning to the kitchen in my bathrobe, a towel on my head turban style, I checked the clock: 8:30 a.m. Still plenty of time to work on the Dreyfus paper, then go in and get dressed for my big day. I promptly buried myself in my work.

Two hours sped by. Then, around ten-thirty or so, Arthur, Lila and Jonna appeared in the kitchen. Lila seemed hung over. Maybe that was from the sleep medication the doctor had prescribed to calm her nerves from the calamity of the past few weeks. Arthur, nattily dressed in his seersucker summer jacket and white shirt, looked very dapper, like Arthur Schlesinger. He said he was planning to work only for the morning and would return home that afternoon. With both hands on Jonna's back, he gently nudged her into the middle of the kitchen. All three broke into a loud and boisterous "Happy Birthday." Jonna handed me a small, neatly wrapped package and a large white envelope, which said, "To Kim, Happy Birthday," in Lila's beautiful penmanship.

I felt myself soften. *Wow, I have to hand it to my family. No matter what is going on, they always make our birthdays special.* And it was true. A complete truce was called on every birthday. The mood of the household would shift from dismal despair to buoyant cheerfulness. It was temporary, but a refreshing lull in an ever-brewing storm.

I read the card. "To Kim—We are so very, very proud of you... Happy Graduation...Happy Birthday...All our love...Dad, Mom, and Jonni."

I carefully opened the little package and found inside a beautiful gold pinky ring with several small rubies on either side of a glimmering small diamond. I was thrilled and rushed from Arthur to Lila to Jonna with hugs and kisses. The commotion of the past weeks over our neighbors' being fired from their jobs seemed to have dissolved. Arthur excused himself to leave for work, then turned around and came back to the kitchen.

"You know, Kim, I wanted to tell you that I'm very proud of this extra-credit work you're doing on your essay. Is it going okay?"

"Yes, Dad—thanks for asking. I'm going to be showing it to the Study Group later this week to get their comments."

"I'm curious, Kim: I know that you really love French history, but what made you write about Dreyfus?"

"It was the whole thing that you've had to go through the past few years, Dad…having to answer all the time about your political leanings and fight about signing loyalty oaths. It's so unjust. I also thought of Dreyfus because of what happened to the McVeys."

Lila looked up, her eyes beginning to fill with tears. The McVeys, an older couple who lived two houses down, had befriended us from the day we moved into the tract. Both Lanny and Joy McVey had worked at RKO as successful screenwriters. One day a couple of months ago, they had been summarily dismissed from their jobs. The studio told them their work was outdated, but fellow writers said it was because Lanny and Joy were suspected of "Red leanings." With only occasional income from freelance work, the couple became nearly destitute. Lila, decidedly one of the least talented cooks in existence, had been bringing prepared dinners to the McVeys for the past month. Each time she returned from their house, we saw the look of panic on her face. Two evenings ago, when she brought back the pans from the previous delivery, she turned to us and said, "Next it will be Arthur. Then who will bring *us* dinner?"

He turned to Lila. "So, you're afraid I'll be unfairly accused, like Captain Dreyfus?'" Arthur said. "And, you feel the same way as your mother, Kim."

"Yes, I guess I do," I said. "And I wonder who speaks for people like you? Dreyfus had Émile Zola to protest for him in '*J'accuse*.'"

"Well, Kim, we also need to look on the positive side. So many people of good conscience are speaking out every day. Just look at Edward R. Murrow and how he's been able to expose this travesty in his weekly broadcasts. Then there was the Special Consul for the Army Joseph Welch, at the Army-McCarthy Hearings—remember when he attacked McCarthy's indecency for falsely accusing an innocent young attorney in Welch's firm of being a Red and attempting to destroy his career? And you have that clipping in your scrapbook from 1947 when we first moved here, when that large group of Hollywood stars flew to Washington, D.C. to support The Hollywood Ten. Many people are willing to do the right thing."

"But those are just a few," I said. "During the Dreyfus Affair, the whole intellectual community of writers and artists in Paris supported him. Even the students at the Sorbonne went out in protest. But, here it seems like not enough good people stand up for what's right."

"You know, Kim," said Arthur, putting his arm around her shoulder, "you can't get into the 'good and bad' or 'good and evil' thing. Perhaps I was too harsh about Elia Kazan. He loves his work, and wants to make more films. If he didn't testify, the studios would've dropped him. And, to boot, he truly believes that communism is an 'evil' thing."

"But Dad, Arthur Miller was his best friend."

"When HUAC has your thumbs pressed in a vise, friendship doesn't seem to matter. Fear for your own survival takes over. Anyway, Dreyfus was the proverbial scapegoat in French society," Arthur said.

"Are you going to be the scapegoat at LACC and UCLA?" My question came out before I could stop it and betrayed the anxiety felt by everyone in the family.

"Someday I'll be able to discuss my own situation in detail. Right now is not the time. It's your birthday, and you should enjoy every minute of it."

The long silence that followed was shattered as Lila slammed her bedroom door.

Arthur looked down, slowly shaking his head. "I'm sorry this enjoyable morning had to end like this, but I still hope you have a wonderful birthday with your friends, Kim." He hugged me, planted a kiss on Jonna's head, and left the house.

As I was about to leave, Lila rushed in from her room, still dabbing at her eyes with a Kleenex, and gave me a Happy Birthday hug. She went right back to her bedroom where we soon heard her sobs.

My friends were gathered waiting at the Circle M Market, two of them in their sweaters, skirts and "bucs." Andrea and I wore our favorite pedal pusher outfits. It was a beautiful July day. The sweltering heat which plagued the Valley would come later in the summer. We chatted as we walked down Coldwater Canyon Avenue.

Ever since I met her, Andrea always had the breaking news of the day. We even dubbed her "The Clarion Caller." Today it was no different. "Did you hear that Roger Bannister broke the four-minute mile in England? We were talking about it this morning. My dad always asks us what we think is an interesting current event of the week."

"What did your gorgeous brother have to say?" giggled Ruthie.

"He's not very sports minded, so he doesn't really care about Bannister, but he has been flipping out about the new Supreme Court ruling, Brown versus The Board of Education in Topeka. He says that will end segregation in public schools. He thinks Chief Justice Warren is the fairest man in this country. He was able to engineer a unanimous ruling with his fellow justices, so my brother says that gives the decision even more clout."

"That's just like him," swooned Ruthie. "I wish he'd come with us today, Kim."

We were all talking so much that we hardly noticed how quickly we got to the Red Car station on Chandler Boulevard—and that there was a critical difference in its appearance. When we stopped and looked around, we realized that the station was empty. Where were all the people usually sitting on the benches under the overhang waiting for the trolley? Why was it so quiet? No Red Cars rushed by. No clashing of brakes. No trolley horns blared.

I turned to my friends: "Something's wrong. Is it a holiday or something? There are usually twenty or thirty people here waiting for the Red Car."

We spotted a white sign, placed over the tracks, with huge black letters. It read: Services Discontinued: Red Car to Be Replaced by Bus Service to Begin August 1, 1954. We had to read the sign three times for the news to set in.

"I can't believe we didn't hear about this before." Ruthie said. "My mother told me she and her friends were taking the Red Car to Hollywood tomorrow for the summer sale at the Broadway. I better call her and let her know."

"Don't call her yet, Ruthie," Robin exclaimed. "There's been some mistake or maybe it's a practical joke."

"It's no joke guys," I said. All of a sudden, Arthur's lecture at UCLA from two years ago came back to me.

Andrea turned to me. "What do we do now? How do we get to the Egyptian?"

"Let's go back to my house. We'll think of something." I led the dejected band back to my home, hoping that Lila's mood of the morning had passed.

When I opened the front door to the living room, Arthur was sitting at his Smith-Corona typewriter. He looked up at our long faces. "I know what the matter is, girls." On the desk beside him was an editorial from the morning's *Los Angeles Times*.

"The last of the Pacific Electric Railway Company's Red Cars rolled down the tracks in El Segundo on June 15, 1954. No one questioned; no one said good-bye. It happened without fanfare and without protest. No one has sought to question what forces were behind this, and what is happening in our fair city."

"Can you believe they've shut down the Red Cars?" Our faces flushed, we looked and felt distraught.

"Dad, I can't believe it. My birthday celebration's going to pieces." I was just about to ask Arthur if he would drive us into Hollywood when he broke into a loud diatribe.

"Behind the scenes of this tragedy is a merger of sinister proportions, a calumny which deprives many of us of our rights to make free choices."

That's right; humiliate me in front of my friends. You always do this. My birthday celebration is destroyed and I have to hear a lecture from you. My freedom has been taken away from me. How am I going to get a break from you and your pontificating, and Lila's moods? And how are we going to get to the Egyptian?

Arthur approached me, reaching out to touch my shoulder, and put his arm around me. "Well, you're lucky. It turns out that I'm not going to work this morning after all. I'll give you a ride to Hollywood."

Our faces lit up.

"Really, Arthur? That would be super." I knew the price of the ride would be more of his lecturing on the way over, but Marlon Brando was worth it. And sure enough, as soon as we turned onto the Cahuenga Pass and headed toward Hollywood, Arthur began again: "The public is in the dark. They can't protest. It's already too late. The busses will take over and the Red Car will be just a memory." With each swerve in and out of traffic, my friends and I clung to each other and the seat.

"But what about the press? Didn't anyone get wind of this while it was happening?" Andrea asked, hoping Arthur could concentrate on her question and his driving at the same time.

Her ploy didn't work. Arthur simply wasn't capable of doing both. As he turned to Andrea in the back seat to answer her question, he barely missed a large white truck veering over the white line. "The press was notably silent about it, and even if they hadn't been, the public was too consumed with their backyard barbeques and daily lives."

As always, I was torn between admiring my brilliant father and being embarrassed by him in front of my friends. At home it was different. There he was emotionally uninvolved. With my friends, he became the pontificating university professor. Still, I thought, he was driving us all the way to Hollywood, for which I was grateful. He even offered to pick us up later.

From now on we'll just have to take busses to get into the city. But the Red Car was only fifteen cents. Well, I'm off to UCLA this fall anyway, and the first thing I'm going to do is get a job and buy a car—no matter how old or used. But what are the rest of the people in the Valley going to do?

Arthur was quiet now. "I want you to have a good birthday, Kim. It's your last birthday at home before you leave for the university." I looked at him and smiled, amazed that he had even put this together.

Arthur let us out at the curb right on the corner of Highland Avenue and Hollywood Boulevard. It was 1:00 p.m. and he arranged to meet us right before 7:00 p.m. at the same spot. Hollywood Boulevard was crowded with tourists and the working lunch crowd. He waved good-bye to all of us as he slowly pulled out into traffic.

We crossed Hollywood Boulevard and immediately saw the huge movie poster of Marlon Brando's face, so handsome and brooding, staring right at us from the outer lobby of the Egyptian Theater. I took Andrea's arm, Andrea hooked her arm into Ruthie's, and Ruthie hooked hers into Robin's. We were relieved to immerse ourselves in my birthday celebration and forget about the loss of the Red Car.

The movie was compelling and Marlon Brando was gorgeous. But my mind wandered. I kept thinking about the Red Car. Did my funny dream and my flying through space mean that I wished to fly away whenever I need to? Had my dream somehow anticipated the demise of the Red Car? That's silly! As I munched my Good 'N Plenty during the movie, I turned to Andrea who was sitting on my left and whispered, "I have a feeling our lives are going to change in a big way."

Andrea, her eyes filled with tears, was intently watching Marlon Brando lead a whole group of strikers down a wharf, his eyes black and blue after being beaten by the mob. Still looking straight ahead at the screen, she said, "You're too serious, Kim. Who else but you cares this much anyway?"

Chapter 10

1957

I had a sinking feeling when I took the receiver from my roommate Jeannie. "Yes?"

"Kim," the voice on the other end began, and I immediately recognized it was my Aunt Marion. "Kim, can you come home right away? It's your mother—she's not right…"

"Not again. What did she try this time?"

"Pills. If you hurry, you can get here before they take her to the hospital." Marion's voice trailed off. I could hear a lot of commotion in the background. Marion returned to the phone. "Are you there, Kim?"

"Yes, Marion, I'm here." *Another call about my mother at the worst possible time.* I'd have to miss work again.

"I'll have to call and change my work schedule. I'll be there in less than a half hour."

I was a filing assistant for the noted musician Henry Temianka, and I loved working for him. I hoped he would be willing to let me make up the work time next week. I needed the money to get through UCLA. The hours I worked for him paid my rent and grocery bills and allowed me to be independent. In no way did I want to rely on my parents for support. *I hope Dr. Temianka doesn't get discouraged with me. I feel like*

I'm always straddling two worlds, one normal and smooth, the other chaotic and bumpy!

As I dialed Dr. Temianka's number, my hands shook. I hoped my voice would hold steady. When he heard it was me, he responded with kindness. "Dr. Temianka, I hate to do this to you on such short notice, but my mother's been taken ill again and I must rush to the Valley."

"I'm so sorry, Kim, but it's okay. You go take care of your mother. We can handle what has to be done today." I breathed an internal sigh of relief. Dr. Temianka was always so understanding. There were times when I was working with him that I got sidetracked and started reading letters in his file cabinet from other luminaries such as Benjamin Britten and Ferde Grofé. Even when he reprimanded me about this, he did so in the gentlest way. He and his wife were always warm and kind-hearted.

"Thank you for understanding." *I'm lucky Dr. Temianka is so easy-going.* "I promise I'll be in tomorrow." As I hung up the phone, though, my hands were still shaking, and my mind was racing, just thinking of the familiar chaos I now had to face.

I said a quick good-bye to my roommate Jeannie and hurried downstairs to the underground garage to my white Chevy parked in the corner. I tried valiantly to start it. It coughed and sputtered, and finally caught hold, unlike my mind, which was flooded with uncertainty. Once on the winding road over the Glen, my car went its usual forty miles per hour and no faster. One phrase Marion used reverberated in my head: "Your mother's not right."

When has my mother ever been all right? I thought bitterly. *There's never been a 'right' with her, only alternating hysterics or days upon end when she would not get out of bed.* I could not count how many peanut butter and jelly sandwiches I'd made for Jonna and me to take to school all through our childhood. We envied our schoolmates whose carefully wrapped bologna or chicken sandwiches, accompanied by thoughtful bits of potato chips, and tender pieces of fruit, had been packed by caring, loving mothers who only focused on them.

Almost in sympathy, my car's engine gave a slight moan. I pounded the steering wheel with my left hand, not so much to urge on the car, but to steel myself against the trauma that awaited me.

I was halfway up Beverly Glen and should be home in ten minutes. Will that be enough time? I had to admit, I was really worried. No matter how much I inwardly griped when my family called with a crisis, I always went. The all-too-familiar push-pull molded itself like a cloak around me.

I hope I'll get there in enough time to see Lila and offer her some comfort. Even though she strongly supported the idea of higher education for me and Jonna, I knew Lila saw me as the one person in the household who truly cared about her. My leaving for college had been quite a loss for her. Her depression worsened in the months leading up to my departure, and I felt guilty for deserting her. The morning I left for UCLA, Lila was nowhere to be seen, her bedroom door closed. It was too painful for her to say good-bye.

Please God, let me get there on time. Let her be okay. I was so preoccupied I barely noticed the large oak trees and scarlet colored oleanders lining the road toward Ventura Boulevard. This was my favorite route home.

I floored the gas pedal and coaxed my used 1948 convertible up the last incline on Beverly Glen, my voice overriding its protests at the load I was putting on it. *Come on baby, I know you can do it!* At the top of the grade, I eased up on the gas and held my breath as the car headed down toward the Valley. My short curly hair blew in the breeze created by the downhill rush.

Sometimes I wished I'd gone to Berkeley so I would be out of reach. Then no one would be able to call me at all hours of the day and night expecting me to be the rescuer in a family where traumas are a dime a dozen. *And when all this is happening, where in the world is Arthur? He's nowhere to be found.*

I was getting really close now. I drove through the old neighborhood, drew in a deep breath, and girded myself for what was to come. When

I arrived at the house on Oakwood, the oleanders in our front yard swayed in the May breeze, their pink and white blossoms brightening the front lawn. The bushes made the small frame house look deceptively peaceful—except for the ambulance backing out of the driveway.

As I carefully parked my car at the curb, I saw a group of people on the front porch: Aunt Marion, Jonna, and Arlene Costas, a neighbor. I could see that I had arrived too late to comfort my mother, but she'd probably be too out of it anyway. Now I had to figure out to avoid Aunt Marion. Despite the commotion, she was meticulously dressed, as usual. *Look at her. How did she have time to coordinate that outfit? Always looking so beautiful and poised, when my mother barely manages to get out of bed in the morning. She's usually the contact when something like this happens, and when she calls our home, it's always to speak to Arthur.* It was hard for me to conceal my suspicions as I walked up the front sidewalk.

I turned away as Marion leaned in to hug me. "Where's my dad? Did anyone call him?"

Aunt Marion began picking some lint off of her aqua sweater, which perfectly matched her blouse and skirt. "We tried his office at the university, but no one knew where he was. I guess he's at the University Guest House again."

"Are you guessing, or do you know?" *The sicker my mother gets, and the more she complains he's never at home when she needs him, the more he stays at the University Guest House. He claims his work is piling up.*

"Kim, what do you mean?"

"Did you call there?" I demanded. I saw the hurt look in Marion's eyes and realized, after the words were already out of my mouth, how sharp my voice must have sounded. I tried quickly to cover my tracks. "I'm just upset about all this, Aunt Marion."

"Of course you're upset." She touched my arm tenderly.

"Who found her?"

"Jonna. When she came home from school, and found her collapsed on the floor, she ran over to Arlene Costas' house and Arlene called me."

I pulled away from Aunt Marion's touch. As always, I was torn between appreciating her as a concerned adult who tried to help out, and my confusion about her intimacy with our family—and Arthur in particular. Was Marion a rescuing aunt or an intruder? All of Lila's and Arthur's friends were introduced to Jonna and me as "aunt" and "uncle," to the point that we didn't know who our real aunts and uncles were. But this aunt, or whoever she was, was often at the house whenever Arthur was home. I remembered that in New York she was also a confidant of Lila's, but after she moved to California, it became clear that she was most interested in Arthur.

Just then I caught Jonna's eye, as she stood huddled next to Arlene. Her eyes lit up when she saw me. She ran to me, and I put my arms around her. Aunt Marion and Arlene stepped inside the house to give us a few minutes alone.

"Oh Jonna, I'm so sorry I wasn't there for you!" Jonna threw her arms around my waist and burst into tears.

"Kim, it was so awful. I didn't know what to do. She fell down and I couldn't lift her. I didn't do anything wrong, did I?"

"No, Jonna, you did the right thing," I said, trying to console her as I stroked her head. "You called Arlene and she got help."

My words failed to soothe Jonna, whose shoulders heaved as she swallowed and tried to catch the tears pouring down her face. "I could have helped her sooner. I just stood there and looked at her and hated that she always felt sorry for herself and made my life so horrid."

Jonna choked, and I became frightened that she was going to stop breathing. I patted her gently on the back. "Jonna, you can hate her as much as you want. But just remember, you didn't make this happen. She's sick. There's nothing else you could have done."

I wish I knew how to help her. She's so thin and frail. I can never make a difference in her sadness. She shouldn't have to be alone with Lila. And where is Arthur? How could he abandon them? But maybe I'm not much better. I'm usually so bound up with my classes and my friends that I don't really take enough time to be her trusted big sister.

"Why don't we go inside and we'll have some lemonade or something?"

Too spent to resist, Jonna leaned her small frame into my shoulder and allowed me to lead her back into the house. Marion and Arlene Costas were already in the kitchen preparing cocoa and coffee.

Marion turned as I entered the room. "They've taken her to Gateways Hospital. Do you want me to come with you?"

I felt like I had to go to the hospital, but I also wanted to stay with Jonna. Marion's offer to come with me gave me an unaccustomed sense of relief.

"Thanks, Marion, but let's wait until we know what the situation is." I went to the telephone and called Gateways Hospital where my mother had been taken twice before when she attempted to end her life. I noticed that I had already committed the number to memory—more proof of how accustomed I was to my mother's crises. I cupped my hand over the phone, "You know, maybe that would be a good thing, Marion. They don't seem to take me seriously there, like I'm a kid or something."

Marion looked at me and smiled, saying under her breath, "kid or something…?"

I asked for the admitting nurse and was surprised to hear her call me by my first name.

"Do you know what she took, Kim?"

"I'm not sure," I replied, "but my aunt found a bottle of empty pills. Maybe this time she needs to talk to a psychiatrist. I have a friend whose father takes some medication for his depression and…"

"I'll have Dr. Prager, the admitting resident, call you and he can discuss it with you. Is your father there, or some other adult?"

"I'm the adult!" I snapped. "Talk to me!" From my peripheral vision, I saw Aunt Marion start to get up. I held up my hand to stop her. "I'm the one in the family who takes care of this."

The nurse assumed a maternal air. "Don't worry, Kim, we'll take care of it. You just leave your mother to us."

I hung up the phone and went over to the couch to check on Jonna, who was now fast asleep. I also had to call the business office of Gateways to make the financial arrangements before my mother could be permitted to stay there. Before that was possible, I had to call my cousin, Nora, who helped us twice before to pay the Gateways bills until Arthur could pay her back.

Cousin Nora's soft and welcoming voice had a sing-song quality to it. She asked how our family was and how I liked UCLA.

"Classes are going fine for me. I wish I could say the family is fine too, Nora. That's what I'm calling about. My mom's in the hospital again."

"Oh Kim, again? I'm so sorry. How can I help?"

"Well, you were so great when she was hospitalized twice before—I mean, when you loaned me the money for the admitting fees. I'm afraid I have to ask you again. But this time, I'm going to pay you back myself, because it took Arthur such a long time to do it before."

"I'd be glad to help, but why are you the one calling? Where's your father?"

I felt Nora's twinge of anger toward Arthur and almost wanted to protect him. "He's around, I suppose. But I need this money fast because I don't have the time to look for him."

"This isn't the exact moment to talk about it, honey, but someday I'm going to sit down with Arthur and have a heart to heart."

Nora's remarks about Arthur embarrassed me. Many times, Lila had told me that her older sister Rose, Nora's mother, had strongly opposed their marriage. Evidently Aunt Rose saw Arthur as a self-serving and ambitious malcontent, a revolutionary who was certainly not a good match for her baby sister. She rarely visited us at our home because of her animosity toward him. I guessed that some of Aunt Rose's antipathy might have rubbed off on Nora, even though she was always warm and generous toward Jonna and me.

I squirmed a bit and I tried to change the subject. "How are you doing, Nora?"

"I'm doing all right. My idea for a screenplay about the Army-McCarthy Hearings didn't go over too well with the studio execs. They're absolutely frantic that someone will label them "Reds" so they want to avoid the subject altogether."

"Nora, what a coincidence. You're writing about the Army-McCarthy Hearings, and, speaking of McCarthy, I was supposed to take part in a vigil tonight at UCLA to support Arthur Miller. He was found in contempt of Congress for his refusal last year to name names when he was called to appear before HUAC. Now, with Lila ill, I can't do that."

"I'm so sorry you have to miss the vigil, and even sorrier you have to deal with all this."

Once again, I wanted to change the subject. "Well, someday I'd like to write about this McCarthy situation, Nora," I said.

"I hope you'll have a better climate than exists today and you'll be able to do that in the future. For now, the studios have taken up arms against anyone who dares to defend the Hollywood Ten or writers like Miller. But, if you ever do write about McCarthy, I'd love to read it, honey. Right now I'm just sorry your life has to be disrupted by your mother's illness. Kim, you are so intelligent and motivated, I know you'll be successful in anything you attempt." Nora's voice was soft and soothing.

I was taken aback by her confidence in me, and one of my deepest wishes came to the surface. "Well, maybe some day you'll let me live with you at 'The Fun House of the Stars.'" That's the name Nora gave her house at the top of Sunset Plaza. "I could become a studio researcher for one of your projects, or write a book, and you could make a movie of it."

"I'll be waiting for that book, Kim."

"Thanks, Nora, but right now I have to move quickly to be sure Lila stays at Gateways. That's where they've taken her."

"Why don't we do this Kim? I'll call my secretary at the studio and she'll send a check posthaste. I'll also call Gateways and let them know the check is on the way."

"I don't know what to say, Nora. I'm so grateful to you. You always come through. I promise I'll pay you back, even if it's only ten dollars a month."

"This isn't for you to worry about, Kim. For the moment, you can rest assured Gateways will be paid."

Marion stood behind me listening to the whole conversation. She remained silent, and watched me as I reached for my scarf and headed for the door, my eyes brimming with tears. "I need to get out for a little while—take a walk or something. Can you stay here with Jonna?"

"Of course, you just go. The walk will do you good."

I walked down Oakwood Avenue toward my old haunt, the flood control pipe. The trees were full and alive with lush leaves. They were barely reminiscent of the scrawny twigs they'd been when I moved to this tract years ago. The Valley, in harmony with the trees, also grew and flourished. Since my teenage years, there was a proliferation of new homes and the addition of two churches in the tract. A light breeze came up and I thought how pleasant May and June could be before the sweltering summer weather descended on the Valley. As I crossed Van Noord, the last street before the Pipe, I thought how different my life was now compared to my early years in the Valley.

For me, UCLA was stimulating and challenging. Life there was radically different from my life at home. Living with three other girls was often complicated, but it was a complication I relished. Having three roommates was a lot like having three sisters, but all my own age. This time I wasn't the oldest and I didn't have to watch over anyone. It also made me feel less alone.

Because I lived with my roommates, I usually came home to a light, fun atmosphere. We enjoyed each other. We shared a tiny house on Barrington, a mile from campus, and split the $75 monthly rent four ways. With whatever little money I had left over after rent and car expenses, I'd buy a new record album, Odetta or Pete Seeger, or a new book for my already growing collection. My books were like my friends. They traveled with me everywhere.

Wow, I can't believe I'm in my sophomore year already. I'm actually making it work. Now, I've got classes I love and a job I love! But I wish I could just be wholeheartedly devoted to being in college. It wears me out to be so divided inside. When I'm at school, I worry about Lila and Jonna. When I'm home with my family, I can't wait to get back to school. I'm always off balance, so I never feel good about my accomplishments. I'm tired of these constant doubts about whether I'm doing enough to help my family.

I picked my way through the underbrush, my feet scuffing up gravel and dust as I headed for the same spot where Andrea and I had always met to share our dreams. I lifted myself onto the round, steel edifice and carefully walked to the middle of the Pipe until I found exactly the right spot. My spot. I sat down, wishing Andrea were there with me to talk about what was happening in my life.

When I came back from my walk, Jonna was already in bed. The blinds were drawn shut and the bedroom was very dark. I sat down on Jonna's bed, gently nudging her to wake her. "I wanted to say good-bye, Jonni."

No response. I looked at her inert form and all of a sudden felt a chill go down my spine. Jonna was acting just like Lila did when she was depressed—escaping to a dark room, withdrawing under the covers.

"I know it's hard for you, but I have to get back to UCLA and go to work. Tomorrow I'll go down to Gateways to see Lila. I will leave my work phone number. You can call me anytime after one, okay?"

Still no response. I felt the same pangs of guilt all over again that I felt when I left for college. Who was I supposed to show allegiance to? I felt that if I kept trying to save Jonna or Lila from drowning, they would pull me under and I'd drown too! Then, my thoughts would quickly shift. How can I leave Jonna? If something happens to her when I'm gone I would never forgive myself.

"Jonna, I'm going to ask Marion to stay with you the rest of the day and tonight." I leaned over and planted a kiss on the back of Jonna's head. "Bye now, I'll call you. I'll be back soon to visit." I slowly wrenched myself out of the room, knowing that if I spent another minute in that dark place, I'd never get back to UCLA and my commitments there.

Marion agreed to spend the night and be sure Jonna got off to school the next day. She walked me out to my car, and then put her hand on my shoulder. "You have to stop worrying about everything. I'll stay for a few days and be sure Arthur hears about this and makes some arrangements for Jonna." At that moment, I was really grateful. Maybe Aunt Marion wasn't so bad after all.

As I drove back over the Glen, I pretended I was on the Pipe again, as though I were continuing one of my many conversations with Andrea. I began to speak out loud, knowing that even if someone were to see me, the windows of the car were closed and I couldn't be heard. I was virtually screaming. "Andrea, I'm going to make four promises to myself. They'll also be my new set of wishes. Someday, I'm going to be independently wealthy and never have to beg for money again, and someday, I'm going to find someone to love and we'll love each other so much and have such an affinity for each other that I'll never be stuck in the same kind of relationship Arthur and Lila have. And someday, I'm going to study the causes of depression and find out what makes Lila tick, so what has happened to her will never happen to me." I imagined my legs dangling from the flood control pipe, above the long drop to the concrete below. I saw myself sitting there for the longest time looking out over the construction site for the new buildings at Valley College. Soon, my fourth wish came.

Someday, I'm going to find out where Arthur goes at night, and why he doesn't come home anymore.

I drove on until I reached the end of the Glen and turned right on Sunset Boulevard. In my head, I envisioned Andrea, her head shaking back and forth: "Forget the last wish, Kim. Bury that need to know. No one will ever find out where Arthur goes at night. Just concentrate on you and your other wishes. Your shoulders aren't large enough or strong enough to carry the weight of your own future and the weight of your family's woes as well." In my daydreams, I often engaged in the kind of fantasy where I could attempt to see the battling forces inside of me. I made Andrea the voice of reason, invoking her image to remind me of my right to focus on myself. This fantasy worked for a short while, only to be followed by long periods of shame and guilt and frequent telephone calls to the Valley—to Jonna, to Lila, or to Marion, with whom I had long telephone conversations about my family and their troubles. Marion would end each of our phone conversations in the same way: "Kim, you have only one life to lead; only one time to go around in this world. Now, stop worrying and concentrate on you, your future, your life at UCLA, and your career afterwards. You are too young to take on so much responsibility for all of them."

"But, if not me, who?" I asked. "Who is going to make sure something awful doesn't happen to them?"

After a long silence, Marion said, "The person who is responsible and should stop running away from that responsibility. That's who! And I am going to find him and confront him with that."

I remembered my fantasy and Andrea's response. "Don't bother, Marion. No one knows where he is, or where he goes. So, how will you find him?"

"I'm bound and determined, darling, and when I do, I'll set him straight."

Whatever Marion's relationship was with Arthur, I thought, I'm beginning to see that she has good intentions towards me. Marion tried, but Arthur was unavailable. He had one excuse after another. He was rarely home, and when he was, he was too distracted to even hear her.

I *did* hear her. And when Lila was released from Gateways but still sank into further depression, I arranged for Jonna and me to speak by phone every few days, just so she knew I was there. I was more determined than ever to follow Marion's advice. Her support gave me the strength to dive into my studies, my job, and the stimulating friends and activities which made UCLA my isle of refuge. Who could have known that the woman whom I suspected of intruding on our family and of having an illicit relationship with my father would become my female champion?

Chapter 11

1958

F ree! My three roommates and I flew out of the lecture halls after
finishing the last of our mid-terms that early spring day. We
almost danced back to the apartment, excited about our evening plans.
As a reward for getting through mid-terms, we were going to a popular
folk music club to hear one of our favorite singers, Odetta.

I opened the apartment door and gasped: "Wow! This place looks
like a tornado hit it!" Books and papers were strewn everywhere. Paper
plates recently filled with potato chips and Tabasco sauce and an empty
carton from last night's pizza dinner were brushed into a corner, ready for
dumping in the trash bin downstairs. Almost on cue, the four of us started
bustling around, putting books back into bookcases, and throwing papers
and magazines into the garbage can that Jeannie had brought up from
the basement and planted in the middle of the kitchen.

In the middle of stuffing my two weeks' worth of laundry into a
pillow case, I glanced at the clock. Five o'clock already? I stuck my head
out the bedroom door. "Hey guys! We have to leave at seven-thirty and
it's already five! Who wants first dibs on the shower?"

Jeannie's response was a mad dash to the tiny bathroom. In seconds,
the sound of clunking pipes announced her shower. One by one, each

of us took breaks from the cleaning frenzy to use the shower in our one and only bathroom. Right after my shower, I walked into the living room, where my roommates were sitting on the couch, laughing aloud at Jeannie Nelson's antics. Tall, blonde and extremely attractive, Jeannie was dating Hassan Ambari, newly arrived from Iran. She was mad about him, and was parading around in the tiny living room practicing what she would say to her conservative Orange County parents about her dating a Persian.

"I know you're concerned about his background, but he's the descendant of a sheik, and his parents have so much money they might even be willing to invest in your company. What do you think of that, Dad?" Jeannie paused in her dramatic enactment.

"Jean," interjected Robin, "does it have to be a sheik? Sheik sounds like he belongs in a Rudolph Valentino movie. How about a member of the royal family? You know—the heir to the monarchy or the Shah's cousin, something like that."

"Good thinking, Robin. My dad says the Shah brings fortunes to American businesses. That should impress him."

Rhoda and I laughed. "Jeannie, we both think you're overdoing the hiding bit," I said. "And seriously, we're tired of lying to your folks every time they call."

"I know, guys, I know. I'm practicing how I can tell them and..."

The phone rang. Jeannie stopped in mid-sentence as Rhoda and I rushed to answer.

"Oh hi, Mrs. Nelson, how are you?" My voice was the epitome of innocence. Jeannie's alarmed look made me want to laugh.

Mrs. Nelson's shrill voice coming through the phone could be heard by everyone in the room. "I'm fine, Kim. Jeannie tells me how well you are doing in your studies and how helpful you are to her. I hope someday you'll come and stay at our beach house. Is she there, by any chance?"

"I'm sorry, Mrs. Nelson. You just missed her by less than a minute. She's at the library studying for her last mid-term exam which is tomorrow morning." I tried to keep my voice modulated as Jeannie jumped up and down in front of me. She waved her arms frantically, like a sailor on an aircraft carrier guiding in a jet plane for landing, her lips forming words she wanted me to say:

"Worried…test…many tests…weekend impossible…not coming home."

After gracefully saying good-bye to Mrs. Nelson, I put down the phone and turned to my roommate. "Jeannie, we can't continue to be your shield. You should bring Hassan home and introduce him to your folks, or have them call you at a prearranged time on Sundays so you can be here to take their calls."

Rhoda and Robin nodded vigorously in agreement.

"Okay," Jeannie said. "It's just—well, you guys have met my parents. You know how straight-laced they are. But I agree it's not fair to put that burden on you. I'll tell them this week when I'm home for spring break."

At this point, Rhoda noticed the time. There was one last flurry as we hurriedly put on sweaters and touched up our hair. Finally, the Barrington Bunch, as we called ourselves, went downstairs and waited in front of the apartment house. Eddie Randolph, our friend who lived in the apartment house adjacent to ours, was driving us in his Volkswagen bus to Hollywood.

Two years ago, as a freshman, I had seen Odetta perform at a rally in Royce Hall, and became an ardent fan. My roommates shared my passion for her throaty voice, and between us we had every one of her records in our collections.

When Eddie pulled up in front of the apartment house, we all piled into the back, which was strewn with papers and his surfing paraphernalia. We loved riding in his bus, even though it was notoriously underpowered. It gave us a chance to smile and wave at the drivers who always tried to pass and get around his slow moving vehicle.

From Westwood to Hollywood only took us about a half hour. Eddie pulled the bus up to the alleyway in front of the coffeehouse located on a short cul-de-sac, which ran between Ivar and Cahuenga.

One by one we got out and made our way to the entrance, brimming with anticipation. We paid the cover of one dollar and fifty cents and pushed open the door to Cosmo's Alley. Waves of thick, dense smoke engulfed us, and at first it was hard to make out the interior. A huge room, adorned with large posters of Woody Guthrie, Pete Seeger, and The Weavers, greeted us. Most of the forty or so tables were occupied by four or more people, laughing, talking, and making a din so loud it was impossible to hear. Trying to adjust to the smoke and noise, we scanned the room looking for empty seats. The chaotic atmosphere here thrilled me. I felt transported to another world.

As we strained to find seats in the crowded room, Jeannie briskly tapped me on the shoulder. "Don't look now, but there's a guy over there in the corner who's looking you over."

"What? Where?" I asked.

Jeannie tilted her head in the direction of a tall, dark-haired man smiling at the two of us. He gestured to four empty seats at his table. I shrugged. Why not? It looked like we wouldn't be able to do any better with seating.

The four of us approached his table, and I gasped as I immediately recognized his face. He was the guy that so impressed me when I visited Arthur's class that day at UCLA. I'd thought about him often, and even asked Arthur about him from time to time. Now, he stood up and graciously welcomed us. "Good evening, ladies. To my surprise, he waved me to a chair right next to his. "It's Kim, right? We met at your father's Poli Sci and World History class—I think it was about four years ago? You probably don't remember my name. I'm Lucien Rahbar. May I offer you a cigarette?"

A little flustered, I nodded yes to all of his questions, sat down, and accepted the cigarette right away. In a most gallant way, he then pulled out chairs for each of my roommates. I smiled as he lit my cigarette, then the cigarettes of everyone at the table. I couldn't take my eyes off his face, particularly his large brown eyes and long eyelashes. His aquiline features gave him an Italian look–the look of a Marcello Mastroianni.

"So you like Odetta too," I said, smiling at him.

"I could listen to her from morning to night."

Odetta, her enormous Martin guitar resting on her lap, now sat in the middle of the stage and softly strummed the opening bars of "Freedom," one of the songs that had made her so famous. Lucien and I, along with the rest of the audience, became silent and listened reverentially to her powerful voice. Coming out of the gospel tradition, her luminous sound seemed to bore through the crowd:

"…but before I'd be a slave, I'd be buried in my grave. Oh Lord, Oh Lord, set me free…"

Lucien leaned over to me. "Every time she sings that I feel like crying. She sings for all oppressed people."

I felt warm all over, even a little weak, as Lucien brushed up against me. *He's so expressive, not like the 'macho' guys in my classes. I wonder why he's here alone. Does he have a girlfriend?*

Odetta finished "Freedom," sang a few other songs, and ended the set with her version of "Joshua Fit the Battle of Jericho." Loud applause greeted her exit from the stage.

Everyone in the club then ramped up their exuberant conversations. Jeannie leaned across the table toward Lucien, "Do you by any chance know Hassan Ambari?"

"Yes I do," Lucien replied. "Hassan and I were at the same boarding school in England when we were kids."

The rest of my roommates chimed in. They seemed to take an immediate liking to Lucien, and each of them attempted to engage him in some way. I was impressed by his old world courtly manner. None of the guys I had dated were anything like him.

"So where did you live in Iran, and what was life like there?" Rhoda asked.

"Do you find the United States very different than Iran?" Robin wondered.

Lucien good naturedly answered their questions. "We lived in Tehran, a very beautiful city." His eyes brightened with the memory.

"My parents live in a section much like parts of Beverly Hills. There are palatial homes, and, of course, as in your city, sections for the not so fortunate."

"What do your parents do?" asked Jeannie.

"My parents both do important work for the Shah. Their work wouldn't permit them to come with me to the U.S. I miss them terribly, but we write to each other frequently."

I noticed a flicker of sadness move across Lucien's face as he talked about his family back in Iran. As the conversation went on, I found myself responding to his openness by sharing more about myself and my background.

As involved as he was in talking to my three roommates, Lucien's eyes kept tracking back to mine. No matter who I was talking to, I felt him looking at me. Each time our eyes met, I felt a surge of heat and a building excitement wash through me. This strong attraction occurred so quickly, it took me off guard.

As Odetta finished her last song of the evening, "This Old Hammer," we all rose in unison, applauded, and urged her to do an encore. She declined, and, cupping the tips of her two hands to her lips, blew the crowd a parting kiss. Eddie, who had been hanging out at the bar, appeared at our table. "Come on guys, let's get going…got a paper due for chemistry tomorrow."

Lucien turned abruptly away from his talk with Jeannie and looked directly at me. "I have a car here. I could drive you home if you like."

I hesitated, looking back and forth between him and my friends. I was torn.

Jeannie jumped in. "Kim, you go on with Lucien. We'll ride with Eddie and we'll see you at home." My other roommates nodded in agreement. I was relieved. They had gotten the message.

Lucien got up and pulled my chair back as I stood. "My car is parked on the next street. I could go get it, or we could walk there."

"I don't mind the walk…it will give us time to talk," I said. I felt a flutter inside my stomach, a tickle. *He doesn't seem like a stranger. I feel like I've known him a long time.* It was a perfect Los Angeles evening, the kind of March weather that attracted people from all over the country. As we walked toward where he said his uncle's new Pontiac was parked, we talked nonstop.

"Odetta embodies everything I want to stand for," I said.

"And what is that?" Lucien looked down at me.

"She doesn't just express her views about injustice; she's a social activist. I heard her speak at the Congress of Racial Equality meeting and she predicted there'd be a huge civil rights awakening all over this country. She was even called to speak at the White House on the plight of Negroes in this country. I love her courage."

Lucien pondered what I said. "What I like most is that she can speak for her race and for all women as well. She can do this in America, Kim, but she couldn't if she were in my country." His hand rested tenderly on my shoulder. It felt comfortable and right and I wanted it left there. He looked sad when he spoke of Iran and his home situation.

"You're right, Lucien, it's a wonderful country. In my view it's the best country in the world. But it's like...well, it's like a relationship with people you love. There are many traits you value and treasure, and others you dislike—even find reprehensible. But you love them anyway. America has its own issues with censorship, women's rights, and racial prejudice."

"Well, why don't we solve these problems over coffee at Zucky's?" he said, smiling.

"Zucky's it is," I nodded, and then continued: "My family takes those problems very seriously, Lucien. My dad says that what our country has gone through—you know, with the HUAC hearings and the damage done to so many Americans by McCarthy and his cronies—is like the repression suffered under Franco in Spain. Arthur even compares this time to Nazi Germany and how people stood passively by and let Hitler come to power. People in this country didn't do a lot to protest McCarthy either."

"I don't know about that, Kim," Lucien said. "I have always, ever since I took his course, respected your father's opinions and analysis. But I'm now reading about increased support for people who appear before HUAC. I have also read about how McCarthy was discredited and your own Senate censured him for his behavior in 1954."

Wow, I thought. I'm impressed. He really keeps up on the current political scene, and he states his opinions so openly. His openness made it easier for me to express my own views. "I hope you're right, Lucien, I'm usually an optimist, but what happened scared me, and still does…I mean, the whole blacklist business, doing that to people of the caliber of Lillian Hellman, Arthur Miller, and Dalton Trumbo. Even my own father, a few years ago, was under suspicion by his dean because he refused to sign the loyalty oath."

We had been so engrossed in conversation that I hardly noticed the blocks we walked to his uncle's car. Lucien opened the car door for me, waited until I was seated inside, and then leaned down. "We'll get to all that later, Kim, but right now I'm glad we could enjoy this evening together." He quickly went around to the driver's side, got in, and started the car. We drove down Sunset Boulevard, then swung over to Wilshire and headed west into Santa Monica. Lucien said Zucky's was his favorite hang-out.

"Another thing we have in common," I said. "Zucky's is my favorite too."

He continued to talk about his life in Iran well after we entered a crowded Zucky's, and found a corner booth in the back of the restaurant. We talked the night away, stopping only to order more coffee or relight our cigarettes.

I never thought I'd become an avid smoker after watching Lila throughout my childhood furiously puffing away, draining each cigarette of its life, crushing it out, then quickly lighting another. Irritated as I was by the constant smell of smoke and the multitudes of butts left in ashtrays all over the house, when I got to college, it seemed the most natural thing to do. I took up the habit and most of my friends did too.

Lucien continued to talk about his life in Iran, the words spilling out of him like a rushing waterfall. I listened intently, breaking in periodically with questions.

"You said that your parents worked for the Shah and weren't allowed to come to the United States to be with you. So, what is the nature of their work?"

"My father is a renowned physicist who was partly responsible for Iran's success in beginning to harness uranium. He begged the Shah for permission to come to the U.S. with me. The Shah would not relent because my father was considered too valuable to the Shah's regime and had to remain in Iran. My mother is a highly educated poet and writer, but she wouldn't think of leaving my father. Although they are respected in Tehran, they were forced to remain against their will."

My cigarette remained poised in the air. "But the Shah let you come to the U.S.?"

"That was the only deal my father could make. He promised the Shah that I would return and voluntarily serve in the Shah's government. My father realized that once I came to the U.S. I might never want to go back to Iran. And, he was right: I don't. My father desperately wanted me to go to the U.S. Promising that I would return was the only way the Shah would concede. My father also feared if I remained in Tehran—outspoken as I was against authority—that I'd bring danger upon myself. You're so fortunate, Kim, to live in a wonderful country where dissent is tolerated. You even have a father who is a respected university professor."

"It looks better than it is, Lucien. Even with my father's job at LACC and his lectureship at UCLA, he and many of his colleagues have been afraid all these years to speak out for fear of being called up before the committee. Even though Murrow says that dissent is true patriotism, dissent has come to mean disloyalty during the McCarthy Era."

"But your father didn't seem the least bit hesitant in expressing strong views," Lucien recalled. "I really admired his fighting spirit for a country he said he loves, with an awareness of its injustices as well. He gave us a lot to think about."

"That was four years ago, Lucien. He speaks less openly now, Lucien. I don't know how confident he is about continuing to air his stronger views. My father and some of his colleagues at the university have had visits from the FBI, and my mother always suspects that our phone might be tapped."

"I can see how much you admire your father, Kim."

"He's always talking to me about politics and unions, and I've learned a lot from him. But…well, while he may give a lot as a teacher, he doesn't give too much at home. And my mother, well, she has a lot of issues." I crushed my cigarette in the ashtray.

"To look at you, I would never know you had a moment of grief." He gently placed his hand over mine. "You seem, as you Americans say, so upbeat."

"I'm not all that upbeat. I just know how to put on a good face. The truth of the matter is I worry about my mother and sister. I feel like I should be doing more to help them."

His eyes never left my face. He took my hand and caressed it. His touch drew me into a whirlpool of feeling. I could feel myself being drawn in. Talking to him about things I rarely mentioned to others gave me a sense of comfort. And yet, I also felt myself wondering, can this be real? Should I surrender to this feeling or resist it?

"Family obligations can be very confusing."

"How do you get along with your family?"

"I wish my parents could be here, but I feel a certain relief that they are where they are. They smothered me and were much too restrictive about my daily activities, but now my Uncle Parviz is no different. He doles out each penny, and he, too, is strict and watches my every move. Speaking of which," Lucien looked at his watch, "Do you know what time it is? I'll be in real trouble with my uncle." It was four o'clock in the morning; more than five hours since we'd left Cosmo's Alley!

"You're right. We'd better go or my roommates will think we eloped."

Lucien laughed. "That wouldn't be the worst thing in the world. I don't want this time to end. Promise me you'll see me tomorrow night. Beckett's new play, *Waiting for Godot,* will be at Royce Hall. I'll get tickets and it will be our first actual date."

"I'd love it, Lucien, but my sister Jonna is coming tomorrow to see me. She does that every few weeks. She comes from the Valley, and I don't like to miss her visits."

"I'd love to meet her. She can come with us, Kim."

I hesitated, feeling the tingle again. I wanted to see him as much as he wanted to see me, but Jonna might be uncomfortable. "It's a deal, Lucien."

As we drove back through the deserted streets, we moved in and out of pools of light shed by the street lamps. Santa Monica and Westwood had never looked so dreamy to me. It seemed like the city belonged to us. When we arrived at my apartment, Lucien again got out, opened the car door, and walked me to the entrance. We were reluctant to say good-bye and talked for a long while at my door. I thought of inviting him in, but realized there would be no place to be private or do whatever else we wanted to do. I was so excited and it was the "whatever else" that left me feeling anticipation, frustration, and just a little bit of anxiety too.

He leaned in to kiss me good night and towered over me. He placed a hand on either side of my head, and pressed me back against the door jamb. A surge of warmth traveled from my head to my toes, as I felt his body against mine. His kiss was sensuous and lingering. And I wanted more. It was hard for me to let him go, but with my hands on either side of his cheeks, I gently pushed him away. We were going too far, too fast. "You better go."

Lucien cupped my chin, kissed the tip of his forefinger, and placed it on the tip of my nose. "I don't want to leave you." He slowly walked toward his car, turning around several times. "See you tomorrow at Janss Steps, five o'clock. Then to Mario's for an Italian dinner and on to the play."

"I can't wait," I called out. He got in his car, blew me a kiss, and drove off.

When I got into bed, I tossed and turned. I couldn't contain my excitement about meeting him again. I was still awake when the first rays of sunlight peeked through the blinds. Finally, I jumped out of bed, made coffee for myself and my roommates, and was sitting at the kitchen table dreamily staring into space, when Jeannie entered.

"You look like someone just fed you a chocolate éclair with whipped cream," she said, as she affectionately tussled my hair. "No need to ask how the evening went after we left you."

"Jeannie, I can't believe it! I never met anyone like him. We talked the whole night away."

"When are you going to see him again?"

"Tonight! He's got tickets for *Waiting for Godot*. He's perfect."

The day moved as slow as molasses. I bounced around the apartment, dust rag in hand, counting the hours one by one. When I called Jonna to ask her to the play, she opted out. She claimed she had a headache. Jonna always claimed to have a headache when she didn't want to do something. Despite my pleas, she remained resolute, saying she'd rather spend the evening with two friends who were coming over to watch an interesting program on television.

As much as I was anticipating my date with Lucien, not seeing Jonna made me uneasy and I felt a need to check in with her. So I persuaded her to drive in from the Valley and meet me at the Village Coffee Shop for lunch. When we met that afternoon, she seemed enthusiastic about her new high school classes. I was reassured that she was all right—at least for the moment. She also told me that Lila had calmed down quite a bit after her last episode, and was even being nice to her at home.

Secretly, I was glad I was going to have Lucien all to myself that evening. I could hardly wait to be with him again. My hands almost shook as I put on my lipstick and did my hair before I went to meet him. The play was compelling and we wound up at Zucky's again talking about the meaning of Beckett's play, then, somehow we wound up talking about Vietnam.

"Politics intrudes into everything. My buddy from the Physics

Department said that he's worried this so called 'advisory action' in Vietnam will turn into an all-out war."

"I hope not," I said. "Maybe we should be out there starting to protest! Beckett says we all just sit in a deli like Zucky's waiting for someone else to take care of everything."

"Too early for protest, Kim. We have to see where this goes," Lucien said gravely.

On the drive back to my apartment, Lucien stopped and took my hand. "I know this sounds silly after only two days, but I feel like we've been together for a long time."

The following morning, I was the first one up again in the tiny apartment kitchen, already drinking my first cup of coffee when Jeannie sleepily stumbled in.

"Hi, I didn't hear you come in last night. Did you have a good time, like I even have to ask?"

"I'm crazy about him. I've been thinking that instead of giving up the apartment as we planned to do, I'd like to keep it for the summer. If you and the others could stay on, great; if not, I'll try to find another way. I mean, I feel this is an awful time to leave. I want to be with him."

"Of course you do, Kim. I know what you mean. I feel the same way about leaving Hassan. Maybe our folks would let us stay through the summer. I need to do some work for my psychology thesis, and you could do more work on your fellowship application."

"Right. I hope your parents agree, Jeannie. As long as I pay the extra expenses, mine won't care. They're too absorbed in their own stuff. I have an idea how to pay the additional rent and incidentals. I'll call the athletic director who hired me to do some tutoring for some of the football players."

We poured ourselves a second cup of coffee and got out a notepad to calculate the costs of spending the summer in Westwood.

The remaining spring months passed quickly with the frenzy of finishing the semester. In the middle of June, Jeannie and I deposited our two roommates at the Greyhound bus station in Santa Monica, one bound for Eugene, Oregon, the other for Orinda in the Bay Area. As agreed, Jeannie and I would continue to live in the apartment until the end of August. Rhoda and Robin would rejoin us when they returned in the fall. And so it began: a summer that only three months ago I could not have imagined for myself. Lucien and Hassan quickly became a part of our routine. When I wasn't at my jobs or doing fellowship work, I was either part of the foursome of Jeannie, Hassan, Lucien and myself, or, alone with Lucien.

Lucien became a soothing balm in my otherwise frenetic world. Gradually, I had less need to make my weekly calls to Andrea. She couldn't possibly understand what Lucien meant to me, because even Andrea didn't know how bad things still were in my home. For so long, my mother's emotional condition and my father's strange disappearances left me feeling fearful that everything could land on my shoulders. Now, there was a ray of hope I hadn't felt before, that my life could be better. I'd never known what it was like to be in love, but now I knew. My life had changed dramatically because of Lucien. I thought of him day and night and I needed him as a constant presence in my world.

Our relationship deepened even before it turned sexual. In all ways—in mind, in body, and in spirit—we were together. Even our political beliefs were aligned. I marched beside him when he picketed for National Committee for a Sane Nuclear policy (SANE), the organization formed in 1957 as a reaction to the Eisenhower administration's heavy reliance on nuclear weapons development as well as to a general anxiety about the destabilizing effects of the arms race. As I became part of Lucien's crowd, my world expanded. I'd never known so many students from foreign countries.

As our love intensified, I began to change. I no longer needed to run ten steps ahead of the mounting sadness I felt about leaving my mother and sister behind. Something in me had eased. Every once in a while, I did feel a little flicker of anxiety, especially when it seemed that we had gotten so close so quickly. But those thoughts were easily dismissed because I was, overall, so happy to have found not just love, but a soul mate.

For hours, we sat together while I read him my writings and he recited his poetry, or we sang folk songs together. We shared our dreams with each other. He wanted to follow in his father's footsteps as a physicist. And like my father, I wanted to become a history professor at UCLA. We became each other's champion. For the first time in my life, someone cared about me—my thoughts, my interests, and my dreams.

One afternoon, as I walked to our appointed meeting place, Lucien's tall, lanky frame suddenly appeared before me, his black wavy hair shimmering in the afternoon sun.

"A penny for your thoughts." He laughed, and kissed me on the tip of my nose.

"You. Us. How good we are. And how much I miss you when you're not there."

"While I drink my morning coffee, I write you letters in my head. I have great fantasies about us."

"Tell me?" I nestled against him.

"We're making love on a tropical island and I hear my uncle's voice. I tell him it's no use, that we're each other's forever."

"He worries you a lot, doesn't he, Luc?" I asked.

"Of course he worries me. He forbids me to see you. He wants to pull us apart." Lucien held me very tightly, leaned down, and kissed the top of my head. "And I certainly won't let that happen. You mean too much to me. Life with you has made me whole."

I moved closer to him. "He can't pull apart two people who belong together. If he only knew how much we've given to each other. I can just about endure anything. Like last night when Jonna called, you were by my side, totally there."

"I hope you weren't too scared, Kim, although her threat to run away or to kill herself last night would frighten anyone. Let's tell her she can always be with us if she needs to. It might help her."

"I'll tell her that, Luc, but just having you there relieved me. I didn't feel alone and helpless as I have in the past. When you calmed her down on the phone, I felt maybe things could change."

"You need to feel it's all right for you to focus on yourself and finish what you need to do. You have a right to do that, Kim. You can't make Jonna better. Only a professional can do that. It doesn't help her in any way if you fail. Someone in your family has to have some success in changing their life. You can be a model for her."

I nuzzled into the folds of the leather jacket his uncle gave him some weeks ago for his twenty-first birthday, and thought of the lavish birthday dinner I wasn't invited to. I pulled away. Something gnawed at me.

"What's the main reason he doesn't approve of me? Why am I not welcome in your uncle's home? What is it about me? That I'm American? Too free-spirited? Jewish? Does he blame me for your increasing rebellion toward his rules?"

Lucien looked into my eyes. "My uncle is traditional, Kim. We are Iranian and he insists that I marry an Iranian. Everything you said is correct. You are American. You are too independent. You are Jewish. He worries that I'm becoming too American, that I'm his responsibility and he's failing to guide me in Iranian traditions. And, he knows that my wish to move into an apartment near campus is to be with you."

"So what can we do?"

Lucien beamed. "I've already figured it out. I have a big surprise for you. Today, Dr. Fowler, the Physics Chair, asked me if I would like to live in his guest house rent-free in exchange for taking care of his lawn and his animals. I told him I was seeing someone and could she join me from time to time. You know what he said, Kim?"

"Tell me."

"Who could expect a handsome fellow like you to spend time alone? She can join you whenever she wants."

We decided that I'd stay in my place during the week to honor my agreement with Jeannie, and stay with him on weekends. Jeannie was very pleased. When I moved out for the weekend, Hassan moved in.

"Together, we will plant a beautiful garden," Luc said.

Unfortunately, the only thing that would be growing in my garden would be weeds. And it wasn't just Jonna's occasional anxious calls that disturbed us. As the summer wore on, I slowly became aware of another disruption of our tranquility. Lucien and I had noticed a dark green sedan slowly cruise by now and then. It seemed to follow whenever we were out walking. When we stared at the car, it would pull away. The windows of the sedan were darkened, so we couldn't see inside. We thought it odd, but chalked it up to being either a university security car or an immigration vehicle.

It was Jeannie who first became alarmed. She spotted the same car one day as the four of us were leaving the UCLA bookstore. "Hey, what do you make of that? That's the same green car that's been cruising up and down our street for the last two weeks. This morning it stopped in front of our apartment building."

"I wonder what they're looking for," Hassan said.

"Well, we can't ask them because we can't even see who they are," I replied. I felt very nervous.

Lucien remained very quiet, and I could see by his furrowed brow that he was as nervous as I was.

We approached the apartment and noticed that the green sedan was now parked about fifty feet from us. We stopped in our tracks, turned around, and started to walk back to the bookstore. The car sped off. Lucien said he'd call UCLA Security to find out about the color of their patrol cars. He left with Hassan and Jeannie for class.

I went back to my apartment and heard the phone ringing as I fumbled with the key. I was in a rush to get to the ringing telephone, hoping it was Arthur. He had left a message for me at my Institute job saying he needed to talk to me, that it was urgent. But I never reached him. Probably he was calling about a problem with my mother again. *Hurry up, hurry up—if it's him, he'll always call back, right?* Finally, the key turned the lock and the door swung open. I dumped my books on the couch, raced to the phone, and flopped onto the overstuffed couch nearby.

"Where in the world have you been?" Arthur growled. "I've been trying to get you since early morning. I thought you were going to be around more after you finished your finals."

I could envision Arthur's fingers tapping impatiently on his desk, his lips pursed in an annoyed grimace.

"I'm sorry, Arthur. There's been so much going on. I'm preparing for the fellowship, trying to keep up with my job at the Institute, and I've had to line up another job to make enough money to stay here in town for the summer."

"Okay, okay, Kim. There's been a little trouble, and I think you have to be a bit careful about who you talk to or who you're seen with."

My heart began beating rapidly. I'd kept the details of my new romance from my parents—not that I shared that much with them anyway. I was worried they might interfere somehow. Was it Lucien that Arthur referred to when he said, "Watch who you're seen with"? I hadn't even told Andrea about Lucien yet, but for a different reason. I wanted him all to myself. He was too special to me. In some strange way I felt that if I kept my feelings about him within me, he'd be mine alone.

"Kim, are you there? Will you say something, please?"

"Arthur, I'm sorry. Why should I be careful? Careful of what? Careful of whom?"

"It looks like I might be called before HUAC. It's not certain, but I think it's a given that there'll be a lot of investigations going on. I don't want Lila, or you or Jonna implicated in any way. Just be careful." Arthur hung up.

My heart began to pound. *Oh my God! It's finally happened! All those years we lived in fear that Arthur would get called—and now it was actually happening! I can't believe the timing. Is it possible that this could affect my romance with Lucien?* I needed to speak to him right away. I ran the eight blocks to the campus to meet him at Janss Steps, as soon as he got out of his class.

When I told him about Arthur's call, Lucien was infuriated. "I found out that some of the UCLA Security patrol cars are dull green. That explains the car that's been lurking around."

"This is surreal. I can't believe they could be tracking me."

"Or me, Kim."

We stared at each other and watched the sun making its slow descent on the horizon. We sat close to each other, our arms around each other's shoulders. Uncle Parviz wasn't our only problem.

The silent tension, as we sat on the steps and stared at the passing cars, reflected our anxiety. Yet, both of us couldn't help smiling as we heard from one of the passing cars, its windows wide open, the strains of Elvis Presley.

"Love me tender, love me true…never let me go. You have made my life complete and I love you so…" Together, we could tackle anything!

Chapter 12

The blazing afternoon sun had scorched the ground, and the intense Valley heat made me feel faint. Numbly, I looked around at the other mourners clustered around my mother's gravesite. My mother's good friend Zee, whom Lila called "my California mah jongg pal," was crying softly and shaking her head from side to side, still in disbelief about Lila's death. Zee's husband Mel put his arm around her shoulders and with his free hand tenderly patted her face. A profound sadness washed over me. Their closeness was in such contrast to my parents' relationship.

Lila had fallen into the filled bathtub one morning last week. She hit her head with such force on the concrete rim of the bathtub that she had died instantly. The emergency techs were not able to revive her when they arrived at our house. We were almost used to Lila's suicidal bouts, but her sudden death in this way had shocked all of us.

I stared down at the gaping hole that would soon receive Lila's body, feeling so disconnected from her and from my sadness. Was it the heat that prevented me from weeping? Maybe I had already cried as much as I could. Her life was full of such missed opportunities, I thought. My mother started out as a spirited young woman—at least that's how she portrayed her past to me—and she had become so beaten down by life, she never realized her potential.

In the rapidly developing Valley of the late 1950s, Eden Paradise

Cemetery had recently opened and Lila's grave was in the new section called "Peace Valley." The nearest grave was more than two hundred feet away. As the funeral services began, it struck me that Lila would lie in death as she had lived in life, isolated and alone, her fantasies of a more colorful life reflected by the many flowers the mourners placed on her coffin.

Together, the small group of friends and family stood solemnly while Lila's coffin was placed on the bier. Jonna was sandwiched between Arthur and me, both of us resting a hand on one of her shoulders. Thank goodness for Lucien's presence. Without him I would have felt utterly alone. Andrea and her parents were back East visiting relatives and weren't able to fly back for the funeral.

"Don't worry, Kim, I'll be giving you a great big hug before you know it," Andrea said through her tears over the long distance lines from Brooklyn. I hated to admit it, but I was actually relieved when Andrea couldn't make it. Lucien's loving presence was enough comfort for me.

Lucien stood to my right, dressed in his one and only suit, which fortunately was black, and which his uncle insisted he wear. Hearing about my mother's unfortunate and untimely death, Lucien's uncle had softened, and temporarily suspended his ban against Lucien seeing me. Now, Lucien held my hand tightly, squeezing it throughout the service to offer his support.

I glanced to my left and watched Arthur, his face red as a beet, clutching Marion's arm. His lined face revealed the exhaustion he felt from the events of the past week. Once again, when he had been needed, Arthur was nowhere to be found. Typical of the pattern since I left for UCLA, the family tried in vain to reach him, then called me to come and manage one of the most difficult situations of my life: my mother's funeral.

He's such a Houdini. He can escape all the traumas of reality by running away and turning to greener and more pleasant pastures, like Aunt Marion, and maybe even other women too. It's his fault

Lila got worse. It was possible she died because she didn't know how to take the newly prescribed anti-depressants she'd gotten the week before. Whatever it was, she didn't get much help from Arthur. She didn't have to die so soon, or in this way. If he had cared enough about her, he could have done so much more to prevent it—or at least been there when she needed some help.

Looking at the kind face of John Follster, the Unitarian minister officiating and our neighbor for many years, I put aside for a moment the anger I felt toward my father. *At least Arthur, in the one thing he did do to help me arrange the funeral, made the right choice of someone to perform the service,* I begrudgingly admitted to myself. Arthur admired John, who was a man of integrity. Also, to Arthur, Unitarianism seemed the closest thing to a humanistic approach to religion, if a religion were needed at all.

Well, I'm completely with him on that score. But how can a man like my father, who's so humanistic and liberal, be so emotionally insensitive?

My thoughts were interrupted when an older, handsome-looking woman, her white hair pulled into an elegant chignon, walked up to me. "My name is Mrs. Barbara Bridlesbee," she said softly. "I want to offer you my most sincere condolences. Years ago when I was back East, I'd often call your mother and she would help me with my dog, Jericho, who has passed on to the far beyond. God rest his soul. It is because of her and her abiding love of animals and birds that led me to own a cat and a bird. I was saddened to read about Lila's death in the obits and I've come to her funeral to bring some precious remembrances."

Mrs. Bridlesbee carried an extremely large shopping bag which clashed with her elegant appearance and her designer suit. She looked like a cross between an older Princess Grace Kelly and a bag lady from the streets.

"I know your mother would have loved to have some small mementos of animals placed in her casket, but she died so quickly that she didn't have time to have that done." With that, she opened her huge paper sack and took out a locked box which she now ceremoniously opened. I watched her as she produced a cellophane wrapped bag filled with dirt, and another with ashes, both accompanied by a long, long feather. "To share a special moment of feeling with Lila, I offer her the ashes of Jericho, my beloved dog, a little dirt gathered from my cat Catania's grave, and a feather from my deceased parrot, Lila Two."

I struggled between a desire to burst into hysterics, and my genuine respect for the woman's sincerity. Mrs. Bridlesbee, apparently mistaking my widening grin for a sign of permission for her to go ahead, approached Minister Follster and requested he hand the mementos to three of the closest members of Lila's family. With a flourish of her hand waving in the air, she said, "I know Lila would have wanted it this way!"

John Follster good naturedly agreed to include the placement of these reverent mementos in Lila's grave and, as the service progressed, to call on family members entrusted with one of the mementos. I got Jericho's ashes, Marion (whom Mrs. Bridlesbee mistook for Lila's sister) got the dirt from Catania's grave, and Jonna got Lila Two's feather.

Jonna looked pale and wan. Her tears seemed to be permanently plastered where they had fallen. She nervously clutched the feather. She was extremely shy, now overwrought, and turned to me, "Kim, do I really have to do this?" Jonna gave the feather a disdainful look. "Do I have to drop this thing into Lila's grave?"

"I'll be there with you, Jonna, when Mr. Follster asks you to drop it."

Arthur was clearly disgusted with the entire interlude. "How could you accept that silly woman's offering?" he hissed at me. When he realized the other mourners were looking at him, he lowered his head and withdrew.

It was slowly dawning on me who Mrs. Bridlesbee was. She was one of the ladies Lila used to laugh out loud about, referring to them as "those old biddies" who entrusted their pets' psychological security to her and Marion many years ago when they worked for a newspaper in New York City.

"Who is that lady?" Lucien asked.

"It's a long story," I whispered. "Lila and Marion met when they worked together on the *New York Daily News*. Their boss was a man named Doc Cogan, who managed the *Dog, Cat and Bird News* section. Lila and Marion wrote a column together called 'Barks, Meows and Tweets.'"

Lucien laughed aloud. I dug my elbow into his side, as people looked askance at us.

"They'd spend hours answering letters and phone calls from concerned pet owners helping them deal with their disobedient dogs, their recalcitrant cats, or their overly-noisy birds."

I laughed inwardly, continuing to whisper, "There was one tremendous irony to this. Neither Lila nor Marion ever owned a dog, a cat, or a bird. So, day after day they used their imaginations to concoct remedies for all of their callers. They simply made them up! It went something like this: 'Mrs. B, to get a dog to listen, you must be firm, consistent, sing to them, and give them a treat when they obey. Your dog is like a child and needs the same type of care and tenderness.' Lila would then get off the phone quickly, lest Mrs. B ask her what she did with her own pets!" Many people, like Mrs. Bridlesbee, became like friends over the years and kept in touch with Lila long after she left the *Daily News* to marry Arthur.

Lucien tried to stifle his laughter. He'd guessed early on that Lila didn't like animals and had never had a pet of her own. The one time he'd brought me home because Lila was ill, he'd brought his boxer, Buster, with him. Lila, in her bathrobe and recovering from pneumonia, met him at her front door and insisted he keep Buster tied to a tree outside. Dogs, she said, were never permitted in her house!

I turned and whispered to Marion: "Do you remember this lady? She's one of the callers from the dog and cat column of the newspaper where you and Lila worked." Marion looked confused, and then said under her breath, "I do recognize her. It's sad to remember that time when there was a Lila full of life and laughter, and so very beautiful."

Oh right. How hypocritical! If she was so beautiful, and so full of life, how could you participate in taking that life away from her?

But, as soon as I had thought these accusatory thoughts, I remembered how Marion had been there to take care of Lila whenever she had a crisis. *I'll never know what their relationships were. It's just that not knowing makes me so suspicious.*

I sensed Jonna's agitated movements as we watched the coffin waiting to be lowered into the grave. She looked down, her eyes darting from side to side, and all of a sudden dropped to her knees and frantically brushed the ground with her hands. I was alarmed. What was she doing? Was she ill? Was she still reeling from the sudden loss of Lila? I gently put my hand on her back. "What is it, Jonni, why are you down there?"

Jonna looked up, wide-eyed and petrified, as John Follster called upon Marion to put Catania's dirt atop Lila's coffin. The feather would be next.

With a look of panic written all over her face, Jonna looked up at me: "I lost the feather, Kim! I can't find the feather!"

I kneeled down to help Jonna look for the feather. Many of the mourners around us, assuming we'd lost a precious piece of jewelry, fell to their knees and crawled around on the ground, intent on helping us find the treasure. As John Follster extolled Lila's virtues and her intense love of animals, Arthur grimaced, like he was going to be ill if Follster spoke of Lila's love of animals one more time. "What a farce," he muttered.

Mr. Follster called me to the casket, whereupon I dutifully deposited the open box of Jericho's ashes on top of the dirt from Catania's grave. I then rushed back to tend to Jonna who, by this time, was near hysterics. We were about to give up on the feather when Mrs. Bridlesbee, puzzled about why the feather hadn't been deposited, bustled over to us. She kneeled down to see what we were looking for and I spied the feather clinging tenuously to her underskirt. Each time she moved, the feather waved in the breeze. I remembered that when Mr. Follster began his eulogy, Mrs. Bridlesbee had moved closer to Lila's casket, and brushed past Jonna. She must have gathered the precious feather in her wake.

Looking up at Mrs. Bridlesbee, I quickly pulled the feather from her underskirt, passing it to Jonna just as Mr. Follster said, "Now the symbolic memento of Lila Two: her feather!" Jonna, her relief evident, walked to the casket and placed the feather on top.

The service ended, and I felt the need to get out of the burning sun. Aunt Marion invited all the mourners at the gravesite to gather at her home for refreshments.

Arthur shot me a look as I immediately shook my head from side to side: "I'll stay here if you don't mind!" I ignored him and began to cry. My mother was gone. She was only forty-nine years old. *She will never see me married, and she will never see my children, my four boys.* The more I cried for my mother, the more resentment I felt toward Marion and my father. I averted my eyes, not wanting to start trouble with them. But as the rest of the crowd prepared to leave the park, my anger, particularly toward my father, flared up inside.

Arthur came towards me, holding out his hand. "Kim, won't you consider coming by to be with the family?"

Marion quickly put her hand on Arthur's shoulder. "She's upset, Arthur. We're all upset. She doesn't have to come if she doesn't want to." My anger toward Marion turned to confusion as she gently took my chin in her hand and turned my face towards hers. "Someday, I hope you come to know what you can't possibly understand at this moment. There's so much you need to be aware of."

"What does that mean?" I cried. "Am I to understand that you let my mother languish alone on many evenings so the two of you could be together?" Turning toward Arthur, I spat out, "So that you could run away from anything unpleasant and avoid helping us by being with her?" Marion recoiled, looking down, shaking her head back and forth.

"Kim," Arthur said wearily, "I know you're upset and grieving right now. We all are. But there is so much you do not know. Please do not jump to conclusions. Your Aunt Marion is not the devil here."

I turned away from Arthur, partly to try and hide my own copious tears and partly because I saw such pain and heartbreak on Arthur's face.

Give him a break—he's been through so much these past six months. It was such a roller-coaster when he thought he was going to be called up before HUAC, and I could tell he had been worried about my safety too, when he warned me about the FBI.

Lucien gently pulled me away from Arthur. But still, I couldn't quite let go of my anguish. Turning back to Arthur, I hurled one more salvo at him: "But why does everything always have to be such a mystery with this family, Arthur? Why?"

Arthur hung his head. He had no answer, of course.

Lucien and I left Arthur and the departing crowd and returned to my mother's grave, hearing Marion's sobs behind us.

I turned back to watch Jonna walking to the parking lot between Arthur and Marion. She swung her head around and looked back at me. My eyes met her pleading look, and I felt a tug of guilt. I had Lucien, but Jonna seemed so alone. I paused, thinking I would go after her, but thought better of it, since I would have to come in close contact with Arthur and Marion too.

Lucien put my arm in his, and led me to the shade of a large elm which would offer us protection from the blistering sun. I leaned into his muscular body for support, my shoulders heaving with my anguish.

"I wish I could sort this all out, Luc."

"It's too hard to sort out. You've gone through your mom's sudden death, her burial, the whole episode between Marion and your father, and now you and your father. And all of this is on top of the upheaval you've all been going through the last six months. There's no better or worse, it's all horrible!"

I buried my face in his shoulder. After a long silence, I made a feeble attempt to lighten the intensity of the day. "The feather took the cake, don't you think?"

"Well, the feather did take the cake, Kim!" Lucien looked at me sideways and then burst out laughing. He laughed until his eyes filled with tears, then became serious. "My uncle says all events have meaning. What possible meaning could Lila's death and the feather have?" He looked at me tenderly, pulling me down with him to the ground. We lay close together, his face against mine.

I whispered, "There is no way to understand the meaning of the unreal things that have happened. The only meaningful thing I have is you. Only you make sense to me, Luc. You've changed my world."

Lucien hugged me. "We'll always be together because we have such a unique bond."

I smiled. "I believe you. Maybe I don't have to look forward to having the continual tension and unhappiness my folks had. As a kid I couldn't understand why people had such awful feelings about divorce. I prayed for my parents' divorce from the time I was five years old. When I came to understand what the word 'purgatory' was, it described my parents' marriage. In one of her rare, calmer moments, Lila once apologized to me for her terrible outbursts. She thought her perpetual tantrums came because she felt that her life and her marriage were so dissatisfying. She always felt trapped and saw her life fly away and get lost—just like the feather. So, I guess we could say that's the meaning of the feather."

"Maybe. But this McCarthy thing didn't help her either. It made her crazy fearing your dad would be singled out. What a living hell for all of you."

I gazed into the distance, trying to mask the intense emotion I felt. "It's hard to describe what it was like for me to see her in that kind of agony. One day I came home from school and found her examining the telephone. She was turning the receiver over and over. I didn't have to ask what she was doing. She was certain our home was bugged, that the

FBI was spying on Arthur. She used to say there was an ominous visitor who lingered in our home and his name was 'terror.'"

Daylight began to fade, casting long shadows over the rolling green lawn. Luc and I still lay together, side by side. I felt drained, and the hot air had evaporated my tears. My limbs felt achy, as if the burdens I had been carrying the last few days were lifting off of me. And then, my memories and words about Lila tumbled out, almost as if I were delivering my own private memorial to her. I couldn't stop talking about her. "You know, Luc, despite the chronic chaos, there were pleasant times as well. On rare mornings, before I left for school, Lila and I would sit together while she sipped her coffee and I tried to eat my lumpy cream of wheat, which she could never make right. She always had a lit cigarette between her fingers, and she had these large dewy brown eyes. She would stare into space at some beautiful but lost life beyond the one she had in the Valley. A dreamy kind of smile would always appear when she was speaking of her past. She'd regale me with stories about her fast life as a single woman—lots of dating and travel, as far as I could gather. When she spoke of her past, there was no hint of the screaming banshee she became when my father got home. She would piece together for me a picture of a person who did not exist anymore."

Lucien stroked my hair. "That reminds me of my uncle, who reminisces and weeps about the elegance of his past life in Iran. His memories center around the glittery pomp and unimaginable wealth he had in the world of the Reza Shah Pahlavi. How different life in America is for him. Uncle Parviz and Lila: two people who never reconciled their old lifestyles, which seemed like fairytales, with their new ones. They both had to face such a different kind of reality."

The relieving cool of evening fell over the cemetery. Still lying by my side, Lucien turned to face me, propping himself up on one arm. He ran his fingers gently over my face. "I've always wanted to make all this go away for you. Maybe someday we can make it go away together."

I looked up at him, stroking his smooth face. "You already make it go away, like a soul mate who makes me forget my past and look forward to better things in my world."

Lucien smiled and kissed my ear lobe. "For me, too. You've opened up my life."

Staring up at a dark sky emblazoned by multitudes of stars, we continued to lie on our backs. Neither of us spoke for quite a while, and then I broke the silence.

"They look like diamonds, Luc, don't they?"

"They do indeed, and one of these nights I'm going to pluck one of those diamonds from the sky and put it on your finger."

For some strange reason his beautiful promise made me anxious. I felt a sudden shudder that made me sit up. Just then, I saw two coeds walking lightly on the grass path between graves in one of the areas near us. I had a flash of jealousy of their ease with each other and themselves. But now I was being defined as part of a couple. Would I become a different person if I got married to Luc, just as Lila had when she married my father? Would I be able to realize my potential? *But Luc is so entirely different from Arthur—so caring and tender. But maybe it's partly the act of marriage that changes people, that makes them feel like the other person belongs to them.*

"What just happened, Kim?"

"It's nothing, Luc, just a shudder of happiness. It's time to leave this place."

Chapter 13

1959

I sat in the dim light of Royce Hall waiting for Lucien. The magnificent auditorium, paneled with walnut, was the oldest building on the UCLA campus and, to me, the most beautiful. Overcome by a feeling of awe, I couldn't believe I had been able to land tickets for the Juilliard Quartet. And here I was, on the eve of my senior year in college, about to hear one of the most brilliant quartets of the century.

Lucien rushed down the aisle to meet me and folded his long frame into the seat just as the lights dimmed. We sat, hand in hand, listening to the strains of Beethoven's beautiful Rasoumovsky String Quartets. The large hall was filled to capacity; so many students sat in the aisles or stood in the back of the large room.

Sitting with his arm around me, Lucien leaned over and whispered into my ear, his curly hair tickling my neck, "You didn't really mean what you said this morning, did you?"

I shot him an annoyed look and pulled away from him. "Please, not here. Let's talk when we get back to the apartment. These tickets for the Beethoven Cycle are for your birthday. They cost me ten dollars, almost a day's salary, and I don't want to miss a minute. I've been looking forward to this concert for a long time."

"Some birthday present," Lucien sulked. "You give with one hand and take away with the other." He leaned forward looking ahead, his chin in his hands, trying to ignore me.

I became immersed in the music and the intensity of the string quartet members. I was impressed by their synchronization, and it seemed to me that the musicians spoke a precious language to each other through the music. Each sat in rapt concentration and their precision was breathtaking. I'd always wanted to play an instrument, particularly the piano, but was too eager to escape my household to spend the time at home practicing on Lila's ancient upright.

Out of the corner of my eye, I caught Lucien frowning. I pulled him toward me and planted a warm kiss on his cheek.

He turned to me, his dark eyes glistening. "Kim, you're all I have. I hope you're not thinking of leaving. My whole life is tied up with yours."

A disgruntled couple in front of him turned and frowned disapprovingly. The woman hissed, "Will you two lovebirds quiet down?" A gray-haired woman sitting next to me, her large black-rimmed glasses perched on the lower part of her nose, added, " Please be quiet, I've been looking forward to this for almost a year myself!"

We both mouthed an apology and settled back to listen to the rest of the concert. I squeezed Lucien's hand and put my finger to my lips. "I told you, we'll talk more when we get home."

When the music ended, the enthusiastic crowd clamored for an encore. Despite the audience's persistent clapping, the musicians opted to make the last quartet their final piece for the evening. Lucien and I lingered in our seats until the crowd thinned.

It was a glorious January evening. We strolled along Veteran Avenue humming some of the beautiful Beethoven pieces we'd just heard. Finally, I broke the silence.

"We're so lucky to be here in Southern California. The rest of the country is having below-zero temperatures, while our evening is so balmy. What a beautiful night, Luc, with all the twinkling stars out—just for us."

Lucien gently put his hand on my shoulder. "I like when you say, 'just for us,' like there will always be an 'us.'" We walked toward Wilshire Boulevard, turned west and rounded the corner to San Vicente where we came to the 7-Eleven, which, true to its name, was open until 11 p.m.

"Do we need eggs, bread, and some milk for the morning?" Lucien asked. I nodded. How natural this all sounded. We were a couple living together. *Am I crazy? Who in their right mind would want to give up this arrangement?* We entered the convenience store.

The fluorescent glare was unexpectedly harsh, the sort of light that was never kind to people's skin color. Lucien laid out two dollars: one dollar for a gallon of milk, thirty cents for a dozen eggs and twenty cents for a loaf of bread. After getting his change from the student who ran the store, we headed to my apartment. We had continued our arrangement from last summer and through this academic year of sharing all expenses and spending the week in our respective places and the weekends at Lucien's "cottage guest house." This evening was an exception. Jeannie was spending the weekend on Balboa Island with her folks, and I particularly wanted more privacy because of what I needed to talk to Luc about.

My stomach did a flip-flop as I started thinking of what I was about to do. I was trying to keep our conversation light until we got back to the apartment, but inside I was having a tug of war with myself. One minute I was convinced that my soul-searching during the past two months had led me to the correct conclusion. But then in the very next moment, I'd think: *No, this isn't the right thing to do.*

Almost as if he were reading my mind, Luc fixed his eyes on me, monitoring my mood, my expression. *That's what bothers me—I feel as if he's always watching me. Maybe it's not in a bad way. I know he cares deeply for me, but sometimes it just makes me feel claustrophobic.* Luc's eyebrows shot up questioningly. I shrugged, and smiled at him as brightly as I could.

Turning west on Kiowa and passing in front of the row of two- and three-story apartment buildings, we came to my building in the middle of the block. Occupied by several of our friends, mostly graduate students, the doors of many apartments were ajar, an open invitation to enter at any time. To save money, we often had potluck dinners, and the cozy, informal atmosphere felt like a big community center.

We climbed the stairs and Lucien reached for the key hidden in the ivy plant next to a Ban the Bomb poster that my friends and I had hung after a Ban the Bomb rally we had attended earlier that month, to support the organization that had started just the year before in England. We wanted the world to know where we stood on issues, were proud of our liberal views, and advertised them whenever we could. I guess I was most definitely Arthur's daughter in that respect.

I went to the tiny kitchen off the entryway to put the groceries away. Lucien dubbed it "La Prison," because it was easy for two people to feel crowded and trapped in the tiny space. I momentarily busied myself, knowing that I was going to have to face him at some point and resume our serious discussion from this morning. I had begun to broach my concerns to Luc, but a neighbor coming over with some homemade coffee cake had interrupted us. I could tell that Luc had been stewing ever since.

The kitchen barely had room for two tiny café chairs and a small round walnut table I'd purchased at the Salvation Army Store. We called the table "La Centre," and used it for eating, serious discussion, studying, even dozing. I began to tidy the top of the table, but sensed Luc behind me starting to pace, gearing up for our talk.

Lucien brushed past me and dropped on the threadbare red sofa, another Salvation Army purchase, his long, slim body filling its near seven-foot length. He remained silent for a long while, staring at the poster of Pete Seeger, which dominated the living room wall. "Okay, let's have it," he said grimly. "You've been so withdrawn for the last two months. What's bothering you?"

"I'll tell you, Luc," I said, stalling for time. I crossed through the tiny alcove to the living room and stood in front of the large bay window watching the glow of lights from Westwood in the distance. I was nervous. Luc's intensity about anything that concerned the two of us always unsettled me. I had to deal with our relationship, because the tension between us had grown and my stomach was in a knot. I had to be honest. *This is the right thing to do. Just don't look into his eyes, because you know you'll just melt, and back away from what needs to be said.*

I began slowly and hesitantly. "The past two months have been difficult for me, Luc. I've had a lot on my mind ever since Lila's death last summer, as you know. And now, with getting ready to graduate and thinking about my future, I've been doing a lot of soul-searching about every facet of my life, and our relationship." I could see Luc starting to fidget, his eyes glued to my face.

"Oh, Luc. This is so hard for me. But I just don't think I can do the kind of growing I need to do if we are a couple."

"But Kim," he countered, trying to restrain himself. "Don't you understand that I totally support all your career efforts? I would never stand in the way of your growth as a person!"

"I think we should face that we do have differences, though. And one of the differences is that you are very traditional, which is understandable, given your upbringing."

"So it's that—my Iranian heritage? My uncle's disapproval?"

"No, Luc, it's not that. I've certainly had concerns all along about your financial dependence on your uncle and his disapproval of me. And you know I've worried that I could be holding you back because of that."

"But Kim, I've made it so clear that I'm devoted to you!" He got up from the couch and ran his hands nervously through his hair. "I don't care if my parents find out about you! They can disown me and that won't change how I feel about you! I'll get a job on my own and apply for a permanent visa."

"Luc, where would you be able to get a job? At the 7-Eleven? Your prospects depend on getting a degree. Plus I've seen how you dislike shopping at the Salvation Army and the other thrift stores. We are so different. I don't mind shopping for secondhand things. I didn't grow up with the noblesse oblige like you did." I saw the hurt look on his face, and realized my remark wasn't really a fair one. I quickly changed the tack in my argument.

"But really, Luc, this isn't about your situation. It's about what I want for myself and my life. Pretty soon I'm going to be twenty-one, and I don't know what I want to do with my life. I want to be free to explore and take opportunities as they come my way."

"What good will *my* life be without you?" Luc shouted. He grabbed a book from the coffee table and threw it against the wall.

I stamped my foot. "I knew this was going to happen! This is why I haven't been able to bring this up until now. You make me feel that you can't be anything without me—and I don't want our relationship to be based on such a heavy burden."

"Kim, just tell me what you want and I'll do it. If you need for me to give you more freedom, I can do that." He started to wave his hands, as if to discount the seriousness of my concerns. Lucien moved closer to me, his body touching mine. I flushed with warmth. He enclosed me in his arms and began to kiss my face, each time kissing me harder, until I could no longer breathe.

Reluctantly I pushed him away. "Luc, listen, it's not just a matter of you changing your ways. It's me. I have a lot of searching to do. I have to start figuring out what I want to do with myself. And the way we are now, I can't do that so easily. I'm a little afraid of our relationship. It's too intense, and I'm not sure I'm mature enough or ready to commit to it. I can't think clearly when you're around."

He looked startled. His mouth hung open, like he'd been struck. The pain in his eyes was unbearable for me.

"Please, Luc, don't look at me that way!" I rushed forward as he began to turn away. "Just listen to me. Maybe it would be better for us to go our separate ways just for a while." My eyes blurred with tears as I thought of Frost's poem, "The Road Not Taken" and the famous lines. Out loud, I recited: "Two roads diverged in a yellow wood and sorry we could not travel both…" Luc's profile was lost in a blurred image of a distraught form moving back and forth across the room.

"I can't believe you're saying all this, and stop reciting Frost! It doesn't help!" Luc buried his face in his cupped hands.

"It's my fault, Luc. I need to go on my own path. I can't have both. I can't have you needing me and wanting me as you do, and also find the space I need to find out who I really am and where to go in my life." I realized I was pleading with him. For what? For his blessing of my emancipation? I did not know.

Lucien slumped on the sofa, still holding his face in his hands. He got up and moved toward me.

"I cannot be without you. You've been everything to me this past year. Everything. I'll get a job. I'll ask Dr. Stevenson when I go to his clinic tomorrow if he'll recommend me for a scholarship. Then I would have enough money to keep a separate apartment, so you wouldn't feel stifled about my coming here all the time. And if you go to New York, I wouldn't insist that we live together."

My heart was pounding. I had not realized that this was going to be so difficult. *I thought we could talk it out reasonably and that would do it. How foolish of me. I'm confused about him, about life, about my future. I just need space.* "Luc, we need time apart. I mean, whether I go to New York or not. And I may not even go to New York. With my mother gone and Jonna having one episode of depression after another, I don't know what I should do. I have a lot to work out, Luc. Maybe I'll apply for a scholarship here at UCLA to the Graduate School of History, get another apartment, and have Jonna move in with me. I'm not ready to give up my dreams like my mother did."

"Kim, please reconsider. How can anything as beautiful as our relationship end? You're being foolish!" Lucien's eyes filled with tears again and his voice started to sound desperate.

I reached for his hand. "I'm not ready for something as close and precious as we have. I feel you and sense you every moment of the day. I told you you've made me feel alive, and I meant it."

"Why would you leave me then? All the more reason for us to be together."

"I'm simply not ready to commit to any long-term relationship now. This just seems like a momentous time in my life. I feel like I'm on the brink of a whole new chapter. I have to find my way and settle on what's best for me. And I have Jonna to think about. Maybe when all this is settled, we can be together, but not now."

"Don't say it! Stop talking! I can't listen any more," Lucien sobbed.

An odd calm began to settle over me. Luc's outbursts were really uncomfortable for me. But they also validated my increasing fear that I could be suffocated by his passion. Over the last year I had seen glimpses of how intense and possessive he could be. I had felt smothered.

After what seemed like hours, Lucien calmed down a bit, then sat down beside me on the sofa and gently took my hand. His eyes were red and almost swollen from crying. "I need to take a long walk and clear my head, Kim. I guess I'm hoping that in those minutes there'll be a magical moment and you'll change your mind."

I looked down and grasped the couch as if it would help me hold onto my resolve. "I won't, Luc. I think this is best. For both of us."

Lucien looked drained as he slowly walked to the door and left. A feeling of sadness washed over me. I would move on in some way or another, but I knew my life would never be the same.

Chapter 14

1963

As I looked around at the soon-to-be graduates sitting in the hall, I felt a sense of pride and accomplishment. My roommate and classmate Arlene and I had arisen early and donned our caps and gowns for this special awards ceremony, scheduled for Friday, November 22, 1963. We would be officially getting our degrees in mid-December, along with the rest of the graduates, but our college was holding this awards ceremony to acknowledge those who would graduate with honors. Wow, I've done it! My master's degree! And with honors. Lila would have been so proud! And I've done it on my terms.

Arlene and I squeezed each other's hands as the dean ceremoniously walked to the podium to begin the morning's proceedings. Since her family was back in the Midwest and mine was absent, we were each other's support team.

We weren't prepared for what the dean now said. "Graduates, family members and friends, I am very saddened to have to tell you that we must suspend this morning's ceremony." A buzz went around the room. Arlene and I looked at each other quizzically: What in the world could be the matter?

"We have just received word," the dean continued, "That President

Kennedy has been shot in Dallas. We have no further details, but in light of these tragic circumstances, we feel it would be inappropriate to continue." Everyone in the audience gasped, almost in unison. All around us, Arlene and I heard people crying in despair, or voicing their disbelief. Arlene and I turned to each other and wept. Then, still in our robes, we walked outside, where the thin November light seemed suddenly bleak and uninviting. We drove back to the house we rented in Laurel Canyon, crying the entire way.

We staggered inside, turned on the television, and fell onto the sofa, staring like zombies at the newscasts: Dan Rather reporting from a grassy knoll in Dallas where President Kennedy's motorcade had passed; a replay of Jackie Kennedy in her pink, blood-stained suit, trying to scramble out of the black Continental convertible; Secret Service agents protecting her and holding back the stunned onlookers, their faces frozen with the horror of what had just happened. The whole world waited.

And then it came. At 11:38 a.m. California time, Walter Cronkite made the announcement that we'd never forget. Reading from an AP wire, he said, "President John F. Kennedy died at 1:00 p.m. Central time, 2:00 p.m. Eastern standard time..." He took off his glasses and glanced at the clock: "some 38 minutes ago." Cronkite paused briefly, put his glasses back on, and swallowed hard. With emotion in his voice, he repeated the announcement and said that Vice President Lyndon Johnson would now become the next president of the United States. Arlene and I burst out sobbing, holding on to each other in a desperate attempt for support.

For the rest of the day, we milled around the house, at a loss for words. The hours seemed to pass in a blur. We took off our caps and gowns and changed into our jeans, but had no desire to go anywhere. At some point, in the late afternoon, we sat down on the couch again to watch the awful footage that kept replaying, of our young president being cut down in his prime. It was as if the world had stopped. I don't know how long we sat like that, but soon the neon glow of the television was the only light in the darkening room. At a certain point, I realized the phone was ringing, but by the time I reached for it, it stopped. Then Arlene said something about needing to talk to her folks in Milwaukee.

I just nodded numbly and wandered to the huge bay window that overlooked the hills of Wonderland Drive, taking in the view of the lush flowers and trees that adorned the canyon below, all bathed in the glow of the setting sun. Arlene and I had been living here for two years while going through the master's program. It had taken me a while after graduating with my bachelor's to chart a direction for myself. I had felt a bit adrift after my senior year. Losing my mother, breaking up with Luc, feeling responsible for Jonna: all had taken their toll. My advisor had suggested I apply for an eighteen-month fellowship in European history. Since it came with a scholarship, I had jumped at the chance. After that, I took a job and worked for a while to gather enough resources to pay for graduate school. I had first heard about the house in Laurel Canyon at the start of my graduate work, and moved in with the grad student who had the lease on the place.

Of the three roommates I'd had, Arlene was my favorite. Good-natured, honest, and kind-hearted, she had little patience with pretense. After ironing out a few pet peeves in the beginning (she'd leave dirty dishes in the sink and I'd leave water droplets on the shower walls) we not only got along with each other, but became close friends. And she was helpful and understanding about Jonna. I was glad she was here with me now.

Jonna. Oh my God. I've been so turned around by this news that I completely forgot about her! She said she'd come to the graduation ceremony and never showed up. *I should've followed up, checked in with her beforehand.* Now I was worried. I needed to call her right away to find out where she was, but Arlene was still on the phone with her parents. Just as I was about to ask her, she hung up and the phone rang immediately. She answered it.

"She's right here, Jonna."

I barely missed tripping over the Turkish ottoman in my race to grab the receiver. "Jonna? Are you okay?"

"I wanted to tell you the good news, but first, congratulations." Her timid voice sounded forced with good cheer. "It's great you are receiving honors and that they're going to let you graduate early. I wish I could've been there…I'm sorry, I…"

"It's okay, Jonni. Are you sick?" I asked.

"No, I'm not sick, but I feel fuzzy. I've been dreaming about Lila a lot and I think about her all the time and I don't want to be like her anymore, but I don't think I can help it. I just am." Her voice trailed off.

My heart dropped to my toes. "You're *not* like her, honey. You're smart and in love and have a whole life ahead of you. Right now, you're scaring me." The long silence made me think I shouldn't have said that, because it might keep her from being honest with me. I didn't want Jonna to feel that she had to pretend to feel more upbeat for my sake. A few weeks ago, her boyfriend Wally told me that he was concerned about her, and that medical school was demanding so much of his time that he wasn't able to be with her lately. I, too, had been preoccupied with wrapping up my master's thesis. Maybe I hadn't realized that perhaps Jonna was getting worse and slipping into a depression. I pictured her nervously fiddling with the engraved gold pendant Lila gave her when she made the honor society in high school. "Is Wally coming over?"

"No. He's at the hospital. I'm not good enough for him. I can't bear to make him live with me because I'm like Lila. He'll just be miserable with me. You're not like her. You're like Arthur—energetic, positive. I have to do what's best for everyone. I just wanted to tell you that I know how much you care, how much you tried…"

I was suspended somewhere. I felt helpless. I needed to do something. "I'm coming right over. We can spend the evening together, just you and me. We'll go to dinner. And you can stay here with me and Arlene." A tingling sensation crept through my hand. It was numb from my tight grip of the phone. I switched to the other hand. "Have you turned on the television today?"

She said she hadn't. I caught Arlene looking at me, dangling the car keys, signaling for us to leave to get Jonna.

"Jonna, I need to see you. I've missed you."

The line suddenly had a lot of static, but I heard her whisper, "You were the only sane person in my life, Kim. A rock." She sounded distant and started rambling, "Don't forget, I love you Kim."

"I'm on my way, Jonna. I'll see you in a few minutes."

Jonna didn't respond. She had tried to hurt herself before, to end her life by cutting her wrists, but it was a half-hearted attempt and she barely scratched herself. This felt more serious, like she meant it. I heard the rum of the car's engine but needed to call the dorm first, to try to reach someone there. There was no dial tone—Jonna must not have hung up the phone. *Oh my God. There's no way to call out from here!*

Arlene was gunning the engine. I tried to think. How can I call emergency or campus security or someone who could get to Jonna before me? I bolted out the front door and missed the two steps, plunging to the ground. I heard a crunching sound in my wrist, and then excruciating pain shot up my arm. I grabbed my purse with the other hand, held my throbbing arm close to my chest, and jumped in the car with Arlene at the wheel.

She raced down Wonderland and toward the Westside to the UCLA campus. I told her I needed to call the police. My voice was hollow with helplessness. Arlene squealed to a stop at a phone booth in front of a store at the bottom of the hill. I called Campus Emergency. *Answer, please answer.* It rang and rang and finally someone answered. With my voice quivering, I told the security officer who I was, that my sister in Clarendon Hall was in grave danger, probably suicidal. He told me that the dorm advisor had already ordered an ambulance and that my sister was taken to the neuropsychiatric hospital on campus. I hung up, and ran back to the car.

Arlene sped down Sunset to Hilgard and through the quiet, peaceful looking campus into the driveway of the recently completed Neuropsychiatric Institute. We barreled out of the car and through the hospital doors. The silence and emptiness of the corridors alarmed me and the shiny overly waxed floors seemed sterile. It felt cold and lifeless. A nurse at the end of the hall beckoned us. "Miss Lebow? Are you the sister?"

Shooting pains throbbed up my arm. I cradled it against me. "Where is she? Where is Jonna?" I glanced at each door as I followed the nurse down the hall, Arlene right behind. The nurse stopped at a room and gently opened the door, edging herself halfway inside, signaling for us to stay put.

I heard the murmur of voices coming from the room. "Let me in," I cried. "I need to see my sister."

Arlene put her arm around me as I braced for what was coming. A dignified, gray-haired man in a white physician's coat with the initials UCLA on the pocket came out, carefully shutting the door behind him. He was so somber, and his brow was knitted in such deep concern, that I knew what he was going to say before he opened his mouth.

"I'm so sorry."

The room swayed and I felt my knees buckle. Arlene held me up and the doctor reached out to help her. "I must see her. I can't be too late!"

The doctor eased me into a chair. He was talking but his words all ran together. *We did everything we could. Main arteries of her wrists. Lost lots of blood. Locked herself in the dorm bathroom. No one could get to her. Too late. Too late. Too late.*

"She was getting married. This can't be," I protested. "She was happy…wasn't she?" *I should've known. I had warnings. Wally even told me.* I wept uncontrollably. I should've insisted she move in with me. Jonna. Poor Jonna. I didn't tell her I loved her.

I needed to touch my sister. Kiss her one last time. Hold her hand and tell her how sorry I am that I wasn't there to save her. I'm all she had and I let her down. I asked the doctor to give me some time alone with her.

Just as the doctor opened the door to let me in, I heard an announcement on the loud speaker system saying all classes and campus events would be suspended for the next week to honor the passing of our President. The doctor and Arlene waited outside.

The door closed behind me, creating a hush. I almost held my breath, because it sounded too noisy to inhale and exhale in this quiet place. The lights were low, but I could make out Jonna's slight frame underneath the sheets. *The nurses must have cleaned up the blood, I thought, because there would have been blood everywhere. Maybe the nurses had cleaned her, put bandages on her wrists, and moved the body to this separate room.*

I quietly walked to the bed and looked down at Jonna's pallid face. There was a blue tint to her skin—she had lost lots of blood, I remember the doctor saying—and it made her dark eyelashes stand out. *My little sister. Forgive me, Jonni, for not hearing your cries. Your burden was always heavier than mine, I know. I remember I used to be so afraid you would fly out of that big window in our apartment in the Bronx, and I wished that California would be kinder to us. Now you have truly flown away from all of us.*

I gently lifted her delicate hand—oh so cold, so cold. How could she be gone? My mind just couldn't grasp her absence. I felt warm splashes on my hand—tears I wasn't even aware that I was shedding. The tumult of the day descended on me, and I bent over her bed, stroking her hair and murmuring, "I loved you. Why couldn't I save you?"

So many other thoughts tumbled into my brain. How was I going to tell Arthur? For that matter, how would I even find him? That was the whole reason I had decided not to invite him to the ceremony—he was always absent. Who, then, would I call? Marion, I guess. Funny how, in these family crises, she was the one we all went to. I sighed. I suddenly felt so sad, not just for Jonna, but for all of our family. We were like a family of wounded and writhing birds.

When I came out, I saw everyone in the hallway bowing their heads in silent prayer. But it wasn't for Jonna. Today will be locked forever in my memory as the day my sister took her life. *The whole world will remember Kennedy, but who will remember my sister, Jonna?*

Chapter 15

1994

The clapping of the waves against the bay window carried me away from a deeper immersion in my dream. I woke up feeling frustrated, as if a story about to unfold from within me had been put on pause. I sat up in bed, looking out at the ocean, searching, but for what?

Padding through the spacious bedroom to the bathroom down the hall, I had an odd sensation in the pit of my stomach. An empty, almost queasy feeling wasn't unusual for me these days, even though I was finally getting used to waking up in my bed alone without my husband beside me.

I threw on my robe and made my way to the kitchen. The grayish morning light, so typical of November in Malibu, cast an eerie light on the kitchen wall, making me feel uneasy. I ground the beans and measured the water for my morning coffee, knowing that the routine would help settle me. The first cup was the awakener; the second, the organizer; and the third would bring me fully to life.

My dream lingered like a half-completed crossword puzzle demanding that each blank square be filled in. I tried to piece it together. Two figures in silhouette faded in and out, like a black and white movie where the camera pans in, then pulls away. Each person had a hand raised toward the other, as if in greeting or, sadly, in farewell. Since Lawrence died, I had dreamt of him often. Was I saying good-bye to him again? Or was my brain simply devising a way to fulfill my wish to see him once again? This had also happened to me many times in the last thirty years since Jonna's death. I often had dreams in which she would appear and seemed to be speaking to me, as if she were trying to assuage the guilt that I had felt when she committed suicide.

But when I more accurately pictured the figures in my dream, I recalled that the man had dark, curly hair, and that he was gently placing his hand on the nape of a woman's neck.

I realized now that the woman was me. In the dream, the man's gesture made me feel cherished and protected. It reminded me of the way Lucien used to make me feel when we walked together, his hand on my neck. As he leaned down to kiss the top of my head, the man in the dream was saying, "Again, it will happen again."

How strange that I'd dream about Lucien now, thirty-six years after we had parted. Maybe it's the loneliness I feel from losing Lawrence and our closeness during twenty-five years of marriage. Since his death, I hadn't been with anyone else or wanted to be. Lucien was my first real love, a true friend and confidante. There wasn't a thought I didn't share with him or he with me. But of course, I admitted to myself ruefully, it was that possessiveness that motivated my breakup with him. Maybe his intensity wouldn't bother me so much now.

Well into my second cup of coffee, I felt a bit more alert and ready to think about my day. I was glad I had rearranged my schedule so that my mornings were free. My classes at UCLA started after lunch time, a routine I had established when Lawrence began chemo, so I could be there with him and we could spend more time together. His torturous illness and death had been a struggle to endure and I was still grieving the loss. At the same time, I was gradually coming to realize that my life was quite rich and full—a house at the beach, a position as vice chair of my department, and many dear, longtime friends. Even Andrea, my oldest friend, lived nearby. We walked on the beach together twice a week unless I was out of town presenting at a conference or she was visiting her children or grandchildren. When Andrea's husband, Lloyd, died two years ago, she and two other friends had bought condos at the beach so we could all be closer. I was able to be there for her when Lloyd passed away, and she had been a real comfort to me over the last year after Lawrence died. And most of all, Andrea was the connecting thread to my past, the one who shared a history with me.

I picked up the phone to call her for our walk.

"Ready?" Andrea asked as soon as she answered the phone.

"All set."

"I need ten minutes," she said. "I'll meet you in front of Allegra." She hesitated. "You sound like you're in a fog. Are you all right?"

How did Andrea always sense my moods? "I heard some big news yesterday. Then had a dream I can't shake."

"Tell me." Always impatient for the latest gossip, Andrea could never wait.

"I'll tell you when I see you. I don't want to go over it on the phone."

The waves washed onto the sand, spreading huge furls of suds at the high tide mark as we made our way along the shoreline from the Allegra restaurant to the Dolphin, a mile away, where we always had breakfast. Andrea looked at me expectantly, her cue for me to get on with it.

"I was getting my hair and nails done at the salon yesterday. Constanza, the heavy set redhead with the throaty voice, is taking Lonnie's place while she's on vacation."

"Yeah, go on."

"Constanza was trying to do what Lonnie told her to do with my hair and Regina was relating stories about her kids while she was doing my manicure. To steer the conversation away from kids, I asked them to help me come up with a pen name for my first novel. You know how I feel about those endless recitations about people's children. Of course, I don't feel that way about hearing news of your children, Andrea."

"Why the pen name? Why wouldn't you use your real name?" Andrea asked.

"That's not the point. It was just an excuse to change the subject. I'll be lucky if I publish a novel by the time I'm ninety. So Regina suggests good-naturedly that I use my maiden name. Constanza, meanwhile, is blow drying my hair and asks nonchalantly what my maiden name was. As soon as I tell her "Lebow," she shuts off the hairdryer and, looking shocked, asks me if I'm any relation to Jonna Lebow. Just hearing her name from a virtual stranger threw me for a loop. When I told her Jonna was my sister, she said they grew up together. She said Jonna was the "light of the neighborhood, everyone loved her, and anyone who had troubles went to Jonna." I tried not to get choked up as I recalled Constanza's recollection of my sister.

Andrea's eyes widened and mine welled up with tears. "And we thought she had so few friends," she said.

I nodded. "The hardest part was when she said Jonna talked about how happy she was at home, that she was proud of her sister and father because they were so smart and good to her. Constanza said she never talked about her mother. I had to stop to collect myself. To think Jonna could put up a stoic front when she suffered so much at home. Maybe it was her fantasy life that kept her going, just not long enough."

Andrea stopped walking and put her arm around my shoulder.

I took a deep breath and stepped back to look directly at her. "And then came the real shocker."

"There's more?"

"She said how sorry she was about Jonna, as she put it, 'her suicide and all,' how awful it was for her and Jonna's other friends, and how awful it must've been for me and my family, that she never knew anyone who took their own life before. And then she said what a major catastrophe it was in those days if you got pregnant."

Andrea was thunderstruck. "Jonna was pregnant?"

"Apparently so, or at least Constanza seemed to be certain. I was so stunned I didn't think to ask her how she knew, plus she assumed I knew and I didn't want to say anything to make her think otherwise."

I took several deep breaths and we resumed walking.

"Did you ever wonder if she was pregnant?"

"Yes, mostly because she and Wally wanted to elope, but I couldn't imagine that she wouldn't tell me so I ruled it out. Why didn't I ask her? How could I not ask her?"

"Don't, Kim. Don't torture yourself with 'whys' and 'what ifs.' You'll drive yourself crazy."

"You're right, Andrea. But this news really does make me question myself all over again. Like: why I wasn't more perceptive when I saw how pale she was the last time I saw her? I should've known she always worried so much about being a burden to me that she wouldn't possibly tell me she was going to have a baby!"

"Of course it makes sense to you now. Hindsight is always more perceptive. But you couldn't have done more for her as a sister. You were always there for her."

I picked up my pace. So did Andrea.

"And what about her boyfriend? He must've known, don't you think?"

"I think so. She probably made him promise not to say anything—that would be like her." I was breathing heavily now. "Poor Wally. He must've felt too guilty to tell me once she was gone."

"How shocking for you to hear all this now," Andrea said.

"It is."

"Well, I don't know how you got through all that as well as you did," she said.

"I had lots of support. Friends, like you."

"Well," said Andrea, "I only came back into your life because Marion called me. You were going to go through that terrible period all alone, I suspect."

"I was in such despair, and I guess I didn't want to burden anyone. Thank goodness I listened to Marion when she urged me to let her call my friends. That was a lifesaver."

I squeezed Andrea's hand. I didn't tell her how the past has often rushed back at me, how painful it was for me when I'd think about

Jonna and the many times I got her out of the house during Lila's rages and our parent's escalating arguments. Andrea knew some of it, but not the frequency or intensity of it.

"We've always been here for each other and always will be," she said.

"Yes," I murmured, but my mind had already drifted from our conversation. Andrea fell quiet too, perhaps suspecting that I was retreating into my thoughts. I knew she really didn't like it when I withdrew, but she had learned to let me have my space when I needed it. As I watched the waves, my dream came back to me. So did thoughts of Lucien. His insight about Jonna and his empathy about my family troubles had always given me such comfort. I wished I could share all this with him now. I wished somehow he would suddenly appear.

The Dolphin Restaurant came into view, its pylons lifting it high above the ocean, the Malibu cliffs looking down from the opposite side of the Pacific Coast Highway. So much was stirring inside me, and the searching, questioning feeling was back. Perhaps something was yet to be discovered, but I didn't know what it was. A restlessness, a yearning to venture out beyond my established routines made me long to embrace a new journey. But I knew there would be time to deal with all this another day. For now, I welcomed the comfortable routine I'd established with my oldest friend.

After we were seated at our favorite table, we ordered breakfast and she chatted on and on about her grandchildren. "Now Kim, I hope I'm not boring you with these stories of the young ones," she said playfully. I shook my head, and meant it. I found solace in listening to her and the joy they brought to her life. Andrea and her friendship always had a way of grounding me.

"You know, I was thinking, we need to get moving on our trip to Tecate," I said.

She nodded. Since the late 1980s, when we needed to do something restorative, we wound up in our favorite spa in Mexico, Tecate. Now, we launched into a lively planning session over our coffee refills.

Andrea seemed relieved when she saw the "old me" return. For my part, I wasn't so sure I was satisfied with the old me anymore. I longed to turn a special page in my life—a turn, I sensed, that the old me wouldn't have permitted.

Chapter 16

1998

We sat atop the rust-colored mesa overlooking the vast sun-swept divide before us. The lush white clouds formed mushroom figures highlighted by the bright Mexican sun. The border town of Tecate lay sleepily in the distance, and downtown San Diego was only a few miles away.

"What a great view!" Andrea exalted. "It's so nice to be away from the crowded city!"

I smiled, my salt and pepper hair lifting in the soft desert breeze. Andrea, intent on knitting a sweater for her latest granddaughter, looked up languorously. "When I'm in Tecate," she said, "I can happily banish from my mind what's happened to our beautiful Valley—the crowded 405 Freeway, the scores of office buildings, and the tangled mass of traffic on Ventura Boulevard."

"Absolutely," I said. "Lately I've been thinking that it wasn't just indulgence behind our move to Malibu–it was necessity. In the old days, it took me only twenty minutes door to door from the Valley to my morning class at UCLA. The last week before I moved, I timed my commute, and it was three times longer."

"How I miss the good old days." Andrea sighed, as she returned to her knitting. "Remember when we used to consider five cars on the boulevard a traffic jam? And even before that when the Red Car whizzed on its tracks over the Cahuenga Pass and took us to Hollywood in fifteen minutes?"

"Remember? Who remembers?" I laughed. "This morning I almost forgot your phone number. For twelve or thirteen years I've been dialing that number; I swear I could have done it with my eyes closed. But this morning, while I'm drinking my coffee, I reach for the phone, and my mind blanks. Bip. There's nothing in it. To tell you the truth, Andrea, it panicked me. I was reminded of how Aunt Marion would talk about forgetting names, then numbers, then where she put her glasses and keys. Aging, she said, was like a rotten plague."

Upset by what she was hearing, Andrea dropped her silver-coated knitting needle on the ground. As the desert dust settled on it, the needle soon turned a rich burnt-sienna color. "Oh merde, my teal green sweater will now be half rust!"

For the past ten years, we had been coming to Tecate to rest, relax and lose weight—the latter an ongoing project. We dined on lush vegetarian meals, took as many exercise classes as we could tolerate, and during our down time, lay on our veranda inviting the fierce Mexican sun to bronze our skin. Soon after our arrival, we followed our now-established ritual: We quickly put on shorts and tee shirts, exchanged high heels for tennis shoes, and headed for Montezuma's Mesa, I, lugging my writing pads and pencils, and Andrea her knitting bag. Once we climbed to the mesa top, we would open up beach chairs and sit for hours talking and reminiscing. It was always so pleasant to end each of our vacation day afternoons on the mesa top. We usually stayed for a week, and were enjoying the luxury of our third day in the relaxing spa community.

"I can't believe how the years have flown by," I mused, as I watched a red-tailed hawk circling above us. "It seems like only yesterday that I was at Lila's funeral, then at Jonna's, then at Arthur's. After that, you lost Lloyd when he had the heart attack. And then, it was my turn again when I lost Lawrence."

Andrea stopped knitting, and gazed into the distance. "I still feel terrible that I was away and couldn't be there for you when Lila died. And how you ever got through the other deaths, I just don't know, like your Dad's and Jonna's. They were the worst."

Andrea did not seem to notice my prolonged silence, and went on talking. "First, Jonna's suicide, and then Arthur's car accident. When Lloyd and I visited him at the UCLA Medical Center, he was so thin he looked like a survivor from Dachau. What a twist of fate—being a professor and so used to talking, then left unable to say anything because of the paralysis in his throat. You must have been so relieved that Marion came over every day to tend to him, because it would've been such a chore for you to care for him alone."

I nodded my head in agreement, but chose not to elaborate. Inside, I felt the familiar rush of all the old resentment and anguish as Andrea mentioned my father's stroke and how helpful Marion was. When she realized I wasn't offering any response, Andrea stopped talking too. I knew that Andrea would have liked more information from me—she always did—but I didn't want to clutter the start of our long-awaited vacation with old baggage. In the silence that followed, I could hear only the lonely desert wind picking up in the canyon and Andrea's clicking needles as she resumed knitting. The slant of the sun signaled that it was almost time for the five o'clock refreshment hour. I said, "Hey, Andrea, isn't it about time we made our way to the dining hall?"

We hiked back down the hill and arrived at the dining hall, greeted by a sea of suntanned faces and the loud buzz of many voices. Almost instinctively, we retreated to a secluded part of the huge room. Just then, a loudspeaker squawked out its message, first in English, then in Spanish, as we snaked along the long line of people headed for the "Dieters" section.

"Senores, Senoras, Senoritas, Dr. Lydia Harkening will be speaking in the Rec Room tonight at 8 p.m. on her newly published book, *What People Hide from Each Other: A Commentary on Secretiveness in Relationships.*

Andrea flashed a raised-eyebrows look at me, laughing at the timely topic of the lecture. It had long been her feeling that I had a whole part of my life about which she knew so little. To avoid trouble, I didn't tell her she was right.

Just then the loudspeaker blared into the large dining room. "We have an urgent phone call for Dr. Kim Lebow. Please come to the registration area immediately."

Surprised, I stood up so quickly my chair fell over backwards onto the floor, my chile relleno falling along with it and splattering on the floor. Two waiters scurried over to pick up the chair and wipe the floor. Andrea quickly gathered her knitting bag and my purse and followed closely behind, as I rushed ahead of her at breakneck speed.

I entered the registration area. "I'm Dr. Lebow. You have an emergency call for me?" The night attendant handed me the phone. I listened but couldn't hear anything on the other end of the line. "Hello? Is anyone there? Who is speaking, please?" Straining, I heard what I thought was Marion's soft, faded voice on the other end.

"Marion, speak louder, I can barely hear you." I turned to Andrea and whispered, "She seems to be pleading with me for something, but I can't make out her words."

Just then, the attendant at the registration desk picked up the base of the phone, turned a switch underneath it, and adjusted the volume. Marion's whisper became a screech.

"Kim, please darling, *I must see you.* So many important things I have to tell you. Please come…I don't have that long."

"Marion? Can you tell me what's happening?"

Her voice receded again, and I could barely hear her words: "I'm at the Bergman Convalescent Home. They rushed me here two days ago. I was having trouble breathing. I still am, Kim…I must see you…you sound far away…but I must see you."

"Andrea and I are in Tecate, Marion."

I put my hand over the phone's speaker. "She sounds just awful, Andrea, like she's very ill. I think I should go see her, just to give her some comfort."

"I'll come too!" Andrea declared, putting her hand on my shoulder.

"Are you sure?" I turned to Andrea. "I feel so terrible about wrecking our vacation. We've waited so long for this!"

"Tecate will always be here. We'll come again." Andrea gave me a little pat, gesturing for me to continue to talk with Marion.

"Okay Marion," I said into the phone. "We'll check out and come right away. Where is the Bergman Convalescent Home?"

"It's in Hollywood, darling. Make it as fast as you can, I…" I could hear the sound of something crashing to the floor. She must have dropped the phone. A strange, brisk voice said, "We're just off of the Hollywood Freeway at Vine" and gave me the address. "Ring the after-hours bell when you get here."

"It might take us four hours to reach Hollywood, depending on how heavy the evening traffic is. We better hurry; Marion had such urgency in her tone. I'm feeling anxious because she sounded so pathetic on the phone."

"What did she say?" Andrea asked.

"She had something to tell me. Something of great importance, she said."

"How did she know where to call you?" asked Andrea, as we hurried back to our room to collect our things.

"I guess my answering service number is still on her contacts list," I surmised. "Years ago, when she first moved to the assisted living facility, she had asked if that would be all right with me."

Within thirty minutes we were packed, checked out and en route to Los Angeles and the Bergman Convalescent Home. The traffic cooperated and in just over three hours we were turning off Vine Street towards a large, white, imposing building. We rang the after-hours bell as instructed, watched the steel gate roll open, and were buzzed into an entrance that led into a long, winding driveway. We parked in the visitor's area and, as we entered the foyer, the first thing that hit us was an overpowering smell of Pine-Sol®. A nurse in a starched white uniform quickly rushed up to us and explained their sign-in procedure. "Just a precaution to protect the patients," she explained, and then ushered us to Marion's room.

The close, musty, urine-smelling room, made more noxious by the sweltering July heat, immediately confronted us as we entered Marion's room. We entered quietly and stood watching her sleeping form on the bed. Marion looked peaceful in repose, propped up with several pillows, her white hair neatly pinned into a chignon. I whispered to Andrea, "Even in her last days, old as she is, she manages to look like an Egyptian princess!"

"You're right. She always looks so well put together."

I slowly moved over to the bed and bent down toward her. "Marion, it's me, Kim. I'm here now," I said softly, gently taking her hand.

Just then, Marion's eyes opened and she smiled. Her painfully thin, spindly arms were blotched and mottled, with dark spots like bruises, and her skin had a bluish tint because her breathing problems meant less oxygen in her blood. She weakly reached up for me and I bent down to give her a hug. She was perspiring profusely. Within minutes, Andrea and I felt the effects of the overly hot room and began perspiring as well.

Marion's breathing was labored and she uttered a slight moan with each breath. I was sad, and realized that her illness had taken most of her strength. She might not have much longer, I thought.

With great effort, she whispered, "Kim, I'm so glad you're here."

"I came as soon as I could after your call."

"You...devoted daughter...I always wanted." Marion then started to cough: a low, guttural, raspy sound.

I was startled, not only by her sudden bout of coughing, but by her words. To my surprise, I found myself beginning to cry. "Marion, I was so fortunate to have you there to help me through so many terrible times in my life."

"So much I want to share with you—about me, about your Dad. Don't know...where to start...so little time."

"Marion, please, don't strain yourself," I said gently. I pulled up a chair to be closer to the bed, and softly stroked her arm.

"Want...you...to understand...mother and father—appreciate them. I know things...why they did what they did."

"Marion, that's kind of you to want to share it, but they're gone. What difference does it make?"

"Kim," she whispered, "things...important...can help you understand... make sense."

I couldn't put together what seemed so important for Marion to say and didn't really understand what she was getting at. Things about my parents? How was this important now, in her state? I began to wonder why we had sped here. Still, I felt sorry for her, because she was in such a weakened state, so we settled in to listen. Marion, propped up on many pillows, began,

"Our families...poor...parents struggled. Lila's family from Austria...Arthur's from Russia...mine...Ger-Germany. We lived in same apartment building, walked to school every day...three close friends." Here Marion paused to swallow. She managed a smile at me, and gently squeezed my hand. She was trying so hard to communicate. But I couldn't fathom why it was important to go over this history. Still, since Andrea and I had made the drive, I just let her talk.

"Lila was a little waif. Depression hard, no money for food...parents sent her to aunts and uncles..."

"How did she make it?" I asked.

"She had me and Arthur. We kept her with us, always together... Lila so positive a person, never felt oppressed by her life. Outgoing, lively..."

"That's strange," Andrea commented to me. "Lila never seemed lively to me. She always seemed exhausted, pale, and depressed."

Marion turned in the direction of Andrea's voice. Evidently she had heard the comment, which was really intended for me. "No," said Marion, shaking her head ever so slightly. "Lila a firebrand. Got us jobs...once at *Porgy and Bess* to usher...and a rebel! Lila joined Socialist Party and Abe...Abraham Lincoln Brigade...only sixteen! She got arrested too."

My mouth flew open. Even though it was hard to make out Marion's words, I got the drift of her narrative. I could barely speak. Her characterization of my mother as a young girl certainly didn't square with my knowledge of her. "Marion, what are you saying?"

Andrea was equally incredulous. "You're kidding!" she exclaimed. "Lila? Are we talking about the Lila who was always telling Arthur not to stir up trouble, afraid his radical views would land him in prison or he'd lose his job?"

Marion opened her mouth to answer, and then stopped suddenly, indicating by her waving hand that she needed water. I left the side of the bed and brought over the swing table that I had spotted in the corner, which had a water pitcher and glass on it. I poured her a glass of water, and cranked up the bed so that Marion could drink in an upright position. I cradled her head as she sipped the water.

Thinking about what Marion had just said about Lila, I shook my head back and forth, like I was in a dream state. "I can't believe it. That overly-burdened, nervous lady who tore her hair out every night in a frenzy, thinking her husband would lose his job and her family would be forever destitute, was a radical herself. Another side to my mother I never knew."

"Parents are people…children don't know, Kim…Maybe you will appreciate her if you knew…"

"I always appreciated her, Marion. She was the saddest person I ever knew and I always wished I could have taken away her unhappiness. But I used to feel so helpless."

"Why helpless?" Andrea asked.

"Because I loved her and wanted her to be happy, but I could never reach her. Sometimes, I felt such despair that no one could make any light within her shine, if there was a light at all. I certainly couldn't."

Tears started forming at the corners of Marion's eyes, and she began to pick at the lint on her blanket. "Something else to tell you…a burden for years. Arthur and I kept things from Lila."

"What things? Tell me, Marion," I said.

"Couldn't tell her that he loved *me*...we had almost a life-long relationship..."

"Relationship? What kind of relationship?" I felt that familiar squeeze of anxiety in my stomach, going back to all those times when Marion would show up at our house, and how she often seemed to know where Arthur was when we didn't. I felt myself jumping to the same conclusions that I had in the past, and the anger rose in me. Then, out of the blue, came the memory of Arthur at Lila's funeral saying, "Your Aunt Marion is not the devil here." I took a deep breath and looked at Marion more closely.

"Please, Kim, try to understand." Marion was getting weaker, I could see. I felt pulled by my sympathy for her and at the same time by my own past grievances. "Lila was our cherished friend. But Arthur loved me more. We kept this secret from Lila. Arthur and I were supposed to live together...after his fellowship at Cornell...but, didn't happen." The look on Marion's face was one of deep grief.

"Marion," I asked, as gently as possible, cognizant of her very distressed look. "Why in the world did he marry her and not you?"

"A twist of fate," Marion said. For the first time her tone sounded bitter. "Begged him to help me look for a place...in the Village. He always stalled. Then, his grave mistake."

"His grave mistake, what does that mean?" I asked.

"One night we had a big fight. He said he couldn't afford to get an apartment with me...I was furious, told him to leave...that night, he went to a rally with Lila, got drunk. He took Lila to his place...that was the night you were conceived, Kim."

I looked around for a chair. I felt woozy. If I didn't sit immediately, I'd fall down. "This is incredible. Lila frequently told me they were very much in love when they married, that I was their 'love child.' Now you're telling me I was an accident that altered three people's lives."

Marion was silent for some time. "He told me Lila was only a precious friend. Said he would leave her. But she got sick and depressed... he couldn't. He was an ethical and responsible man." Her lips trembled and she feebly tried to wet her lower lip with her tongue, tears rolling silently down her lined cheeks.

"Ethical? Responsible? Marion, how can you say that? All the times he left us alone and we could never find him when there was a crisis! All the times my mother needed him and he wasn't there. Leaving Jonna and me so often with a mother who could barely get out of bed in the morning. Not getting her proper help. And now, after what you've told me, how ethical was it of him to stay in the relationship after I was born and to have another child with her? Marion, Please."

"Know...know how you must feel, Kim." Marion started coughing again. I struggled to help sit her upright so she would not choke.

After what seemed like hours, I said, "I'm very sorry for my anger, Marion. You shouldn't have to hear it at this time."

"I felt it too, darling. Arthur and I...fights about broken promises, never honest with Lila or me...never got her help for her illness. But one thing, Kim—he was not with me when he wasn't at your house. In later years, I stayed close...worried about you and your sister. And Lila—she was still my friend. But Kim, you had my heart."

Marion was audibly sobbing now. I raised her a little from the pillow, so I could hug her. I was still shocked, but very warmed by what she had shared. I was also bewildered about Arthur. "If he wasn't with you...then where could he have been?" I asked.

"Don't know. He would disappear and not tell me anything either. Stopped asking after a while...you could never know what it's like, loving somebody so much and cannot have him...willing to watch him raise his children," and here her voice cracked: "Go home to his wife."

"Did Lila ever know?" I wondered.

"Probably, but we were best friends. I loved her, too."

"I believe you. You did a lot for her. You were always there when she needed you, and I'm beginning to understand how much you were there for me..."

Marion became more lucid then. She seemed to draw from some inner resolve to talk more fluidly. "I saw what was happening to Lila and you girls. I'd called his fellow faculty members, to try and find him when Lila, in hysterics, would call me. They all told me different stories. He was at political meetings, or busy preparing a response to his failure to sign the Loyalty Oath, or he was having private meetings with faculty people who had been subpoenaed from HUAC. So many stories. One thing for certain: Arthur only had two women in his life—your mother and me."

"But it seems your life with him was as frustrating as Kim's was," Andrea said.

I jumped in before Marion could respond. "Why did you come out to California if you were so heartbroken by what Arthur and Lila did? Why would you want to be around them at all?"

Marion's voice grew more raspy, her words barely discernible. "…teaching position at the university…secretly hoped that I could be closer to Arthur. Couldn't let go of my wish he would leave Lila. Ironic: he grew distant; I got closer to all of you and Lila. I took Lila to her doctors, tried to help."

"Marion, I feel like I'm in a tailspin. All this makes me wonder what else I didn't know about my parents. Like, why did they have to marry? What about abortion? Couldn't they get rid of the baby—I mean, me?"

Marion shook her head on the pillow. "No, no…late '30s, not legal. Arthur and Lila wouldn't go to Mexico as so many women did. They eloped instead." Marion saw the look of surprise on my face. "You didn't know?"

"When did you hear about it, Marion?" I asked.

Marion's eyes closed. Andrea and I both leaned forward, fearing that she was expiring right then. Then, in an almost inaudible whisper, Marion finally said, "Lila phoned from Atlantic City, told me to 'hold onto my hat,' she was now Mrs. Arthur Lebow." Tears streamed down Marion's cheeks.

"My God," Andrea murmured.

"Hated them both," Marion said. "Lila expected me to be happy for her. Didn't realize they had betrayed me. Said 'couldn't happen to two better people'...something like that."

Andrea looked at Marion sympathetically. "What a thing to go through. I certainly couldn't have been as gracious as you were."

"Didn't feel gracious inside!" Marion said, almost forcefully, as her face flushed. "Felt alone, abandoned...didn't stop crying for a week. Inside, never stopped crying."

"Marion," I said, "give it a rest. This is too much for you."

"No, want to go on...guilty for years...couldn't be happy for them. Should have helped Lila more."

I reached down and placed my hand on her arm. "How in the world could you expect that of yourself? How sidelined you must have felt by both of them. What else could you have done? They cheated all of us, Marion. I'm crying inside with you and for you, Marion, and for all of us. We all suffered."

Marion, now sobbing, locked her eyes with mine: "Maybe you can forgive me? Help me forgive myself?"

"I feel something with you today, Marion, that I never felt before. Maybe it's a bond between us. We both loved and admired my father, yet felt so betrayed and abandoned by him."

"I saw other things: he had to watch his activities. Lila terrified his politics would draw attention to her political past."

"Marion," I shook my head disbelievingly, "It's hard for me to believe my mother had her own political past. She always seemed like the least political person in our household."

"But remember what I told you: She was a rebel; outspoken, marched for the unions...friends were Communists. She saw some of them in California...didn't tell Arthur. Lila was afraid: if she was exposed, Arthur's career up in flames."

A dense silence fell over the room.

I turned to Andrea. "Boy, this puts a different mind-boggling twist on things. Can you believe that my mother, who became hysterical daily about my father's political activities, was actually hiding her own?" I turned back to Marion. The tension in her face had disappeared. Her head rested lightly on her pillow, a peaceful smile on her face. Marion had fallen asleep.

Andrea murmured, "Poor thing. All that talking must have worn her out." She and I stood silently on either side of the bed. I bent down and gently kissed Marion's forehead. Marion seemed to stir a little in her sleep.

The head nurse popped her head into the room. "How is she doing?" she whispered, nodding toward Marion's bed. I motioned that she was sleeping. The nurse said, "Maybe she can get some solid rest now. She was so panicky from the respiratory distress and her fear that you wouldn't come that she couldn't sleep before. She kept talking about how lovely her daughter was," she smiled. "And she was right." I startled. "But, I didn't know she had a ..."

Andrea leapt across the room, "Thank you, that is so kind."

"Oh, I almost forgot," added the nurse. "Your mother left instructions and her current living will and power of attorney papers for you."

She left the room to get the packet Marion had left.

"Andrea, why in the world did you say that?" I asked, after the nurse departed. "I'm not Marion's daughter, you know that. I don't even know if there is anyone living who's related to her or even close to her."

"Exactly, Kim! She has no one. You and Jonna and Lila and Arthur were her family. Don't you remember what she said? She made all of you her family, and I think in her heart she secretly wished you had really been her daughter."

I looked away. The nurse reentered the room, a neatly tied packet of papers in her hand. "Your mother is a very nice lady. I hope that you can come visit her in the next few days. If her condition improves, we can talk about transferring her back to her assisted-living facility. And if you have any questions or concerns, please feel free to call us." She turned and left.

"Andrea," I said, tears now rolling down my face. "I think that Marion thought that this might be her last day. That's why she sounded so desperate when she called. She didn't want to be alone if she was going to die."

"Or," Andrea said, "she wanted *you* here with her when she died, so she could share her last thoughts."

"Maybe both." I gently opened the packet and read Marion's last will and testament. Written in her clear, decisive, penmanship, Marion had left all of her estate, belongings and precious jewelry to me. I was flabbergasted. At the bottom of the will, in a faltering handwriting, she had written: "To the only living survivor of two whom I loved dearly. May she receive this with my love, pride, and gratitude and know that I loved her." I folded the will and slipped it back into the packet.

I wished Marion could know how much she had helped me to put some important pieces in place. Well, maybe we would both have the benefit of more time and I could tell her how much I valued what she had shared with me today. More than the jewels and monies from her estate, she had taken me into the unknown realm of history and given me the richest gift of all: the truth.

Chapter 17

2005

ndrea and I were sitting in the front row of UCLA's Royce Hall in the roped-off reserved section waiting until it was time for me to give my speech. "Don't look now, but that man over there hasn't taken his eyes off you for the last ten minutes," said Andrea. She pointed to the side of the auditorium and I craned my neck, trying to see over a tall blond woman seated right beside me who was blocking my view.

"What man?"

"The man right under the center wall sconce," said Andrea. "He's handsome, gray-haired, with sort of a brooding look, Omar Sharif eyebrows. He seems to think you're pretty fascinating."

The auditorium was filled to capacity, and it was hard to make out anyone in the balcony to the right and left of where we were seated. Just as I thought I spotted the man Andrea was referring to, the entire audience rose at once, cheering and whistling loudly for the first speaker at the political rally. Eric Moretti was now moving across the stage toward the microphone. I lost the nameless face in the crowd and turned to Andrea with a shrug.

"Don't worry, Kim, if it's that important, we may encounter him later." Andrea took out her knitting needles, her constant companions, and settled in her seat to listen to Moretti.

"Ladies and gentlemen," Moretti began, "the country's ruling party would have America believe that we are godless liberals, without a moral compass. Is this true?"

The crowd yelled back, "*No!*"

"What, then, is true about us as Democrats? Are you happy with the direction our country has been taking?

The crowd yelled back, "*No!*"

"Does it bother you that we may have to carry national identity cards?"

"*Yes!*"

"Do you lose sleep over the fact that you cannot dissent openly against the war in a democratic country without being called unpatriotic?"

"*Yes!*"

"Well, now is the time for us to stand up and be counted! We need to show that we truly care about family values, that we trust and respect every man and woman by allowing them to be the masters of their own destinies!"

"*Yes!*" the crowd roared again.

Moretti's voice grew louder, buoyed on by the enthusiasm of the crowd, the cleft in his chin and his flashing blue eyes portending future presidential prominence. "We have just begun to fight, we have just begun to mobilize to contend with each and every vital issue affecting America today, and we have just begun to struggle for a real American morality—a morality not born out of a false use of religion, but out of a true sense of social responsibility and a concern for our fellow man." Every pause in his speech was greeted by thunderous applause.

I took out a mint from my purse to keep my mouth from going dry, and tapped my fingers nervously on my prepared speech in my lap. I'd worked on it all day yesterday, and just this morning had an inspiration to add a portion that I hadn't had a chance to rehearse. I was pretty sure my instincts were right and that it had been the right choice to insert the material. But not having enough rehearsal always made me a bit more anxious. I gazed around the hall, astonished not only by the enormous turnout for the hastily called meeting of the Southern California Alliance for the Preservation of Free Speech, but also by the large numbers of younger participants at the rally.

"Eric's at his best tonight," I whispered to Andrea during a pause for applause. "He and the other young Turks are going to galvanize the party. I hope we see a lot more young congressional members like him. The old Gray Panther loudmouths like me are going to be the envelope lickers for the next campaign."

Andrea laughed. "Your envelope-licking days are behind you. That's for the new breed. You'll bring down the house when it's your turn to speak!"

"So, my friends," Moretti continued, "here's what we all need to do. Write your congressional representatives to let them know how you feel about the neglect of education, the environment, health care, civil rights, and a woman's right to choose! Protest The PATRIOT Act, and get out there and oppose Bush's war. Let's take back America, and make it the country we want it to be!"

I leapt up with the rest of the audience, swallowed my mint, and began cheering loudly. It was a relief to vocalize and shed some of my pent-up nerves. Moretti, as always, was going to be a hard act to follow. He had primed the audience, and I just hoped that I could also deliver and keep the momentum going.

The crowd continued to scream and applaud, turning Moretti's words into a chant: "Take America Back! Take America Back! Take America Back!" I turned toward Andrea and noticed a tall man waving at me from the balcony seating on the side of the auditorium. I squinted, then decided that this time I should put on my glasses to make sure he was waving at me and not one of the other people seated around me. I reached into my purse, pulled out my glasses, and put them on. The man started to laugh. Whoever he was, I had a strange feeling that he understood that I desperately needed my glasses. Without them, anyone five feet away would be a total blur.

Then it dawned on me and I started laughing along with him. In disbelief, I turned to Andrea. "You cannot believe who that is! It's Luc!" I started waving frantically at him, my heart pounding. How many eons had it been since we last saw each other?

Andrea jabbed me in the ribs. "Is that your boyfriend from the olden days that you never introduced me to? He's trying to pantomime something to you. I can't quite make it out, though, can you?"

Before I could even reply, a sonorous voice came over the speaker system, "And now, fresh from our own campus, from our History/Poli Sci department, her many articles effective protests against two of the perils of our generation, The PATRIOT Act and the threat to Roe v. Wade. Let's give a round of applause for our next speaker, Dr. Kim Lebow-Massey!"

The audience applauded. I could see many of my students getting up out of their seats, cheering and whistling. I cautiously walked past those in the front row, checking to be sure they had pulled their feet back to allow me to pass. I'd learned many times before that I needed to be extra careful right before giving a talk, because I never could predict when stage fright would appear and throw me off balance. I turned towards the stage, fastening my eyes on the podium to quell my pre-speech jitters. I was also conscious of needing to suppress the shock of seeing Luc if I was to get through my presentation. I reached the dais, placed my papers on it, took a big gulp of air and turned squarely to face the audience, trying not to look for him in that sea of faces.

"Fellow Citizens..." I began, slowly and deliberately. "Over fifty years ago, there were many among us who lived through a period that was unparalleled in our history. It was called The McCarthy Era, taking its name from the powerful senator who capitalized on our country's post-World War II paranoia about Communism. During a highly publicized period of congressional hearings, he and his powerful committee were able to call up American citizens and impugn their loyalty to their country. Many of these Americans were writers, educators and leaders in their fields. Senator McCarthy's committee used flimsy evidence and the hysterical contagion of that era to ruin their reputations, resulting in terrible hardship for individuals accused of being traitors to our country by consorting with Communists. Their families also suffered. This was a strange form of persecution. It was called guilt by association. Due process of law went out the window."

The audience sat in hushed silence and rapt attention as I continued. "And few raised their voices or objected to this calumny. (I smiled inwardly realizing I'd used Arthur's word.) They didn't speak out against this travesty, for they, too, were afraid of being persecuted. They watched as friends, neighbors and family members had their careers destroyed and watched as jobs were lost due to blacklists, and families went hungry. But still their voices were muted. Only a few courageous ones dared to protest this vile assault on American civil rights and freedoms.

"Why do I speak to you tonight about this time in our history so reminiscent of the Salem Witch Trials? Because, in one of the greatest nations in the world, where the Bill of Rights is thought to be sacrosanct, many of our fellow citizens are now being treated as though their rights do not exist. Think about what is now happening with The PATRIOT Act and you will see how familiar this story is."

As I continued, I noticed facial grimaces and looks of utter disbelief. Many of the students in attendance were possibly hearing this for the first time. Many may never have heard anything about this from their parents. At one point, my eyes connected with Andrea's. I knew that both of us were transported back to our high school years in North Hollywood, sharing unspoken thoughts of Arthur, Mr. Samuels, and so many of our friends whose lives were irrevocably altered by the hysteria of those times.

I looked directly at the students sitting in the second and third rows. I was coming to the portion of my speech that I had just added this morning, and my heart fluttered lightly. "You may have heard stories in your history classes about artists, writers and scientists called before the House Un-American Activities Committee, or HUAC. Lillian

Hellman, Arthur Miller, and J. Robert Oppenheimer were just a few of those called to testify." I could see some of them nodding their heads.

"I want to bring this period closer by telling you a very personal story that will show you how ordinary students and families were affected. Roland Samuels was head of the Social Studies and History Department at the high school I attended in the early 1950s. He was the most inspiring teacher anyone could have had. He loved his profession and nothing gave him more pleasure than to have a student tell him what a difference he had made in their lives. He influenced many students to pursue teaching as a career. His political beliefs favored free speech, equality and helping the poor–beliefs that were probably similar to those held by many of you today. Because of those beliefs, someone in our community accused him of being a Communist. Did this accuser make himself or herself known? Oh no, because that was the way McCarthy operated. He stirred hate and fear based on innuendo and lies. So Mr. Samuels was called before HUAC, but he refused to testify on the basis that it was an infringement of his civil rights. He also refused to give any names of others–that was another one of the committee's most insidious techniques: getting witnesses to name names. As with so many of those called before McCarthy and HUAC, there was never any substantial proof given that Mr. Samuels was subversive in any way. However, after a distinguished career lasting over thirty years, the school board told him that he was no longer welcome as a member of the teaching staff. One of the things he loved the most—teaching young people—was no longer available to him. One day in 1953, he took his own life."

There was a collective gasp from the audience. My words had hit home. After all, these kids weren't that far from their high school years themselves, and it was easier for them to relate to someone near their age than that of their instructors.

"You may not think things have gone that far now, and that this could not happen again," I continued. "But I believe things are dangerously close to those fearful times. The names may be different, but some of the tactics are similar: Keep people in a state of constant fear about terrorism, and they become vulnerable to giving up their civil rights, just as they were during the McCarthy Era. Think about it. Are we on amber or red alert today? Do you know that one of the provisions of The PATRIOT Act dictates that our university librarians can be forced to disclose the books you checked out of the library yesterday? If you keep the public worried about the possibility of another attack, it is easier to manipulate them into giving up their inalienable rights. And they may not notice until it's too late.

"But today, we have a golden opportunity to exercise our most precious rights guaranteed in our First Amendment in the Bill of Rights: our freedom of speech, our rights to peaceable assembly, and our right to petition the government for redress of grievances. Today does not have to be a repeat of the McCarthy Era. Today, we can protest with the one powerful tool we have: our voices—our voting voices, our voices of protest, our voices which say, as did Peter Finch's character in the movie *Network*, 'We're mad as hell, and we're not going to take it any more!' We do not have to languish in apathy and ennui. We can raise our voices and demand change!"

I put down my papers, took a deep breath, and felt, rather than heard, the erupting applause. *Now. Now you can look for him. Where was he? Oh right—just under the wall sconce in about the center of that balcony section.* As my eye found the spot where Luc was sitting, I noticed that he wasn't looking at me. Instead, he was checking his cell phone, its blue-gray glow lighting up the lower half of his face. Was he checking for messages from his wife? His kids? *Get a grip. This is really strange, seeing him here, suddenly, like this. But I still have a job to do.*

I turned to my left and exited the stage as the audience continued its applause. Many of my students gave me a thumbs-up, and a few gave me high fives as I returned to my seat. I had only one thing on my mind—finding Lucien. When I caught his eye, I pointed to the exit in the back of the auditorium. "Meet me there," I mouthed.

"Andrea, I'll be right back," I said, and turned to walk the long aisle toward the lobby, trying not to be conspicuous. That was impossible, of course: students and other audience members waved to me as I walked. I tried to calm my excitement at seeing Lucien again. But it was no use—my heart beat rapidly as I moved up the aisle and saw him walking towards his side exit. I felt like a giddy schoolgirl.

I pushed through the double doors, just as he came down the side staircase. He came toward me and took my elbow and steered me where we could talk in a corner of the lobby.

"How in the world? Luc, how did you happen to come here?" I burst out.

"Oh, it's such a long, long story, Kim. My god, I can't believe it's you…" Lucien reached out both hands and took mine. "I can't believe I'm seeing you in person again, and that you have the same smile!"

"Me too, I can't believe it too…I mean, either…" I was so flustered. "I don't know what to say. It's so good to see you! You look as good as ever."

"Oh, come now," he laughed. "Are you still looking at the world through rose-colored glasses?"

"*Plus ça change, plus c'est la même chose,*" I said. I'd love to go somewhere and catch up."

Lucien and I stood in the corner of the lobby, oblivious to the cheers and poster-waving going on inside the hall, until he took my arm and led us outside the building, away from it all.

The years flew by in a minute and I was immediately transported back in time. The memories flooded back: Walking together on the UCLA quad, his hand stroking my then shiny black hair, his arm around my waist. I began to feel the exact same flush and tingling I had felt then.

"Where are you, Kim?" Lucien's gentle voice brought me out of my reverie.

"I'll tell you where I am," I said softly, my eyes beginning to fill with tears. "Walking along a path with you so many years ago. The maple trees in front of the Chemistry Building are tiny and slim, not lush and full as they are today. It's 1957 and Adlai Stevenson is campaigning for

President. We've just attended a Stevenson rally on campus, maybe on this very spot. The Faculty Center hadn't even been built yet. What I remember most is that we were so in love with each other, and with Adlai as well."

The words rushed out of my mouth. "I'm scheduled to be at the wine and cheese reception, but after seeing you, I know my heart won't be in it."

Lucien leaned down and quite spontaneously kissed my forehead as he had done many times so long ago. "Do you remember the day we heard Adlai speak?" Lucien asked, his tone light and teasing.

"I certainly do! We were heading for the SANE rally put together by Steve Allen and Audrey Meadows. Adlai was going to speak at the Hollywood Bowl. It was October, and that time he was protesting the proliferation of nuclear arms in America."

"Your prodigious memory has not changed one bit in all these years." Lucien looked at me, his eyes glistening with affection. "Are you sure you don't want to go to the reception?"

What am I doing? I haven't seen him for forty-seven years, and I'm reacting like we were back in our senior year. Is he married? Does he think I am? Does he care? Can you really ever go back in time and make up for what you lost? Is it possible to let someone in again, when you've spent decades apart, having totally separate lives?

"I'm sure, but I need to find Andrea. We came together." Suddenly, I heard the rise of the crowd again, through both sets of doors, and realized that the third and final speaker was probably wrapping up. "We better go back in," I said. As we walked down the main aisle, we were now bucking the direction of the throng leaving the hall. We laughingly pushed through the crowd until we got to the front row, where Andrea was standing, calling my name and waving. When she spotted us, she smiled, raising her eyes to the heavens as if to say, "What in the world are you doing?"

Lucien smiled, "So this must be Andrea! I can't believe it! Why don't the three of us go out for coffee?"

I was startled. "Now? This evening?"

He laughed, nodding his head up and down. "Did you finally tell her about us?"

"Not really, but I guess there's no time like the present." Throughout my relationship with Lucien, I'd never really shared the full extent of my impassioned involvement with him with her. I'd kept him stored inside me, like a precious private possession.

He smiled broadly and moved toward me to hug me, but a few of my students intervened, still excited by my talk, pumping my hand and saying, "Great!" "Mind blowing!" Lucien stepped back, waited a while, then gently put his arm around my shoulder in an old but familiar gesture to steer me toward Andrea. Being so close to him, I immediately relaxed, feeling the same sense of peace and comfort I felt so long ago.

Lucien turned to Andrea and beckoned her to join us. One side of me wanted to have him all to myself, to drink in his words and his gestures. But, could I trust myself to be alone with him? Maybe having a threesome would be safer. "All right, Luc. Where should we go?"

"How about Zucky's?"

"Zucky's is no longer there. It closed some time ago."

"So, does that mean that all good things eventually come to an end?"

"I hope not, Luc!"

Chapter 18

Waves rippled up to the shoreline beneath the deck where Lucien and I sat sipping steaming hot Turkish coffee. After our sensuous reunion the night before, I felt a serene comfort I hadn't felt for years. I languidly dipped my brioche into my coffee, glanced over at him and smiled. Here we are, two lovers, drinking in the scene before us, watching kamikaze-like pelicans dive for their own breakfast as the water continued to silently tap the sand.

I could die right now a happy woman. I dreamily stretched out my arms and let them fall to my sides. How long it had been since I'd felt such physical abandon and pleasure. The last few years with Lawrence, sex had been out of the question because of his illness. Now I felt so alive! I was so caught up in my bliss that I didn't notice that Lucien had turned his chaise lounge to face mine.

"Kim," he said seriously, "It's only fair that you know some things about me before we go any further in our relationship."

"Luc, we have plenty of time to catch up on the last forty-seven years. Does it have to be right now? We don't have to 'tell all' right away, do we?"

"I just don't want us to begin under false pretenses."

"What's false about our response to each other? I believe in the truth of that."

I looked away from his face and gazed out over the smooth, peaceful ocean. Carefully placing my cup on the glass patio table, I found myself reluctant to let go of the delicious reverie of this morning. But Lucien's face was so earnest.

"If we are to have an honest relationship with each other," he continued, "I want to be the one to start with complete openness."

I felt a warning signal go off inside my head. *If he's going to be completely honest, then he'll demand that of me too.* I could feel myself resisting the pull of his "truth-telling" proposition.

"Luc, I'm afraid that after you tell all, you're going to cross-examine me and demand that I bring out all my dirty laundry too."

"No, Kim, I'm not that same guy you remember, who needed all of you to feel secure. I guess partly I just want to explain myself so that you know more about who I am."

"Well, it seems to me that you're a very handsome, intelligent, well-seasoned man who, if he hadn't been around the block, would seem suspicious to me," I said playfully.

He took my hands in his and kissed my fingertips.

"Well, maybe now is not the time, but I do want to fill you in—and, I admit, I want you to fill me in too."

"Where do we start, though? It's starting to feel a bit like last night at Junior's with Andrea. It seems so awkward and I don't know, almost like high school. She was interviewing you the whole time, asking you questions about your wife and kids, and all I could think about was, when can we take her home so that I can get you into bed?"

"Yeah, I was thinking the same thing too," he laughed.

"Well," I said softly. "I imagine you do want to tell me about your wife and your family."

"Sort of. I do and I don't," Luc said, his eyes staring at a distant place. Then, he turned to face me. "We were pretty happy for quite a while," Luc said.

"That actually makes me glad, Luc. You and I are people who care. I was happy with Lawrence, except…"

"Except what?" he said, picking up on my reluctance.

"Well, if you must know, there were times when my life with Lawrence seemed just a little bit too…I don't know…careful. We loved and cared deeply for each other and we had a rich life."

"So what was missing?"

"Well, thinking about it now, with the advantage of hindsight, I would say that what was missing was intense passion."

"But that got the two of us into trouble before, didn't it Kim? I guess that's partly why I want to talk about our lives. I don't want to make the same mistakes with you that I did last time."

I had the whole day ahead of me. What was I afraid of? It was hard to pin it down. Mostly, I still wanted to relish the thrill of our reunion, bask in the glow.

"Let's get dressed and walk on the beach," I proposed.

A half hour later, we left the house and started a leisurely walk up the beach. To the backdrop of the waves, I listened to the narrative of Lucien's life.

"After you and I parted, I decided to go into law instead of physics. I thought I could make more of a difference that way. Also, I wanted to get away from Los Angeles and reminders of you. I applied for an extension on my visa and got into Cal. My uncle, as you could guess, gave me hell for choosing law, but I never listened to him anyway. I totally immersed myself in my studies and then, after getting my degree, I applied for citizenship. Two of my best friends, Steve Walsh and Robert O'Keefe and I decided to form our own law firm, specializing in labor law and civil rights cases. We had a dream to manifest the philosophy of law we had learned at Cal. We'd all wanted to give back something, and were determined to do some significant work in civil rights cases for those unable to afford good legal representation. Steve and Robert were both from L.A., so they convinced me to move back down here."

"That fits you so well, Luc. You always were good at putting your beliefs into action."

"Yes," he smiled. "We loved what we did. We took clients according to their needs, not their income, so a lot of it was pro bono work. We

got the nickname of 'the social workers of the L.A. law community'!
A Washington, D.C. firm heard of our successful work and formed a
partnership with us. We were flying high and feeling great."

"And how did your wife feel about you taking on so much pro bono
work? You told me last night that Rachel was always worried about
money, and that your two daughters wanted to go to eastern colleges.
So, didn't you have college expenses for your daughters to save for?"

Lucien smiled, "You've forgotten what an organizer and planner I
was and still am, Kim. My partners and I also shared investments in
start-up companies and real estate. At one point, we invested in several
shopping centers in Arizona, and did very well with all of them. This
freed us up to practice law as we wanted to."

"Your wife must have been so proud."

"Well, at first she was. We met at an ACLU fundraiser, and we were
very taken with each other. You know, she was from Israel."

"How ironic," I said. "Given that your old girlfriend was Jewish!"

Luc nodded. "Yes, I thought about that too. But it wasn't just that
I was trying to recreate my lost love—we were really happy with each
other. But I think, after a while, all my involvement with my work
started to grind on her. Especially when we had the girls, she really
wanted me to spend more time with the family."

"That's understandable. So what stopped you?"

"Obsession—with my clients, with their plights. There were so
many people I wanted to help. Part of it was that when I applied for my
citizenship, it was really hard. So many hoops to jump through. And I
would see people with few resources, just struggling to get by, and no
one to help them."

I turned to him and playfully said, "So you turned into a 'bleeding-
heart liberal'"? I smiled at him.

"No, I wouldn't call it that. But I just couldn't switch myself off at
the end of the day and be completely present for Rachel and the kids."

"Hmmm–sounds like you became a workaholic."

Luc nodded. "Yes, I guess I did. It was so hard to see that at the time.

And later, when things got tougher, we didn't have that foundation of family closeness that might have gotten us through the hard times."

"What do you mean?"

"Last night, in your speech, you were talking about the hardships and restrictions from the Bush administration's response to 9/11. Well, think about it, Kim: Look at my skin, my features. What do you think it was like for me, my wife and kids out in public after that attack? That, plus the added stigma of my practice—defending those falsely arrested and accused because of their racial identity."

Ah, yes, I thought. I wouldn't have given it a second thought, but his dark, semitic looks, I'm sure, would have drawn stares, if not worse. There has been so much fear and paranoia.

Luc's eyes met mine, as if he was reading my realization, and he nodded.

"And then, I refused to give way to the Bush administration and the National Security Administration when they began rounding up U.S. citizens—who happened to be Middle Eastern—without charging them, and accusing them of being terrorists. I wanted to take those cases, because I thought it was important to take a stand. Rachel didn't want me to, and protested against that. You know, some marriages get stronger when the outside world turns against them. In our case, it just unraveled."

"I'm so sorry, Luc. And there was no repairing it?"

"No, I'm afraid that my neglect, on top of the strains after 9/11, just made us more estranged from each other."

"And how about now? Are you in touch with her and your daughters?"

"It's cordial, but she is so distant. And my daughters—well, they have their own lives now—which is great, and as it should be. I just hope we can get to know each other later, when they are adults."

I grew silent, feeling the crunch of the light crust of dried sand under my feet. *Of course it can't be exactly the way it was. How could it? We each have so much baggage that we carry from just living life. But oh, to have the chance to recreate something else!*

"Tell you what, Luc, I'm starting to feel hungry. Do you have anywhere you have to be today?"

"No, just with you, if you'll have me."

"Of course!" I said. "Let me fix us some lunch and then I can fill you in on Lawrence and UCLA."

After a long and leisurely lunch, followed by more passion in the late afternoon, I felt almost drunk with pleasure. And, I had to admit, I felt a little overwhelmed. I was used to a lot of solitude on my weekends.

"Luc," I finally said, as the sun began its descent toward the horizon and we lounged side by side in the chaises. "I'm thinking it might be good to take this slowly." He got a worried look on his face. "No, this is not the old Kim saying she's got to go in a different direction." I stroked his cheek. "It's just that this seems like a lot to process. Why don't we try having dates for a while? There's no other man in my life, believe me, and I still have a full plate at UCLA, so it would really help me to be able to concentrate on that during the weekdays. What do you think?"

The aging lines around his eyes seemed deeper in the gathering dusk. But his face seemed even more handsome to me now, marked with the ups and downs and compromises of life. "Yes, Kim, I agree. I don't want to leave, but I think your plan makes a lot of sense. I'll be aching for you every night."

"And I for you. But at least this time, parting will be a sweet sorrow, because we know it won't be forever, right?"

Later, I helped him gather his things, and walked him to his car. As he drove away, I thought that his face, through the dusty windshield, looked pained. But he managed a cheerful wave—as I did. And then I turned, looking at the setting sun.

My life is full again.

Chapter 19

2006

How could I have been so naïve? Usually, after the weekly meeting of the History/Poli Sci Department with Dean Langer, I lingered with my colleagues to catch up on their news. But today, the Dean's remarks had unnerved me, and I just wanted to get outside to think. It was a sunny day, with a light breeze, and I needed to walk to get rid of my tension.

At the end of the meeting, the Dean had singled me out. "Dr. Lebow, we mustn't draw any negative attention to this department. We are hurting economically. We're in the midst of a highly conservative swing in this university and faculty are not to participate in marches, or protests, or write anything inflammatory that would reflect badly on this department," he said adamantly.

Why was he singling me out? And why now? Is it because I'm up for chair of the department? Surely it couldn't be because of that Alliance rally held last quarter?

And still, I wasn't able to name the feelings of anxiety at this morning's meeting. The Dean said he wanted no trouble. Trouble meant incidents. Incidents meant bad press. No one on the faculty was to have altercations with students over anything. "Anything," he had stressed, "Political!"

I headed to the Faculty Center. I was thankful for the buzz of the room with its intense conversations, because it let me lose myself in thought. I lined up at the counter for my usual coffee and biscotti and grabbed the day's *Los Angeles Times*. I passed the cash register and went to the back of the room and settled myself. I took a sip of coffee and glanced at the headline in the California section which focused on local news.

Los Angeles Times 1/22/06

"Witch Hunt at UCLA"

An alumni group is offering students up to $100 per class to supply tapes and notes exposing University of California, Los Angeles professors who allegedly express left wing political views… The group's founder, Andrew Jones, a 2003 UCLA graduate, says his group is concerned about lecture time taken to press positions against President Bush, the military and multinational corporations, among other things.

…Some of the group's targets accuse it of conducting a witch hunt…One such target, Norm McLaren, whom the association rated No. 1 on its 'The Dirty Thirty: Ranking the Worst of the Worst,' says, "Any sober, concerned citizen would look at this and see right through it as a reactionary form of McCarthyism…"

I almost spit out my coffee. My God, now I get it. That's what the Dean was so upset about in the department meeting! How had I failed to recognize the signs popping up at each department meeting over the last year or so? Planning for the Southern California Alliance for Preservation of Free Speech rally last quarter had been thornier than I expected. What had been percolating for many months now leaped to the forefront of my mind. Many of my faculty colleagues had "buttoned it down," as the saying went. When I approached them requesting that they speak at the rally, many of them had declined. In the past they would have gladly accepted. After all, this was the university, our haven from censorship. Some of my colleagues had tried to talk to me about their fears, and their reticence to participate. I was so embroiled in the planning logistics that I just tossed off the signs of their mounting stress.

I had a sinking feeling in my stomach. I began to examine the Dean's remarks to me. So he *was* uneasy about the rally, which now seems clear. But I seemed to recall that there was also the implication that my progressive friends or associations with certain people jeopardized my future at the university. Just a couple of weeks ago, the Dean commented, "Still seeing that brilliant attorney of yours, Kim?"

That comment had taken me by surprise; but again, I had dismissed it. Now I thought about the department's holiday party. I had asked Luc to join me. I was so proud of him, and so much in the first flush of our reunion that I imagined everyone would welcome him. But when I introduced him to the Dean, I had noticed a bit of hesitation, especially when he asked Luc what his practice consisted of, and Luc explained his work with immigrants, as he put it, "falsely detained under The PATRIOT Act." Was it raised eyebrows I saw, or did I imagine the Dean withdrew from Luc's handshake a mite too quickly?

Of course! What the Dean was alluding to were the background checks they're doing on me as the candidate for Department Chair. It's all in that blasted PATRIOT Act. He might even be implying that my being chosen as Department Chair might be on the line. My mind was reeling, and I felt myself alternating between defiance and compliance. To play it safe, maybe I need to revise the lecture I had prepared this morning. I like it, but the Dean might be taken aback by a title like "The Crucible: Arthur Miller's Answer to Those Who Attempted to Silence Him."

The Dean is no fool. He's got his career and his department to protect. What's driving his criticisms of me are the new Chancellor and his emphasis on the bottom line. But where does the compromising end? Shouldn't we be able to hold the line based on our ideals?

I studied the article again, feeling a familiar gnawing in my stomach, unable to put my finger on the source. But then, there it was: "Conducting a witch hunt…" Suddenly I felt such a yearning to see my father. *Oh Arthur—if you could only see what we've come to again!* I could almost picture him knotting his tie in front of the bathroom mirror as he got dressed for a rally on the UCLA campus to protest Chancellor David Saxon's being sacked. Saxon and thirty other professors were forced to give up their teaching positions at UCLA because they refused to sign oaths stating they were not members of the Communist Party. By 1952, the California Supreme Court struck down the loyalty oath and they were all reinstated. In 1975 Saxon became the President of the entire UC system, the first to come to that post from UCLA. It was like an apology, a vindication of his integrity. I could hear Arthur's resonant voice as he was to leave for the rally, as though he were standing right there in front of me. "Remember what Edmund Burke said, Kim: 'All that is necessary for the triumph of evil is for good men to do nothing.'"

If only I could channel just some of Arthur's resolve. I used to feel so ambivalent about his speaking out, but now I wondered: How strong are my convictions if I'm afraid to speak up out of fear of losing my chance to become chair of the department? Was the Alliance rally the Dean's concern? Was he just trying to let me know this wasn't a good time for me to be outspoken about my politics?

Maybe his point is well taken. I've strived for this position for years. My students have always rated me well. My colleagues on the faculty are supportive. I want it yet I may lose out, not because of my capabilities, but over what may be a creeping disease coming back to haunt: "Guilt by association."

This is why I've been waking up with these weird feelings about the past and the present. Many of the decisions of our government during this Bush administration have been troubling for me. Was this what Arthur and all those people during the McCarthy Era endured? I can only imagine how frightened and enraged he and his colleagues must have felt. To have their voices of protest yanked away in a second? Certainly, in this modern era, the same thing couldn't be happening. But I suspected it was.

Looking up from my reverie, I had a brainstorm: Why not consult the Dons of protest themselves? Maybe, if I read some of the coverage from that tumultuous time, I'd find the courage and the rhetoric I'd need to speak with the Dean. I decided to go to the Powell Library, which held the UCLA Archives. I took out my cell phone and dialed my teaching assistant. I did a quick calculation. *Hmm…my class isn't until 3:30; maybe, I could just dive in here for a little while and do some preliminary searching of my own.*

"Brian? This is Kim. I have something I need to take care of. Would you be able to teach my class this afternoon? I know it's very short notice. You can find the notes for the lecture right on my desk." My Arthur Miller bombshell could wait until next week.

"You bet!" Brian answered, eager to oblige.

When I emerged from the Archives four hours later, the sun setting over the tree-laden campus, I was in a state of complete shock. I momentarily lost my bearings. My head was throbbing; my throat dry. I found a bench to sit on, oblivious to the students rushing back to their cars and dorms. I drew my black sweater closer around my shoulders and stared again at the copy of the student newspaper dated June 13, 1950, emblazoned with the following headlines, "LACC Lecturers Fired for Solidarity Declaration with UCLA Professors." The first paragraph began, "Several lecturers from Los Angeles City College were recently fired by that institution. The reason: A declaration of solidarity with their UCLA colleagues who had refused to sign Loyalty Oaths swearing they were not members of the Communist Party. Dr. Arthur Lebow, speaking for the group, said, 'In a free and democratic society, we all have the right to our own religious and political beliefs. These beliefs are private. We cannot and should not be forced to disclose these beliefs against our will. Each and every American is guaranteed by the Bill of Rights of the United States Constitution the right of free speech and the right of assembly. UCLA asked these principled professors to sign a Loyalty Oath, which is in direct violation of their civil rights. Further, they have denied our colleagues the right to gather together to speak out against these injustices. I would rather take a job in The Broadway's bargain basement, which I intend to do, than continue to work in such a system.'"

I stared at the picture of Arthur standing tall, erect, dark-haired and handsome, with the group of professors, flanked on his right by the ACLU attorney who was to represent them. The last line of Arthur's statement rang in my ears. So much was dawning on me. We knew that Arthur had lost his lectureship at UCLA for two years until the Loyalty Oath was struck down. But now I realized that Arthur had been fired from his main post at LACC, just as David Saxon had been from UCLA. And Arthur couldn't tell Lila because he was afraid it would shatter her. And, maybe, it would have. I wondered why Marion didn't tell me about the job in the department store. Maybe she didn't know, or out of respect for Arthur, didn't want me to think less of him for taking a job that was beneath him. In that moment, I could not have been prouder of the choice my father made so long ago. How he kept it from my mother was hard to fathom. Then, I remembered her complaints that the morning newspaper wasn't arriving. Maybe Arthur was grabbing it each morning before he left to keep her from finding out the truth.

How was Arthur able to keep the knowledge of his firing and his job at the Broadway from all of us? So many questions—and Arthur was no longer here to answer them. At least the question of Arthur's absences *was* answered, which I found immensely gratifying. I knew more about my father in that one decision he made than I'd learned in all the years I'd spent with him.

I could not stop shaking as I sat for over an hour on the bench. In a flash, the frightening moods of the fifties and the Cold War came back to me. I pictured my mother, ashen-faced, pacing across the living room. Teeth clenched, arms hugging herself, muttering softly, "if he doesn't keep quiet, he will bring us to ruin. The FBI will be on our tail." At the time, I didn't know how many other families were going through the same thing. All those people, as frightened as my mother, and so much of their fear compounded by their loneliness and isolation.

I rose from the bench, put on my jacket and walked slowly toward the parking garage. The lights outlining the path to the parking lots switched on. I got into my car and headed out of the parking lot to Wilshire. The traffic was predictably clogged. It was Friday evening rush hour, which I usually avoided by leaving UCLA early or staying in town for dinner. Tonight, I didn't even mind the stop and go traffic. Driving on auto-pilot, I let my mind wander back to the day's events: the department meeting, the *Los Angeles Times* article about the current witch hunt, and my startling discovery in the library's archives.

As I edged my car through the PCH tunnel, I saw the sky over the ocean take on a burnt orange hue with the setting sun. With the day's uproar over politics and the Dean's statements, I hadn't even thought about Lucien, but now I desperately wanted to talk to him. Ever since we had first reunited, he had honored my decision to keep some distance between us. Weekends were ours, but the weekdays I had preserved for attending to my teaching and administrative duties. Now I found myself wishing for a chance to find him at home at the end of a long day. Was I afraid that we'd become too comfortable?

I knew that I didn't want to repeat the pattern I had had with Lawrence. Our life had been predictable—perhaps too much so. It lacked passion and intensity. I often wondered what happened to that person I used to know: my former self. Maybe I'd become too

comfortable financially, unable to venture away from the norm for fear
of losing the stability I'd worked so hard to achieve. But now I could
change my life. The excitement and thrill of love could be mine again
if I was willing to take a chance. To be with Lucien.

The traffic eased up a bit as I approached Malibu, turned left at the
shopping center, and finally drove down the gravel driveway at the end
of the road which led to my house. All I wanted to do was call Lucien.
Climbing the few steps from the garage to the door to my living room,
I rushed to the phone and dialed his number. Busy.

Somehow, changing my location seemed to lift me out of my reverie
that I'd been in during the rush hour drive. With the phone in my hand, I
shuffled to the bedroom, tossed the phone onto the bed, and changed into
my favorite pair of jeans, white top and flip flops. I tried his line again: still
busy. I went back to the kitchen to fix myself some supper. The refrigerator
was filled with leftovers from the past weekend's faculty beach party. I
took out a few chicken tenders and leftover broccoli, plopped them into
the microwave, and proceeded to go through the day's mail. There was
an enormous proliferation of catalogues and advertisements, and only one
letter which interested me, because in the left-hand corner, embossed with
the university seal, was the Dean's name.

On my way to the kitchen table, I took a detour back into the
living room and turned on my already-loaded CD player. The voices of
Joan Sutherland and Pavarotti immediately filled the room with their
magnificent duo from *Rigoletto*. Swaying absentmindedly to the music, I
hit the button to play back my phone messages. I heard Lucien's voice.

"Kim, I know you're busy, and you don't want me to bother you
during the week, but you're the only person I want to share my news
with. Please call me right away. We won, Kim, we won," he yelled. "The
court ruled in our favor. Kim, are you there? I'm sure you're not; call
me as soon as you get in."

I eagerly dialed Lucien's number again: still busy. Distracted, I
opened the letter from the Dean, and almost fell back onto the couch
as I read his terse words.

"Dr. Lebow:

We are pleased to inform you that the Faculty Senate has completed its evaluation and voting. You have been elected to be Chair of the Department of History and Political Science. I will respect that vote and support you in your future endeavors. I do hope, however, that you may see fit to tone down your rhetoric, and reconsider, in light of this new appointment, your past, present, and future associations."

Cordially,
Louis Langer, Ph.D., Dean,
UCLA Department of History and Political Science

I put down the letter. My hand was shaking and I needed something to calm myself. Alcohol was out of the question; it would only put me to sleep. The Dean gives with one hand and takes with the other, I thought.

How dare he? "Past, present, and future associations…" There it was again: "let go of this Lucien character and you'll be okay with the Department." How presumptuous…well, obviously my faculty colleagues don't seem to care…they evaluated me on my merits…on the other hand, with this position I'll be watched at every turn. And along with me, Lucien.

The ringing of the phone startled me, and I trembled as I pushed the talk button. Lucien's voice on the other end rang in my ears.

"Kim, did you get my call? So much news to share with you," he said excitedly.

"I did get your call, and I tried to call, but your line was continually busy. I have a lot to tell you too. Sounds like we've both had quite a day. How about meeting in the morning for breakfast at the Dolphin?"

"Yes, that's good, Kim."

"That way, I can clear my head. There is one thing I'm really clear on, though: I love you, Lucien."

"Ah," I could hear his sigh and could almost hear his smile in his voice. "I love you too, Kim. You're on. I can't wait to see you."

I hung up the phone and collapsed into bed. What an incredibly emotional day. Yet, I felt calm. I began to have ideas about class symposia and guest lecturers that could help my students hone their critical thinking skills. Hmm, Lucien's friends at the ACLU would be helpful in that area, I thought. I jotted down a few ideas on a note pad so I could explore them later.

As I clicked off the bedside lamp, I felt a resolve, not fear. I had decisions to make about taking the position of department chair, and about the major dilemma that my political beliefs and relationship with Lucien—and his activism—were posing in my life. Several things I already knew for certain. I was not going to silence my protests for a prestigious position, and I was going to work even harder to encourage my students to think for themselves, to express ideas and to dissent, if and when they deemed it necessary. Arthur had held onto his beliefs—and at a terrible price for himself and his family. I felt a surge of gratitude for what I had discovered about him today. And now, with Luc at my side, I could live out what Arthur had begun.

Chapter 20

I awakened with a jolt. Where was I? My mouth felt dry and thick. The sheets were tangled around my legs. Had I been calling out? In my groggy state, I realized I had been having my familiar, recurring nightmare. It was always the same. I was in the midst of an ocean, stranded on a raft, with no rescuers in sight, frantic and lost. I pulled the sheets up around me and tried to go back to sleep. Sometimes this worked, especially if I took a few deep breaths, but not this time: I tossed and turned for what felt like hours. Finally, realizing it was hopeless, I reluctantly threw back the covers and got out of bed.

What had triggered the nightmare this time? It had originally appeared during Lawrence's illness. And since his death, I could usually trace its recurrence to something that was happening in my life, some stress I was going through. Well, there was no doubt about the amount of stress in my life right now! My head was still spinning from the news about my appointment, mostly because of the conditions the Dean had attached to my acceptance: to "tone down my rhetoric" and be careful about my associations. Just thinking about it made me upset. And, I had to admit, I also felt a certain tension when it came to Luc: should I keep our relationship in weekend mode, or not?

I shuffled down the hallway and meandered into the living room. What should I do now that I was thoroughly awake? I had four hours until I was supposed to meet Luc. Should I sort through my stack of lecture notes? Work on my new syllabus? Somehow those chores didn't seem very appealing. Whatever I did, I knew as I thumbed through the papers, I'd have trouble concentrating on any task. What then? Write in my journal?

Aimlessly, I went over to the bookcase, lightly passing my hand over the book spines, half drowsy still from interrupted sleep. I had arranged all the important books from my formative years on this shelf. In our house, Lawrence used to laughingly call it "the serious Kim collection." I paused at one of my favorites, Ralph Ellison's *The Invisible Man*.

Fifteen years old—that's how old I was the year the book was published. I remembered reading and rereading it, almost inhaling its importance. Ellison did such an exquisite examination of his identity inside a different colored skin, contrasting his interior self with the person he became to the outside world. As a teenager, I had related to the conflicts between his inner and outer selves. Outwardly, I was an extroverted, open, sociable person. Inside, I was a scared kid from a very dysfunctional family. One part of me craved security, sameness and safety, while the other gravitated to the bohemian, the unpredictable.

Settling myself into the corner recliner, I clicked on the reading light. Over the years I had been drawn to the book whenever I was at a crossroads in my life. I vividly remembered picking up the book during the times when I had to ferry back and forth between my UCLA life and going back home to tend to Lila's crises. Tired from the pulls and demands on me, I took comfort in the book, which was almost like a cherished friend. Returning to it now, I quickly became engrossed in Ellison's prose. As I turned a page, I saw something white flutter down like an oversized butterfly to the floor by my feet. I bent down and picked up a slightly crumpled piece of notebook paper with my own handwriting on it.

May, 1977: an eternity ago. How old was I? I quickly did the math. I was forty when I wrote this. I saw myself in that comfortable home Lawrence and I shared back then. I recalled the quiet side street in the Palisades, lined with elm and maple trees, the nearest neighbor a comfortable distance away so that we always felt a sense of space and privacy. What a beautiful house that was, with our tons of books and articles in white bookcases lining entire rooms, French doors that led out to a backyard filled with flowers and Lawrence's latest plantings. I smiled at that—Lawrence loved to grow his own vegetables.

I held on to the white piece of paper while my thoughts went to Lawrence and our relationship. We did have a good life, a compatible life. We were always busy and involved, getting together with friends, enjoying season tickets to the symphony and the many charitable events we attended. I regretted that we chose not to have children. I think that Lawrence realized, too, how our lives were a little too precise and orderly. I recalled wistfully how I viewed the rough and tumble worlds of our friends with their children, and secretly yearned for that other layer of richness that children would have brought to our lives.

I looked back at the crumpled white paper I was holding. On the top line I had written the title, "Rapture." I began to read and felt an immediate rush.

> *Where are you at this moment in time as I listen to Neil Diamond belting out "Sweet Caroline"? Is your heart pounding in cadence with mine? Is your body falling to that magic place and becoming swollen with desire, only to be released by the unlocking of pleasure? Rapture...that vitality you instilled in me.*

> *Do you remember, as I do, the tears on our cheeks gently dropping onto the pillow we shared...that first time for both of us...our shared euphoria...and the elation we felt because neither of us could ever recall a time, any time, in our lives when we had felt such a sense of unbridled release?*

> *Would there ever again be a moment when we could be so vulnerable, and give ourselves the freedom to just be, to give over, to know, that whatever came, we would face together? Such trust, such comfort.*

I remembered the exact day I wrote the letter. Lawrence and I were returning from France after attending a medical meeting where he had presented a paper. We were driving down Melrose Avenue so we could stop to see a friend of ours whose wife had died unexpectedly. As we passed Ed Pearl's Ash Grove on Melrose where Lucien and I had spent so many evenings listening to Mort Sahl, Lenny Bruce, the Weavers, and others, I suddenly started to cry. Frantically, I tried to hide my tears, but Lawrence noticed and immediately moved his arm to comfort me. I told him I was thinking of Shelby and how much he would miss Sarah. That seemed to make sense to him, because he gave me a reassuring pat on the knee and went back to his driving. That night I crept out of bed, went to my study, and wrote the letter I knew I'd never mail.

> *I long for you and often wonder where you are. Are you driving on a dark road somewhere, thinking of me as I so often think of you? Do you sometimes gaze into space and recall that time in our lives when we strolled down a flower-filled lane, now covered on both sides by years of overgrowth? As we walked hand in hand, we would laugh and in those rare moments, look through rose-colored glasses. Our mutual 'La vie en rose.'*

> *Do you cry from time to time, wishing that what we had could happen again? But even being a little scared that it would, and knowing that no matter what life handed us, we would always have those memories of…Rapture.*

The tears ran down my cheeks as I sat alone reading. Some of the letters on the page began to blur, so I quickly grabbed the paper and placed it on the window ledge where the morning sun might dry the blotches.

I got out of the chair and walked to the living room bay window, looking out over the beautiful Pacific, and its foamy, undulating waves which were just now catching the pinkish-yellow reflection of the rising sun.

Luc is back in my life and this time I'm not letting him go or running from him. What I wrote in that letter, about being a little scared that it could happen again, shouldn't stop me now. I cannot deny that side of myself any longer, nor can I go on sacrificing what I truly feel and what I really am for the sake of conformity. If that is the cost of accepting the Chair position, I don't want it. Now, all I can think of is being with Lucien. I don't want to live without him, nor do I intend to.

Just thinking those words, I finally found a sense of resolve. Something in me gave way as I looked at the waves nestling up to the shore, and I felt at one with the world. I couldn't predict what was going to happen, but at least I knew that I was willing to take the risk. I sighed happily, and went to the bedroom to get ready for my meeting with Luc.

When I arrived at the Dolphin, the breakfast crowd had already filled the inside of the restaurant. Luc was sitting in the lobby.

"Hi Luc," I called, as I waved to him. He spotted me and his face broke into a wide smile. He quickly got up to greet me. I felt a lump in my throat, and I put my arms around him and fell onto his chest.

"I'm so glad you called me, Luc. I'm tired of missing you so much. I can't stand being apart from you, even during the week. I want us to be together, weekdays *and* weekends—always."

"I'm here," he said, hugging me closer to him. "I'm here with bells on," he laughed. "Now perhaps we can stop this indecisiveness and be happy by being together."

"You're so right, Luc. I intend to give up my struggling, let you be who you are, and let myself have the one safe harbor where I can be anything I want to be."

We sat down in our booth and I was reminded of our first time at Zucky's so long ago. Today, as we did then, we talked endlessly, interrupted only by the waiter announcing he was going off shift. He cleared some of our empty plates, and gave us a look indicating that he expected a larger tip for the amount of time we'd occupied a table at his station. We stayed on for lunch and continued our "catch up." By the end of lunch, we'd made numerous decisions, most importantly, that we belonged together.

Luc moved some of his things to my beach house that night. I can't say that I didn't momentarily gulp as the moving truck pulled up the next weekend and Luc showed me the papers canceling his lease on his apartment in town. I reminded myself: you are embracing change, remember? You have let new things into your life! Be glad.

And, for the most part, I was. The new arrangement not only worked well, but it began a new phase for me. We saw how much we had to share with each other the forty or so years which had separated us. In between our lovemaking and not being able to keep our hands off each other, I discovered that I could enlist Luc's help with the decisions I faced. The Dean had given me a month to make up my mind about accepting the position of department chair, so Luc and I spent countless hours going over alternative scenarios.

Luc asked for my advice too. He grappled with how to meet the challenge presented by the National Security Administration, which he was convinced was trying to discredit him because he was defending several clients whose civil rights had been violated.

Luc's conviction in keeping a steady path as he worked on his controversial cases so impressed me. Yet, it was also obvious these cases caused him grave concern. One morning, after our daily long walk on the beach, he told me that he was concerned that his legal battles with the government would jeopardize my new position—if I made the final choice to take that position. When we finished the walk and lay in the sand, the sun beating down on us, he told me that he was worried that his being on the Terrorist Watch List initiated by the Bush administration after 9/11 could also affect me.

Luc had already told me about the four clients from Lebanon and Iran, all of them new citizens of the U.S., who he was representing. Two were successful entrepreneurs, two physicians. The Iranian entrepreneurs ran an import-export business in fine perfumes and silks, and were, according to Luc, men with warm, loving families who were opposed to the current Iranian regime. They had been accused of using their business to launder money that would be sent to Al Qaeda. But there was no evidence against them. The only reason they had been accused of terrorism was that they made no efforts to hide the fact that they were practicing Muslims.

We'd been over the cases several times before, and both of us agreed that the current rush to imprison Middle Easterners without charging them was like incarcerating the Japanese American citizens in California during WWII.

"Luc," I asked, squinting into the sun, "has something else happened?"

He admitted that the government prosecutors had just a day ago brought up his Iranian background. "I think it's a thinly-veiled attempt to threaten me and implicate me in what they are falsely accusing the four of doing: aiding and abetting terrorist causes."

"What do your partners Steve and Robert say about all this?"

"Well, of course they're supporting me. And they've started to gather affidavits attesting to my loyalty just to have in our back pocket if the Feds try to pull something. And they've made some calls to colleagues. It appears that some of the Department of Justice attorneys are really disgusted by these McCarthyesque tactics, but what they think is that the higher ups are tacitly encouraging this."

"What higher ups?"

"You can't go any higher, if you get my meaning."

A silence fell between us. I gently placed my hand on his arm. "Luc, don't worry about me or my position. You do what you think is right. I don't want to feel that I am responsible for your capitulating or not going the distance."

Two weeks before Lucien was to appear in court to defend himself and his clients, I made my final decision about the Chair position. I knew exactly what I would say to the Dean. In the time leading up to the decision, in addition to admiring Luc's determination to bring justice to his clients, I thought a lot about Arthur and the legacy he left me. "Honor your principles and stand up for your beliefs," he would have said, just like Mr. Samuels, just like Arthur Miller.

That night as we were having dinner, I felt a sense of well-being. Somehow, facing the truth of my convictions had freed me and given me a pathway to follow. Lucien seemed to sense my state. "Where are you, Kim?"

I didn't say anything for a while. Just looked at him.

"I admire whatever it is in you that makes you fight so strongly for what you believe. In a way, it reminds me of that same trait in my father. For the first time, so many of my experiences from the past are melding together and making sense: Why I so admired people like Arthur Miller, Helen Gahagan-Douglas, and Ralph Ellison. What impressed me most about them was their need to be honest with themselves at all costs, and, above all, I was moved by their integrity."

"Of course," Luc said. "I figured that's why you've talked so much about Mr. Samuels over the years, because he could stand up to the faculty at your high school in the heart of the Red Scare and defend anyone's right to their beliefs, no matter what their beliefs were. He had real conviction."

"Yes, that's true, he did. And you have a bit of that too, don't you?"

"You do too, Kim. You're just beginning to own it. I always saw you as outspoken and unafraid, even when it meant saying things that were unpopular," Luc said.

"I guess that's true to an extent. Perhaps I realized how much more I could say, and do in certain circumstances. Or the many times I did nothing. But now, a new day is dawning. Don't you think pooling our protests would be divine?"

"Imagine 'divine' coming from an atheist," Luc laughed.

My letter to the Dean was short and to the point. "Pleased as I am to be selected by you and my colleagues as incoming Chair of the

Department of History and Political Science, I wish to attach one important condition to this great honor you bestow upon me. While I promise to give my all to ensure the standard of excellence in the Department, I must assert that my beliefs and my politics are my own. My associations are of my own choosing and must be allowed to stand. If these terms are acceptable to you, I commit myself to do the most effective job possible to achieve the aims of our Department, and I will be more than pleased to accept the position of Chair."

As I composed the letter to the Dean, Ellison's concluding lines rang in my head: "In our lives, the ending of one phase heralds the beginning of another." I now knew why I had selected *The Invisible Man* off my shelf after my nightmare. My wish for a kind of honesty and authenticity within myself and in my actions was reflected by Ellison. Lucien, I knew, would help me in that regard. Arthur already had.

Chapter 21

2007

It was late in the afternoon when I pulled into my garage, climbed out of my car, and breathed a sigh of relief to be back at the beach. I was weary from my busy work day and from the grind of my daily commute to and from the university. In midsummer the smog and traffic always seemed doubly oppressive. How different it might have been if L.A. had kept the Red Car and developed a good transit system, I thought wistfully.

Luc's car wasn't in the garage. He probably had a late meeting with his partners about the Department of Justice case. They'd been working pretty hard on it the last two weeks. I snatched the mail distractedly from the mailbox, and entered the house, dropping the pile on the hall table. I glanced at the answering machine, thinking Luc might have left a message. But there was no blinking light. Oh well, I thought, this will give me a chance to have a little down time by myself, starting with a nice cool shower to wash off the city grime.

I dropped off my briefcase in my office and headed for the bedroom. Hmmm, Luc must have really been in a hurry this morning. Several of his dress shirts lay strewn on the bed covers. I gathered them up to hang them up in the closet. Funny, this feels like such a domestic chore. Who would have guessed a year ago that Dr. Kim Lebow would be happily gathering up her lover's clothes and hanging them up for him? Not I, certainly!

The closet was in even worse shape than the bed. It looked as if we'd been the victims of thieves riffling through our possessions. Trousers were half off their hangers, and the closet floor had plastic dry cleaning bags and shoeboxes all over it. A shiver went through me. Had someone been here? Maybe I should check the rest of the house. Warily, I crept down the hallway, opening each door part way before I entered. Nothing else seemed disturbed. I continued on to the kitchen. I couldn't shake the feeling that something was amiss. I shrugged. Well, at least I can get my shower. Just as I turned to leave the kitchen, I saw something taped to the microwave.

It was an envelope. Lucien had written "To Kim" on it. I pulled it off and opened the envelope, tearing out the letter impatiently.

My dearest Kim,

With much sadness and regret, I have decided that I cannot risk subjecting you to any possible repercussions while I am under investigation, however unfounded that investigation might be. Perhaps things will abate. Perhaps the anti-terrorist, anti-Muslim fervor will die down and my clients will be seen for who they are: law-abiding American citizens who have done nothing wrong. This complicated case will require every ounce of my energy and focus which I cannot dedicate unless I am alone for a while.

You have always supported my quest for justice for the underdog and have said that you would stand by me, whatever the cost. But after much thought, I know I couldn't bear to become a hindrance to your hard-won accomplishments at the university, if it should come to that. And I do believe, down the road, that your association with me could interfere with your appointment to Chair of the department. We both know how politically sensitive our higher learning institutions have become.

My darling, do not imagine that my decision has any bearing on something you have said or done. You are the love of my life and our time together has been so deeply gratifying. I can never express how happy I have been with you. I will always love you, but this is something for me that I must do. I must have more space during this tumultuous time.

Please forgive me for leaving without speaking to you in person. It's perhaps a coward's way, yet for me it was the only way. I wouldn't have had the strength to leave if we were face to face. Please do not try to find me. I will try to be in touch from time to time.

Hopefully, in the future our paths will cross again. Until then, my love, trust what I believe is best for us right now and know that I will miss you with every fiber of my being.

Tenderly,
Luc

P.S. Sorry to have left such a mess.

I looked numbly down at the paper in my hand, and let it float to the floor. I felt disembodied, detached, like I too was going to float to the floor. I started to feel dizzy, and instinctively reached for the kitchen counter to steady myself. How can this be? Why didn't he talk to me about this first? Why just leave like this? My mind started to race with what-ifs. Was he going to be incarcerated? Would he be able to contact me when he wanted to? I blinked, looking at the letter on the floor, not able to take in what he had just done to me—to us.

I found my way to the counter barstool and collapsed into it, bracing my head in my hands. It was as if all color and light had been sucked out of the room. I blinked again. This couldn't be happening to me. All that we had recaptured—gone in an instant.

I don't know how long I sat there slumped at the kitchen counter. Gradually, I became aware of the gathering dusk, although to me it felt like gloom. I looked up at the clock and seeing it was nearly 8:30 p.m., caught myself thinking, "I should get something started for dinner. Luc will be starv—oh, that's right. Luc won't be coming home for dinner."

What was the point, then? I certainly wasn't hungry. My stomach roiled with pain. Maybe I should lie down on the couch. The living room was also dark by now. I switched on a corner-reading lamp, and then went to the couch to lie down in the near dark. I must have dozed off, because at some point, I woke up. It was night by then. "Who's there?" I called out frantically. "Luc? Are you home?" As soon as I heard my words, the memory of his note came back. It was then that my sadness overcame me. In the semi-dark, in the quiet, I started to sob. I shouted, "No! You cannot leave me! No! Come back, come back!" No answer came. I started shivering uncontrollably.

Trembling and crying, I stumbled to the bathroom and turned on the shower. Shedding the day's clothes, now wrinkled and soggy with tears, I stepped naked into the shower, the water droplets reminding me that I was still here, still alive. After my shower, I toweled off and went straight to bed, pulling the covers high over my head, hoping that this would induce sleep. But it was no use: I tossed and turned.

The next morning, I awakened to bright streaming sunlight. I squinted and immediately felt my skin tighten over my puffy eyelids and cheeks. I gingerly touch them, as if to smooth out my skin. I raised myself up onto my elbow and looked at the clock. Nine o'clock. I felt as if I had a hangover. My muscles ached, and my stomach felt raw. I did not feel rested. What is the point of getting up? Without Luc, I had little reason to greet the day. But I knew I had to get some kind of movement going. Slowly, I swung my feet to the floor and reached for my robe. Everything around me looked unfamiliar. I caught sight of the disheveled closet, and my heart fluttered all over again. I felt as if I were suspended in time, as if things were happening in slow motion. I tried to gather my thoughts. It would be good to have a little bit of breakfast, I guess. When I got to the kitchen, I thought, "I have no idea how I'm going to survive this."

Then I remembered something a grief counselor had told me after Lawrence had died. "Imagine," she said, "that you do not have to think about a whole day. Just think about one or two small little things that your hands can do—like make the coffee, or put some bread in the toaster. Break things down into their smallest incremental steps and you will find that you can go on, step by step."

So that's what I did. I filled the coffeemaker with water. I ground the coffee, I pulled out two cups—oh no, I realized, I was automatically thinking about the routine that Luc and I had established. Here it comes again, the wave of recognition. No, Kim, you don't need two cups this morning. Okay, start again: get the cream from the fridge, make some toast.

While the coffee brewed, I shuffled slowly out to the hallway to retrieve the mail I'd dropped there after work. I cleared a spot on the dining room table and started to sort our piles of mail. I glanced absentmindedly at the top letter on the stack of mail, and noted it was from the Los Angeles Conservancy. I also noted the postmark. That date—July 30, 2006— rang a bell. But I couldn't place why. My brain was dull and throbbing. I got up and brought my coffee to the table, and had a couple of sips. Better. I opened the letter and my association with the date became clear to me: July 30—of course! That was the date, sixty years ago to the day, when my family moved to our house in the Valley. I pored over the Los Angeles Conservancy letter, and I also realized that it wasn't long after July 30 that I first became a rider on the Red Car.

Dear Dr. Lebow,

As you may have heard, Congresswoman Lucille Roybal-Allard has recently secured $100,000 in federal monies for a study to assess the value of restoring the historic Red Car trolley to help revitalize the downtown Los Angeles core. To conduct this study, and also explore the reintroduction of the Red Car to Los Angeles proper, the Los Angeles Conservancy is currently recruiting a panel of experts and involved citizens.

Your article, "Good-bye to Public Transportation, Hello to Blight!" attracted the attention of our Board. We, too, believe that the traffic problems and resultant smog and respiratory diseases in our city stem in part from the lack of a truly viable transportation system. With what we now know about Los Angeles' unique geographic situation, the inversion layer formation and global climate change, we believe it is imperative to reexamine the feasibility of introducing a new kind of public transportation system. The Conservancy believes that in bringing this panel together, our collective efforts will begin to make a difference in the quality of our citizens' lives.

We need strong voices for this panel and believe that you would make an excellent addition to our study team. Please let us know when we can set up a meeting to discuss your possible participation.

The chairperson of the Conservancy had signed the letter. I realized that for the moments I was reading the letter, I had forgotten about my pain. I even felt a bit of excitement. Me! They were asking me to work with them on a project to restore the Red Car. Old positive feelings of anticipation that I used to have when I boarded the Red Car as a teenager welled up in me. Now, they were attempting to bring it back and I wanted to be a part of it.

I caught myself again wanting to call out to Luc, to tell him my good news. But of course the house was empty, silent, and I was alone. No partner with whom to share my news. I felt almost like fainting. Again, I told myself to get a grip, to proceed slowly. The entire weekend was ahead of me, like a great chasm I was falling into. I glanced out at the deck, where our two chaise lounges sat, turned toward each other. Without his presence, the rooms and furniture seemed less animated, as if they needed his spirit to signify "home." But I knew this was my grief at work, my brain coloring the surroundings. I began to realize that if I stayed in the house all weekend I'd go mad with loneliness and pain. I needed contact.

As soon as I dialed her number and she (thankfully) picked up the phone, Andrea's voice had a soothing effect.

"Hi, Kim! What's up? You usually don't call me on weekends. Is Luc out of town on business?"

"Andrea, Luc has left. He taped a note to the microwave and I…I was wondering if you might have some time to walk and talk?" I couldn't keep my voice from trembling.

"Kim, I'm there. Where do you want to meet? Usual place? Just give me an hour to finish my laundry and we can have a walk and an early lunch."

"Thanks, Andrea."

Good. Now I only had an hour to fill. Surely I could manage that. I went back to the bedroom, resolutely shutting the closet door so I didn't have to look at the reminder of Luc's leaving. I picked out some jeans, a top and a sweater in case the fog rolled in, dressed and fussed with my hair. Then I went back to the dining room table to sort through the rest of the mail. Methodically, I set out piles for household bills, personal mail and a pile for Lucien. Just seeing his name on envelopes made me wince. I bit my lip, and went to the kitchen to clean up.

An hour later, when Andrea and I met, she silently embraced me, rubbing my back in sympathy. I brought out the now wrinkled letter he had left me, and let her read it. As I watched her poring over his words, I realized that throughout most of our relationship, I wouldn't have been this forthcoming with Andrea. But I felt so alone and needed her support more than I needed to be "strong Kim." I needed her to know what was going on, so that at least one other person was in my court.

"Oh Kim," she murmured sympathetically. "He is trying to do what he thinks is the honorable thing to do, don't you think?"

"Yes," I managed to say. "But doesn't he realize that I'd back him no matter what?"

"I think he does, Kim. But he also doesn't want you to have to pay that price."

"How can he do this to me? I don't even want the Chair position now. It doesn't seem worth it!"

Andrea put her arm around my shoulder. "I think you do, Kim, and I think that deep down you know that he's hurting as much as you are. This will take time to get through. Just know that I'm here, no matter what."

I turned to my oldest friend and hugged her again. "Well," I sighed, "I hope you're ready for many more gab-fests!" I tried to manage a weak smile—and almost succeeded.

I could see tears in Andrea's eyes too. Almost simultaneously, we both turned and began walking vigorously toward the Dolphin. The walking felt good. I took a deep breath, and then another and another. I kept walking, tears streaming down my face.

At the restaurant, after handing me some Kleenex, Andrea suggested we order a big omelet and split it. When the food came, I realized I was ravenous, and dug in willingly. My spirits rose as I listened to Andrea chatting about her youngest grandson's T-Ball adventures. As I perked up, I realized I had something else to talk about: the Conservancy letter.

As I sketched out the point of the letter I'd gotten, Andrea's face lit up. "Kim!" she exclaimed. "This is fantastic! They couldn't have come to a better person–you've been a champion of the return of the Red Car for as long as we've been friends!"

I nodded. "It's true. Do you realize it's been over sixty years since we rode that car into Hollywood for our outings?"

"So, what are you going to tell them? Are you going to take them up on their offer?"

"I don't know, Andrea. Luc's leaving is such a blow. I don't know if I can cope with that and taking on a new project at the same time."

"You know what I think? I think it would be the perfect antidote for you. It's something you care passionately about, and you know you're going to have lots of open time now that he's not there."

I felt a lump forming in my throat again. But I knew Andrea was right. She had good instincts.

"Andrea, do you think you'd have some time to read over my response to them?"

"You bet!" Andrea's pert little smile reminded me of the enthusiastic young girl I had met so long ago. "Of course, I'm not a literary or historical genius like you-know-who, but I'll do my best!"

I dug back into my omelet, feeling heartened and less fragile for the moment. When we parted, Andrea made me promise that I'd call her if I felt panicky. "Don't worry about what time it is," she repeated twice.

It was now late afternoon on Saturday. Just about twenty-four hours since I had been dealt the blow of Luc's departure. I went back to the house, and put on some music, and walked through the house crying aloud. In between bouts of sobbing, I read and reread the Conservancy letter. It seemed like the only redeeming thing in my life right now. I even talked to Luc's absent form. "You see, darling: I have something that I can contribute, to try to right a situation too." Somehow I knew, deep down, that he would have supported me in this endeavor as well. In our months together, he had consistently encouraged my teaching, my writing, and my political involvement.

That night I slept deeply, waking periodically from dreams of longing for him. In my dream he said, "Don't worry, Kim. I am all right. And you will be all right too. Someday we shall be together again." Even though I woke with tears in my eyes, I felt a bit better the next morning. I decided I would work on composing my answer letter to the Conservancy. If I got far enough with the draft, perhaps I'd call Andrea to get her feedback. It felt good to delve into the writing; it was something my brain knew how to do. After three drafts, I was ready, I thought, for some outside input.

Andrea was more than game. "Kim, why don't you come for dinner and then you can read what you've written out loud to me?" That sounded like a great idea to me. Even though I had managed to distract myself as I wrote, I wasn't looking forward to another long evening in the house alone. When I got to Andrea's, she had whipped up a marvelous pasta with pesto sauce and had uncorked a bottle of wine.

She sat on her couch as I paced in front of her and began to read, waving one arm in a circle for emphasis.

"As a teenager, I was free to go beyond the confines of what was to me the often boring and dusty Valley to find new and exciting experiences 'over the hill.' My vehicle for doing that was by boarding the wonderful Red Car—often with my dear friend. Arriving every forty-five minutes at the station on Chandler Boulevard, it was our ticket to liberation.

"The Red Car embodied the spirit of freedom and unity which linked the Valley with all parts of the larger city beyond. When it suddenly rolled to a final stop in the mid-1950s, my friends and I were shocked. We missed it terribly and were extremely puzzled that such an efficient and effortless form of transportation for so many of us was gone. I can even remember, with great surprise and sadness, the picture in the *Los Angeles Times* in June, 1955 of the Red Car pulling into the station in El Segundo for the last time.

"Only when I became an adult and read about the history of our city did I begin to comprehend what was behind the dismantling of the Red Car. The alliance of Standard Oil, Firestone and General Motors that led to its demise was connected to the financial gain of these three companies. Their profits proved to be an incalculable loss for so many people in the Valley and in Los Angeles.

"For me, personally, taking that Red Car to town filled me with hope and inspiration. It opened the door to a new and exciting world on the other side of the hill. Every time I rode the Red Car across the Cahuenga Pass, I would think about all of the unknown places I wanted to explore.

"My dream would be to bring back the lines that ran from the

Westside to the ocean, the Valley to the City, and Pasadena to Union Station. That's my hope. Reestablishing those lines would unite all of the outlying branches of our city. What an answer to freeways which are practically parking lots, and what a relief to the strain we all feel. Maybe, the new Mayor will put his weight behind the Roybal-Allard project and try to do something about it."

I put down my draft, realizing that my voice had risen as I read. I looked expectantly at Andrea, who was smiling broadly.

"Wow, that's wonderful, Kim! I think you've hit on all the important points. You'll be the perfect spokeswoman on that planning committee. They'd miss out if they didn't use you!"

"Do you really think so, Andrea? I hope you're right, and that they will choose me. The more I worked on this today, the more I realized that I *should* be part of that project. I had always believed that the end of the Red Car set the Valley apart from the rest of Los Angeles. It also led to a sort of provincialism for many Valleyites that still exists. The hope that we could bring the Red Car back thrills me."

Andrea nodded. "You know, I always thought that you and your father put too much store in the notion of the Red Car being part of a general trend. But in the years since, I think that you were right. What amazes me is that I don't remember any big protest. I know we were really upset, especially that day of your birthday. But I don't recall any letters to the editor and things like that."

"No, I don't think there was much protest. People didn't seem to realize what was going on. My father did, though. But very few people got it. So, freeways were built left and right, a lot of new cars were sold, and little was said about the trolleys that totally vanished."

"But was that all bad? I remember my dad being really excited about taking us on family trips and the roads getting built."

"Yeah, I guess people in Los Angeles were like most Americans at that time, interested in improving their own lives and living the American dream. They were not privy to nor would they have cared too much about what was going on."

"It was such a different time, wasn't it?"

"Yes, it was. My father liked to remind me that the Red Car closed just one year after Arthur Miller was brought before HUAC. It was smack in the midst of the McCarthy Era. People still idealized their government, and they had no idea that our elected officials could be untrustworthy."

"Well, you know I've never been one to be super-political. But, the fact that the Conservancy is exploring whether we should restore the Red Car seems like a positive direction, doesn't it?"

"Yes, maybe something *is* beginning to happen. Times are better now. A lot of people are tired of the conditions in L.A. At least people feel free to voice complaints about traffic, noxious air, and 'politics as usual.' When I think of McCarthy and HUAC, any protest or dissent was frowned upon and considered disloyal. So many good people kept quiet because they were afraid."

"Do you think it's different now, Kim?"

"Well, it seems to me that the current dialogue about The PATRIOT Act, global warming, inadequate health care, and the government's indifferent response to what's happening to our air is reaching critical mass."

"Well, if that's true, it's because of people like you, Kim. I admire your courage in speaking up so much. I just hope other people are as open to change as you say they are."

"The letters to the editor in the *Los Angeles Times* may be a sign. They always give me hope. Did you see that editorial last week in the Times by Carolyn See called 'Streetcar Desire...'? She was talking about traffic, too many cars, gridlock, and even suggested bringing back streetcars."

"No, I missed that editorial. But that's great that she wrote that. Now, my friend the crusader, what do you say we do some damage to this pesto?"

Andrea was such a good balm for my distress over Luc's leaving. She knew me so well, and could steer me in the direction of more lighthearted conversation without it seeming too superficial. When she suggested I spend the night, I agreed. I didn't have any classes till noon the next day and could easily manage the drive back to my house and into the campus before then. As I left the next morning, she gave me another hug and said, "Don't forget to mail that letter right away!"

A week later, I was on my way to my first Los Angeles Conservancy meeting. The bumper to bumper traffic on the 101 was as frustrating as the level of mucky smog which permeated the morning air. *Just too many rats in the maze*, I thought. I was due at the Conservancy's downtown offices at 9:00 a.m. and the turtle's pace traffic was an obstacle to my being on time.

A huge semi with the words WALMART on its side suddenly cut me off. I slammed on my brakes and was about to lean on my horn, but decided it was best to swallow my anger and turn up the radio instead. Why get upset over what had become an everyday occurrence? I had enough on my mind without worrying about traffic. Luc's absence caused a stab of pain whenever I thought of him, or read an article about which he would have had an opinion. I had even taken to talking out loud to him almost daily when I was alone at the house. Somehow it seemed to help. I felt I could conjure his support and loving encouragement by talking things out.

I turned into the parking lot of the building on Hill Street with four minutes to spare, and parked my car in the stall marked "Los Angeles Conservancy Officers." I tucked my written report, "The Reprise of the Red Car" under my arm, and hurried to the Conservancy offices on the third floor. Well, I thought, this is it! Another Red Car chapter!

Short of breath, I hastened to an empty seat. I greeted the seven other members of the Conservancy Board for the Revitalization of Los Angeles: L.A. Red Car Project already gathered around a shiny, oval oak table. I felt elated. Even though I'd lost Luc—which I hoped was a temporary situation—I'd been given a second chance to help redo a vital area of my past life: bringing back the Red Car.

Chapter 22

2007

I set my coffee cup down on the counter and glanced at my watch. Time to go. I would be lucky to get downtown on time. As usual, I had dawdled over my morning coffee and the paper. I hurriedly started to gather up my briefcase and Conservancy papers.

Today was the last Conservancy meeting and I was a bit edgy about my presentation. It was a public hearing, and would be very different from speaking just in front of our core panel. Today, a lot of people were expected. Developers and car dealers would be out in force for sure, and the press would likely be there, too.

As I dashed toward the garage, I found myself wishing that I still had Luc in my corner. This last year without him had been terribly lonely for me. I had contacted his partners at one point—against my better judgment—but they had firmly refused to give up any information about him.

I pulled out of the driveway and headed toward Pacific Coast Highway, hoping for the predictable late-morning let up in traffic going east.

On the drive downtown, I felt a rush of pride as I reflected on our committee's accomplishments from the last few months of meetings. With the solid endorsement of the mayor, construction would include street level trolleys and later, underground metro lines similar to those in San Francisco, Quito and Rio de Janeiro—an enormous boost toward reducing traffic congestion and providing low cost transportation to Angelenos. It wouldn't solve all the problems, but it was a step in the right direction.

The study panel had concluded that if it were financially feasible, the line would initially link downtown, Hollywood, and West Los Angeles with the San Fernando Valley. Future projections called for the extension of the line to the beach communities as well. The Red Car might once again become a reality. It was a reality, however, that did not appeal to everyone, especially to the business and development interests opposed to the revitalization of public transportation. Well, I thought, I guess it's only natural that the ones against the return of the trolley will try to sway opinion.

The main conference room was filled to capacity. There were perhaps eighty-five or more in attendance. I caught the Chairperson's eye and could see she was irritated that I was late. As point person, I had studied the history of the gradual abandonment of the streetcar system in March of 1963. She and I had agreed that I'd be first on the agenda to highlight the reasons to resurrect the trolley system now. She had saved a seat for me next to her, and I hurriedly settled myself and arranged my papers. The meeting convened with a few words of introduction from the Chairperson regarding the panel's purpose; she then nodded to me and I went to the podium. Less nervous now that the moment had arrived, I began to speak with a calm, measured delivery.

"There are many positive reasons to resurrect the Red Car. Based on the recommendations of this committee, linking the metro area to the Valley with a streetcar system would increase commerce on both sides of the hill, increase mobility by reducing traffic congestion, and improve air quality. And there is another less obvious reason. In the last twenty years, there has been a growing movement in the San Fernando Valley to secede from the City of Los Angeles. If we were able to link these major areas of the city, it would go a long way to defuse the resentment felt by many Valleyites toward the L.A. city government. We believe the next logical step in this process is to hear from our constituents. In view of the effects on our citizens, we strongly recommend the public be informed of these proceedings at every step and encouraged to voice their concerns, as is their right. Public buy-in would be a powerful incentive for our potential funding agencies. The vision of an L.A. reunited could become a long-awaited reality."

As I took my seat, the Chairperson then nodded to the next scheduled speaker, who launched right into his objections. "We at the Downtown Development Association are concerned that this plan will be a detriment to many in our city. For example, we have bus and taxi companies which depend on city business contracts. They would suffer financially if the trolley system diverts their riders. And I also see no reason for the public to be needlessly bothered and encumbered with details of these meetings. Press releases would only cloud their thinking and delay the process," he asserted.

Well, I thought, it was no surprise that the DDA group perceived this as a threat. Score one for the opposition.

Next up was a representative from the Hollywood Restaurant Owner's Association. "I remember when the old Red Car line brought hundreds of people every day over the Cahuenga Pass to enjoy dinner and entertainment in Hollywood and Westwood," he countered. "I think that Hollywood's decades-long decline can be partly blamed on the loss of business that used to come directly from the Valley's streetcar riders. The sooner we make this a top priority, the better off Los Angeles will be!"

I wanted to run over and hug him. I could see audience members nodding in agreement. The Chairperson and I had discussed the lineup of speakers, and had agreed to alternate between speakers from both sides of the issue, pro and con. It was the only fair approach. But we also hoped that, by alternating speakers, any strong current of opposition might be diffused.

A reputable downtown car dealer was now at the podium pointing out the dangers of a trolley system. "Just like the current Metro Link trains, streetcars are difficult to control since they're run mostly by a centralized system. They can be a lot more hazardous than automobiles. The original Red Car trolleys went out of business because of numerous accidents and lawsuits. That's the last thing our city needs to be saddled with again!" He sat down then jumped back up. "And I agree we don't need the public in on this." He chuckled. "So few get involved anyway, it's not worth the time and effort to give them the option."

My frustration was mounting. I wanted to jump up and tell him how wrong he was. But then, I heard Luc's guiding words playing in my head. "Remember, Kim, if you let your emotions control the situation, you may not be as effective as you want to be." I quickly murmured in the Chairperson's ear and asked whether she might recognize me for another comment. I saw her pause. It was, after all, not on the agenda for me to interject additional points.

"Dr. Lebow, do you have something to add to the last speaker's comments?"

"I do, Madame Chairperson," I said evenly. "Just to keep the record straight, the dismantling of the Red Car was due to many factors. History shows its disappearance was not, in fact, due to public apathy about public transportation. There were strong corporate financial interests—notably Standard Oil, Firestone and General Motors, as well as the L.A. city government—which all agreed to promote more upscale transportation through automobile ownership. Needless to say, this did result in lucrative city contracts for freeway construction, along with the subsequent need for gasoline and tires. Los Angelenos, just as other Americans, did gain a new level of transportation freedom. However, who gained the most is now debatable. And we now know that this private transportation boom introduced other health and quality of life consequences. Our next speakers will address these effects. I did, however, want to reiterate that at the time, the public was misinformed about the reasons for the switch to automobile-centered transportation and that we must foster transparency in our process the second time around." I caught the subtle nod and smile of endorsement from the Chairperson.

The EPA representative presented a summary of the latest scientific data on pollutants and smog. He was followed by a research physician based at the UCLA and Cedars-Sinai Medical Centers who had studied the increase in lung disease, asthma and other respiratory illnesses caused by carbon emissions. "Those afflicted with such illnesses range from early childhood to the elderly, which is much more far-reaching in terms of harm to the general public than the remote possibility of trolley accidents," he noted. "The trolley should be the stepping stone on a path to an even broader plan to expand public transportation throughout the metro area in the future."

And so it went. A few more detractors spoke, as did others who endorsed our panel's findings. The meeting adjourned about an hour later. I felt heartened, even encouraged by the direction it had taken and admittedly, the part I had played. I knew that the sixteen-year-old Kim inside was still as fiery and passionate about causes as ever. But today, another Kim had taken the lead, thanks to those who had guided me and supported me. I felt gratified that I was serving my community to advance a cause that I truly believed in. Instead of chasing the Red Car, maybe I'd actually be riding in it again.

I needed to stretch my legs, and headed to the food court to grab a bite and a noontime coffee pick-me-up. While I was waiting in line, an elderly gentleman with a shock of thick white hair, a ruddy well-tanned face, and a warm smile approached me. He leaned slightly on his cane. He seemed to recognize me, but I was drawing a blank. "I'm Eugene Franks," he said, extending his hand. "You were probably too young to remember me, but I was a friend and colleague of your father's."

I scanned his face and tried to place him. It was difficult to go back in time to retrieve all those faces from the tumultuous McCarthy years. But then, wait a minute. "Weren't you a history professor?" I asked.

He nodded. "I'll be darned. You do remember."

I paid for my salad and cappuccino and motioned him toward one of the umbrella-covered tables on the patio. I helped him get situated in a chair. "Do you want a coffee or something to eat?" I asked.

"Oh, no thank you," he said.

I took a sip of my coffee, picturing my childhood house in the Valley, the living room packed with people eating the dinner that Lila had fixed. I tried to envision a younger Eugene Franks, without his white hair, in that crowd. "I seem to recall a lot of people sitting around listening to broadcasts on our Philco radio," I said. "And, I definitely recall that my father spoke of you often."

Eugene had a wistful look, as if he were hearing it all over again. "Oh yes, in fact, you might remember that very famous broadcast when the Hollywood Ten voiced opposition to the HUAC hearings." I nodded.

"We were all in sympathy with those blacklisted writers," Eugene continued. "We knew the shame they must have felt when they lost their jobs, and couldn't find work to support their families—just like your father."

And for some, the shame was so unbearable, it caused them to take their own lives, like Mr. Samuels, I thought.

Eugene put his trembling fingers on my shoulder. "I so admired your father for his convictions. I just wanted to tell you that I saw him today in you."

Tears welled up and I hugged him gently. "Thank you, Eugene. That means a lot to hear you say that. I've thought of him often lately. Perhaps our current political climate is reminding me of those days, and of him especially."

"I didn't have your father's courage, I'm sorry to admit. I could've stood by him, but didn't. I was too afraid of losing my job. And even now, I'm ashamed whenever I think about it again."

"Life sure isn't black and white. How would we know what we'd do under such circumstances until we're faced with it? I resented my father for years for not being there to take care of us, and mostly dumping the responsibilities on me. He never told us he was fired and working evenings as a sales clerk in the Broadway department store. I thought he was having an affair."

"He didn't tell you the truth—of course you'd think the worst. I think many of us knew his dilemma, but then, we didn't feel that it was our place to talk about it, which was the least we could do. All of us were too afraid and we didn't go the distance in supporting him."

"You know, I understand so much more about that time now. It's so easy to fall into judging others. Maybe getting older has helped me accept that Arthur strived to do the best he could under very difficult circumstances."

Eugene fumbled in his jacket pocket and handed me an envelope. "I think you might be interested in this event."

I scanned the invitation. It was from the regional ACLU which was sponsoring a sixtieth anniversary reading of the original 1947 radio broadcast, "Hollywood Fights Back," as well as acknowledging the tenth anniversary of the Screen Writer's Guild's reinstatement of the blacklisted writers whose names were removed from film credits during the McCarthy era. "Why Eugene, you've been staying in touch with this issue all these years too, haven't you? It's tonight, isn't it?"

He smiled sheepishly. "Seems like fate that we would meet again, today of all days. Don't you think?"

I suddenly wondered if he had come to find me for this express purpose, but it didn't matter. "Yes, it does. I had heard about this event too. I'm a member and on their mailing list. But I hadn't planned on attending because I thought I would be too exhausted after today's Conservancy hearings." I saw Eugene's face fall, and quickly amended what I was saying.

"You know, since we've run into each other, and since it's such a vital meeting, I simply must go. After all, it is important to remember the past, right?"

"...for those who cannot remember are destined to repeat it," he recited.

"You sound just like my father," I laughed. "How about if I pick you up this evening and we'll go together?"

Eugene's face lit up. I suggested we grab a light supper at my favorite haunt, The Literati Café in Westwood, beforehand. Eugene agreed and let me walk him to his car.

Meeting Eugene had brought back the ghosts of my past. But this time, those ghosts did not bring dread or sadness. Encountering him had occurred at a time when I understood so much more. I now had a clearer vision, given what has happened in our country once again since 9/11, of what courage it took to speak out and why my mother was so consumed with fear. Even though it felt strange, all of a sudden I remembered something my mother had said, and realized how it had influenced me throughout my lifetime. "Dream if you wish," she would tell me. "Dreams are fun, but always remember: a dream is just a dream until you make it a reality. It's the action that counts."

What a debt we owed to people like my father and Luc, who had taken action and were not swayed from standing on their principles. If history does seem to repeat itself, maybe it gives us the opportunity to learn a little more with each go-round, to get involved, question authority, and make changes. That era had taken a toll on so many. It occurred to me how fortunate I had been to be deeply and personally involved in these critical turning points. I've been able to watch people close to me respond with such personal heroism in the face of overwhelming threats. And their examples have given me the courage to forge a path for myself. I silently thanked Mr. Samuels for watching over me, and hoped, like the proverbial acorn, I had come to land closer to my father's tree.

About the Author

Ellen Ruderman is a psychotherapist in Encino, California, and the author of many academic publications. This is her first novel.

Breinigsville, PA USA
19 November 2010
249560BV00002B/14/P